INADVERTENT DISCLOSURE

USA TODAY BESTSELLING AUTHOR
Melissa F. Miller

Brown Street Books

Published by Brown Street Books.

For more information about the author,
please visit www.melissafmiller.com.

For more information about the publisher,
please visit www.brownstbooks.com.

Brown Street Books ISBN: 978-0-9834927-4-0

Cover design by Clarissa Yeo

Book Layout & Design ©2014 - BookDesignTemplates.com

For my sister Theresa, my brother Trevor, and Kevin,
true stewards of the earth,

and

for my children, Adam, Jack, and Sara,
who will reap the benefits.

ACKNOWLEDGMENTS

My first book was a labor of love. This second book carries with it the weight of expectations—both yours and mine. As such, it was, in some ways, more challenging to write. As always, I could not have written it without the abundant good humor, constant love, and occasional tough love of my husband and first reader, David Miller. I also want to thank my friends and family, whose support and encouragement have been phenomenal. Although I cannot name everyone who has inspired and supported me here, I would be remiss if I did not thank Missy and Geoff Owen and Beth Henke for their friendship, both generally and specific to this venture. I also wish to thank the real Gavin Russell, whose generous donation to the Amelia Givin Library earned him a place in these pages. And, of course, I thank the fine folks at Brown Street Books. Finally, my sincere thanks to each reader who wrote me a note or stopped me on the street to ask, "So, where's the next book?" Here it is.

PROLOGUE

Springport, Pennsylvania
July 29, 1974
The height of the oil crisis

The sisters sat on the wide front steps of their soon-to-be old house and watched. The older girl, almost twelve, had willed herself not to cry, but she couldn't stop her cheeks from burning with rage. Her sister, two years younger, wasn't able to quell the flow of tears down her cheeks, which were also bright red, but from shame, not anger. The repo men studiously avoided their eyes as they walked back and forth between the house and the van, loading it with their bikes, their ice skates, even the old stuffed bears that still slept on their twin beds out of inertia more than any need.

When she saw them taking her microscope kit, along with the specimen slides she'd spent the whole last year collecting and mounting, the younger girl lost what little control she had over her emotions and let out a pained wail. The cry drew the attention of their mother, who had been taking great care in loading the trunk of the borrowed station wagon with her family's heirlooms—the only possessions they owned that their father hadn't pledged in a fruitless attempt to save his oil-fired furnace business. Their mother laid her grandmother's jewelry box on the cloth she'd had to borrow from the family's former maid along with the car—even their linens had been taken by the note holder—and rushed over to the steps.

"Stop it," the older girl hissed, annoyed that they were drawing the attention of creepy D.J. McAllister across the street, whose smirk gave away his feigned ignorance of what was happening to his neighbors. One thing the girls wouldn't miss about their house was the presence of Daniel, Jr., or D.J. nearby. His good breeding, as their mother liked to call it, wasn't strong enough to outweigh his teenage hormones, and it totally grossed them out the way he leered at their mom in her hot pants.

The girl struggled to catch her breath between sobs. The older girl was about to give her arm a good, painful pinch to distract her, when a white satin-covered book peeking out of the crook of one of the men's sweaty arm caught her eye.

"Mom," she shouted, as her mother came over to put a comforting arm around her still-bawling sister, "they're taking my diary!" She had the little gold key hidden in the pocket of her jean shorts, but everybody knew all you needed was a bent bobby pin to pop the cheap lock. That book contained her private thoughts. Including the way looking at creepy D.J. sometimes made her feel funny. She'd die if anyone ever read it. "This is bullshit!"

"Language," her mother said in a firm voice. Then, a second later, "No, you're right, this is bullshit." She marched over and tapped the repo man on the shoulder.

He turned. "Yes, ma'am?"

"Do you really think it's necessary to take my daughter's diary? It has no resale value. This is just cruel."

They watched while the man weighed this, looking at the shiny white book in his arm. He shrugged and handed it over. "You're right, I guess."

The girl ran up and snatched it from her mother's hands and clutched it to her chest. Her mother didn't even try to remind her to say thank you. Manners were worthless in their situation.

The man's eyes shifted to the younger sister, still crying on the stairs.

"I guess it's only fair if she gets to pick out one thing to keep, too, huh? It's not their fault, after all."

"No, no, it's not," their mother agreed. "This is their father's fault."

She motioned for the girl to come join them, and she did, still sniffling.

"What do you want to keep?" the repo man asked, eager to get this over with.

"My microscope, please," she muttered.

"Ah, jeez, that looks expensive."

"It's really not," her mother explained, "it's just a junior kit. She's worked so hard on her slides."

Her mother reached out and traced a finger along the man's bare arm.

"Please?" she said her voice breathy and low.

The man glanced over at their father, who sat staring up at their mansion, oblivious to everything but his own pain, and then back at their mother.

The girl held her breath and hoped he'd say yes. Finally, he did.

"Okay, sure."

She ran over and grabbed the microscope and her slides from the carton on the curb before he could change his mind.

Her mother's hand lingered on his arm. "How can I ever thank you?"

He looked away and continued down the steps like it had never happened.

The girls hugged their mother tight, and they walked together to the glider under the big red maple tree in the front yard and waited for the nightmare day to end.

~ ~ ~ ~ ~ ~ ~ ~ ~ ~

As it turned out, that nightmare day was just the beginning. Within three months of losing the gracious Victorian mansion with its turrets and hidden passages, they'd go on to lose the double-wide trailer their parents had rented on a patch of weeds outside of town. While their mother had taken in sewing and done babysitting to earn what money she could, and they'd traded riding lessons and the latest fashions for nasty hand-me-down clothes from the Salvation Army, their dad had just sat in a lawn chair in front of the trailer and done . . . nothing. Until two days before Halloween, when he'd finally done something: He'd drunk most of a bottle of Wild Turkey, then he'd pointed the barrel of their neighbor's hunting rifle into his mouth and pulled the trigger.

"The coward's way out," their mother had shouted when she found his bloodied, faceless form, already swarming with ants and grosser insects by the time they'd returned from the food pantry with their bags of government cheese and generic soups.

With no life insurance proceeds, thanks to the suicide exclusion, they couldn't pay the rent, let alone afford to bury the man who'd led them to this place. They moved into a cramped studio apartment with thin walls and low water pressure, where they lived for free in exchange for their mother acting as the super for the building. The three of them slept in one room, which they called the bedroom despite it lacking a bed. They ate meat once a week, on Wednesdays, right in the middle, and the girls learned how to sew well enough to turn their thrift store donations into something resembling fashionable clothes.

The older girl wrote every day in the white diary, until the day she turned eighteen and ran off with the man who would turn out to be her first of several husbands, leaving it behind on the dresser she shared with her sister and mother. Her sister never left the microscope behind. When she went off to college in Ohio on a scholarship, the microscope was nestled on the bottom of the one cardboard *box she took with her, wrapped in a sweater her mother had crocheted.*

1.

Firetown, Pennsylvania
The present day
Monday, 4:30 a.m.

JED CRAYBILL STARED UP AT his ceiling and waited. Tall orange flames licked the sky, reflected in his bedroom window. The flares of gas whooshed as loud as any airplane. With each *whoosh,* the floorboards shook and his bed rocked back until the headboard hit the wall behind him.

He'd known for months that this night was coming: after a well pad was completed, the controlled burn off of surface gas began. The fires would burn day and night for days, maybe better than a week. All the while, the smell of methane would fill the sky like a low-lying cloud and seep in through his walls.

The gas company had been busy since the fall, working to create a well pad on the edge of his neighbor's lot. First it was the incessant buzz of chainsaws, as they downed the old walnut trees. Then the chippers. Next the bulldozers came, and with them, the huge lights, so they could work through the night, moving the earth so it could be leveled. Trucks rumbled along the road, gears shifting, doors slamming, loud voices calling to each other, around the clock. All working toward this day.

He was just glad Marla hadn't lived to see it. She'd always been a light sleeper. The slightest noise, even the wind in the trees, used to wake her. Toward the end, the only respite she'd had was a sound sleep.

He was the opposite. Even the flares, with their noise, light, and stink wouldn't have kept him awake if he'd been able to fall asleep in the first place. But he had bigger problems than his idiot neighbors letting the gas company rape their land, and he couldn't seem to quiet his mind.

He lay there and waited for the weak April sun to peek over the mountains and paint the sky a faded pink. Then, he'd shower, dress, and make his stand.

2.

Clear Brook County Courthouse
Springport, Pennsylvania
Monday morning

JUDGE PAULSON GLARED DOWN FROM the bench at the attorney opposing Sasha McCandless's motion to compel discovery.

"The Court will not tolerate such behavior going forward, Mr. Showalter. Your client will produce the electronic messages it has withheld by the end of this week in digital format or face monetary sanctions for discovery abuses. Are we clear?"

Drew Showalter bobbed his head but didn't meet the judge's eyes. "Crystal, your honor."

The judge turned to Sasha. "Anything else, Ms. McCandless?"

She glanced down at her legal pad. She'd made and won all of her points. But, she saw no reason to squander an opportunity. She drew herself to her full four feet, eleven and three-quarters inches in height and said, "Your honor, VitaMight requests that this Court award it its attorneys' fees and costs in preparing and arguing this motion."

Maybe she could get VitaMight's commercial landlord to foot the bill for her prep work, not to mention the seven-plus hours round-trip travel time they'd have to pay her for driving all the way up to northern Pennsylvania to argue the motion. VitaMight would be impressed.

Judge Paulson, however, was not.

"Let's not get greedy, Ms. McCandless. Denied. We're done here, counsel."

He made no move to leave the bench, though.

Showalter ducked his head, tucked his lone folder under his arm, and hurried past Sasha, mumbling that he'd forward her the files.

Sasha smiled, savoring her victory, while she crammed her binders and legal pads back into her leather bag.

She paused long enough to think that, just maybe, if Showalter had placed as much importance on preparation as he apparently did on traveling light, his argument might not have been so laughably bad. His claim that his client, a commercial properties investment trust with diverse holdings, lacked the ability to search its e-mails was a pretty pathetic defense. Almost as pathetic as his client's abrupt decision to terminate VitaMight's long-term lease of a distribution warehouse for no apparent reason.

And that uncharitable thought, she later decided, was her undoing.

If she had just shoved her papers into the bag and gotten out of the courtroom a few minutes sooner, she wouldn't have been at counsel table when the red-faced old man came shuffling through the wide oak doors. But she hadn't, and she was.

So, when he banged through the bar separating the gallery from the well of the courtroom, she had the bad luck to be directly in Judge Paulson's line of sight.

"Harry, you old bastard! What do you think you're doing?" The elderly man crossed the well, waving a fistful of papers at the bench.

The deputy leaning against the wall next to the American flag made a halfhearted motion toward his gun, but the judge waved him off.

"Mr. Craybill! Step back!" Judge Paulson leaned forward and warned him, but the old man didn't stop.

"I'm no more incompetent than you are. Who's responsible for this?"

Judge Paulson caught Sasha's eye and motioned for the man to stop talking.

"Mr. Craybill, do you have counsel?"

"What?"

"An attorney to represent you in your incapacitation hearing, Jed."

"You know damn well, I can't afford an attorney, you no-good . . ."

Judge Paulson spoke right over the tirade. "Ms. McCandless, congratulations. The court hereby appoints you counsel to represent Mr. Craybill in the hearing on the county's motion to have him declared incompetent and have a guardian appointed to handle his affairs."

She opened her mouth to protest, and Craybill wheeled around and glared at her.

He turned back to the bench and said, "Her? She can't be old enough to be a lawyer, for crissake, look at her."

Sasha's cheeks burned, but she saw her opening and took it.

"Your honor, it sounds like Mr. Craybill here isn't pleased with the appointment. And, frankly, your honor, I have no experience in elder law. That, coupled with the fact that my office is nearly four hours away in Pittsburgh, leads me to regretfully decline your kind offer."

"It's not an offer, Ms. McCandless. It's an order. Old Jed here'll come around. He might even say sorry for insulting you." The judge stared at her over his half-moon glasses.

She caught herself before a sigh escaped. "Yes, your honor."

The judge turned to the old man and said, "Now, tell your new lawyer you're sorry, Jed."

The man muttered something that may have been an apology, although Sasha was sure she heard "featherweight" and "child" in there somewhere.

Looking pleased with himself, the Honorable Harrison Paulson unfolded his legs and stood to his full height of nearly six and a half feet. He headed toward the door to his chambers.

"Your honor," Sasha said, as he walked away, "when do I need to return for the hearing?"

She figured she could get that information from her new client, but she hoped if the hearing were less than two weeks away, the judge would grant her a continuance right then and there.

Instead, he checked his watch, turned back to her, and said, "In about an hour." He pushed through the door and disappeared into his chambers while she struggled to keep her mouth from hanging open.

Sasha's new client lowered himself in the empty chair at counsel's table and tossed the petition seeking to have him declared incompetent on the table in front of her, while Sasha stood staring at the space the judge had just vacated.

An hour? How was she supposed to get ready for an incapacitation hearing in one hour? Sasha prided herself on her composure in the courtroom. But her calm demeanor came because she over-prepared. In the sort of cases she handled, the victor almost always was whichever party's attorney was more prepared. So her rule was to prepare her case until she was sure she could handle every foreseeable issue, answer every question the judge could conceivably ask, and remove any doubt about her client's argument and then prepare some more. An hour was barely enough time to read and digest the petition and whatever exhibits came with it. She checked the clock. Make that fifty-nine minutes.

She flung herself into the empty chair and skimmed the petition's opening paragraph to find the statute under which the county was acting and then thumbed the citation into her Blackberry. She scanned the statute, reading as fast as dared to take in the gist of the act without getting bogged down in the details. Once she had an understanding of the requirements the county would have to meet to have Craybill declared incompetent and a guardian appointed, she powered off her phone and looked at the man sitting next to her.

"Let's grab a bite and you can fill me in on what's going on," she said as she gathered her papers and headed out of the courtroom. She'd left Pittsburgh before five a.m. and was going on nothing but black coffee.

Craybill eyed her. "We don't have any health food places in town."

"How about a diner that serves breakfast all day?"

He managed a small grin, like it was a struggle to remember how to smile. "Yeah, we got a diner."

He followed her out of the courtroom.

3.

THE DINER SAT ACROSS THE square from the courthouse. Craybill led her to a worn faux leather booth in the front window of the building.

Through the streaked glass, she could see the late morning sun glinting off the statue of Lady Justice that stood atop the courthouse's clock tower. She squinted at the clock's hands.

"We need to be back in court in forty-five minutes. Does this place have fast service?"

He shrugged and looked around. "You see a crowd?"

They were the only customers.

A waitress appeared, pen already poised over her order pad. The name tag on her white shirt read "Marie." She mumbled a hello and said, "What'll it be?"

Sasha looked at the tabletop. Napkin dispenser, salt and pepper shakers, and a plastic tower holding sugar packets were lined up under the windowsill. No menus.

"Do you have menus?"

Marie sighed and launched into a spiel she didn't seem to relish. "No, honey, I'm afraid we don't. Bob's Diner is about to have new ownership. The Café on the Square is having menus printed to highlight our new, locally-sourced, farm-fresh cuisine."

Craybill barked out a laugh. A look from Marie cut it short.

"Uh, okay," Sasha said and took a shot at a dish she assumed every diner in America served. "I'll have a feta and spinach omelet and whole wheat toast. A side of bacon."

Marie scribbled it all down. Sasha felt like she'd just aced an exam.

"Drink?"

"Coffee. And a glass of water."

Marie stopped writing. "You don't want the water, honey."

"I don't?"

"No, you don't. Our locally-sourced water is brown and tastes like crap."

Craybill swallowed another laugh.

"Oh. Then, I guess I don't," Sasha agreed. "But, isn't the coffee made with that water, too?"

"Sure is. That tastes like crap, too, but at least it's supposed to be brown. You want it?"

She didn't have much of a choice. If she didn't get some more caffeine flowing through her bloodstream, she'd have a pounding headache within the hour.

"I guess so."

Craybill clucked at her decision then told the waitress, "I'll have oatmeal. Tell that inebriate in your kitchen to make it with milk, now. You hear? And an orange juice. A tall one. My lawyer's paying."

Marie nodded her approval. "This little thing's your lawyer, Jed? Who you suing?"

"Nothing like that, Marie. Just a misunderstanding, but we've gotta be in front of Judge Paulson at eleven o'clock, so make sure our food comes out quick, you hear?"

Marie tucked her order pad into her apron pocket, slid her pen behind her ear, and headed off to the kitchen without making any promises.

"What's wrong with the water?" Sasha said to her client.

"What?"

"The water. Why does a place called Clear Brook County have brown, foul-tasting water?"

Craybill frowned. "Are we gonna talk about the water or this bullshit petition?"

"Sure, okay."

She really did want to know about the water. Growing up, her father and brothers used to drive up from Pittsburgh every spring to fish in a lake outside of the town, while Sasha and her mother went to the ballet back in Pittsburgh. Her brothers would come home with coolers full of trout and pictures of water so blue it actually glittered. But, her client was right, they didn't have time. She needed to walk through the petition with him— mainly so she could judge for herself if she thought he was mentally incapacitated, as the county's department of aging services claimed in its papers. Sasha took out her legal pad and looked through her notes on the requirements to have a person declared incapacitated.

"First off, do you understand what this petition is all about?"

Craybill nodded, "Yeah, those rat bastards at Aging Services want to put me in a home." He rapped his knuckles on the Formica tabletop for emphasis.

Sasha shrugged. He wasn't far off.

"Well, the petition says you live alone and have no known heirs. Is that right?"

"Yup," he nodded, as Marie returned and placed a tall, hard plastic cup of orange juice on the table in front of him. A saucer holding a chipped white mug of coffee, steam rising off it, followed.

Marie looked at Sasha. "You're not going to want to take that black, hon." She set a pitcher of cream down beside the mug. "I'll be right back with your food."

Craybill took a long drink of his juice. Sasha contemplated her coffee; it looked like coffee. She picked it up and sniffed it cautiously. It smelled like coffee. She poured a liberal dose of cream into the mug, just in case.

"So, no kids, no nieces or nephews, no one?" she said.

"Right," he confirmed. "My wife, Marla, died last year. We never had children. My brother Abe, rest his soul, he was, you know, queer. Marla has a sister, but they didn't talk, because of Abe. I don't know if she's alive or dead or had any children, but as far as I'm concerned, she's no one to me. No, it was just me and Marla."

He looked past her, out the window and smiled to himself. Sasha scribbled a note.

"What's her name?"

"Who?" He turned back to her suddenly, like she'd startled him.

She tried to keep the impatience out of her voice. "Marla's sister."

"I just told you. She's no one to me. If she's even alive. Petty, small-minded witch that she was."

Sasha exhaled slowly. "Look, I understand why you and your wife cut off contact with her sister if she had a problem with your brother's sexual orientation. But, the county's required to list any known adult presumptive heirs, and they haven't listed her. Now, did Marla cut her sister out of her will?"

"Yup. That's more or less an open secret round these parts."

"I assume she's not named in your will?"

"You got that right."

"Okay, then, I guess I don't need to know her name, strictly speaking, but it could be useful to know if she's out there somewhere."

She looked at him calmly, willing him to just tell her his sister-in-law's name.

He stared back at her.

She took a sip of her coffee. It was hot and weak, like diner coffee usually was, but the cream hid anything beyond that.

He thumped his hand against the table again. "Rebecca. Rebecca Plover."

She wrote it down.

"Great. Thanks."

Marie was back, bearing a bowl of oatmeal in one hand and the omelet, toast, and bacon in the other. Sasha waited until the clatter of dishes had stopped then asked for some hot sauce.

Marie pulled a small bottle out of her apron pocket and handed it to her, and then she slapped the bill face down in the table.

"You all pay that whenever you want, but I sure don't want to make you late for court."

Sasha watched her walk away while Craybill dug in to his oatmeal.

She glanced back at the clock. Twenty-five minutes left to interview her client, eat, and prepare some kind of argument.

Her stomach churned. There were attorneys who practiced this way. She wasn't one of them.

Until just a few months ago, she'd been practicing at Prescott & Talbott— one of the largest, oldest, most prestigious law firms in the state. Her experience was in complex litigation. Businesses suing each other over broken deals, companies being sued by shareholders or customers. Big, messy, complicated cases that took years to go to trial. She was good at that. Hell, she was great at that.

In contrast, she had no idea how to represent the alleged incapacitated person at a hearing in Orphan's Court. Truth be told, she'd rather go into the kitchen and sling out breakfast orders. Which was saying something, considering she couldn't scramble an egg.

Fake it till you make it, her late mentor, Noah Peterson, used to tell her. His death was a large part of the reason that she'd left the firm and was now sitting across a sticky table in a run-down diner four hours from anywhere.

She shook her head. No time for this now. She pushed thoughts of Noah and Prescott & Talbott from her mind.

Craybill watched her, with a blob of congealing oatmeal clinging to his lower lip.

She dabbed at her own lips with her paper napkin, but he didn't take the hint.

"You have a little, uh, oatmeal," she said, pointing to her mouth.

He narrowed his eyes and wiped his mouth.

"So, what? Some oatmeal on my lip? Does that make me a drooling idiot?"

She resisted the urge to massage her temples and smiled too brightly.

"Of course not. I'd want you to tell me, though. Moving on. The petition says just after the first of this year, the Department of Aging Services received an anonymous report that you were unable to care for yourself. Any idea what that's about?"

He scowled. She waited while he rolled back through the months. It was early April now, so it'd been over three months since the report.

"Well, shoot," he finally said, "I did fall out back. Can't say for sure when it was. There was snow on the ground. I was chopping firewood and . . ."

She cut him off. "You chop your own firewood?"

"Yeah."

She checked his address on the petition. Rural Route 2, Firetown.

"You don't live here in town?"

"No. I have a place in Firetown."

He said it with a short final syllable—Firetin.

It sounded remote.

"You live alone out there?"

"Since Marla died, yeah."

"Okay, so you fell . . ." she prompted him.

"Uh-huh. Got distracted watching a truck bounce down the road that runs by my place, a water truck going way too fast for conditions. Anyway, I slid on a patch of ice, I reckon. Bruised my hip and twisted my wrist."

She took notes as fast as she could, in her own abbreviated style. She'd come up with it in law school and it had served her well in practice, too.

"So, did you seek medical treatment?"

He shrugged. "Not really. I mentioned it to Doc Spangler when I ran into her at the gas station. She took a quick look, out by the pumps, and said it was probably a sprain. I wrapped it in an ace bandage for a while and took some Tylenol for a few days, but that was it."

"Is Doctor Spangler your personal physician?"

She chased the last bits of egg around her plate with a piece of toast while he explained.

"She's the only doctor right in town. I guess that makes her my doctor. But the last time I went to see her for a real appointment, was, I don't know . . . four or five years back. I'm healthy as a horse. She took care of Marla, though."

Sasha looked down at her notes. She was willing to bet the doctor, as a mandatory reporter under state regulations, had felt she was required to report the fall to the Department of Aging Services. Aging Services. What a name, she thought. It sounded like they helped you get older.

She looked up at the clock tower once more. Fifteen minutes until show time, and she had no sense of who her client was, what he wanted, or whether he was completely out of his gourd.

"Okay, the way the statute works is the lawyer for the Department of Aging Services will explain to Judge Paulson why they think you aren't competent to care for yourself. They have the burden of proof. Now, they've asked for plenary, or complete, guardianship, which would give them the right to make decisions about your finances, your health, everything. The statute prefers a limited guardianship, which means the Judge can appoint a guardian to help you out with specific issues, like money, if he thinks you need some assistance but aren't completely incapacitated. Are you with me?"

She watched his eyes, looking for comprehension, but all she saw was anger. And lots of it.

"Listen, girlie. I don't want any help. I want to be left alone. I want to die in my own goddamn house when it's time. Are you with me?"

Sasha nodded. She felt a swell of compassion for the old man, but she wasn't going to make any promises.

"We'll see what we can do, Mr. Craybill."

She put a twenty down on top of the bill and started packing up.

"Let's go."

~ ~ ~ ~ ~ ~ ~ ~ ~ ~ ~

Five minutes before the hour, Sasha and Jed settled in at the same counsel table they'd vacated an hour earlier.

Technically, Sasha should have moved to the defendant's table across the room because she was no longer representing the moving party. The movant—the party with the burden of proof—customarily took the table closest to the jury box. It was one of those formalities that no one told young lawyers about until they unknowingly violated it.

But, Jed had eased himself into the chair before she'd had a chance to explain the seating arrangement, and, from what she'd seen, practice in Springport seemed to be on the casual side. Not to mention, the breach of protocol might just get under opposing counsel's skin. Always a plus.

The courtroom door eased open, flooding the room with light and the sound of chatter from the hallway. A thin, tanned man with a neatly trimmed beard slipped through the doors. He wore a navy suit and a red and blue striped tie. His wire-rimmed glasses reminded her of a professor, which Sasha assumed was the intended effect.

He stopped beside the table. His eyes flicked from Jed to Sasha and then back again.

"Mr. Craybill," he said, nodding at the old man.

Jed ignored the greeting.

Sasha stood and extended her hand. "I'm Sasha McCandless, Mr. Craybill's court-appointed attorney."

He pumped her hand in a quick, firm shake.

"Marty Braeburn," he said. Then he gave her a little frown. "I wasn't aware Judge Paulson appointed counsel."

Sasha smiled. "I was appointed this morning."

"Ah," Braeburn nodded. "Where did you say you practice?"

"I didn't. My office is in Pittsburgh. I was before the judge this morning on a discovery motion in another case."

"Pittsburgh," Braeburn repeated, clearly speaking to himself.

He glanced up at the clock mounted above the bench and then said, "We have a few minutes before the hearing starts. Let's step out into the hall, shall we?"

He looked meaningfully at Jed, who had been glaring at him without blinking.

Sasha whispered to Jed that she'd hear what Braeburn had to say and be right back.

He shifted his eyes from the county attorney to hers and nodded. "But no deals," he whispered back.

Braeburn held open the gate separating the well from the gallery. As she passed by him, he said in a friendly voice, "Oh, by the way, I didn't want to embarrass you in front of your client, but you're sitting at the wrong table."

She allowed herself a small smile. The fact that Braeburn had bothered to mention it was proof it nettled him, and his tone told her he had decided she was inexperienced and inconsequential. Just the way she liked it.

A scene from some Monty Python movie flashed into her mind. She'd briefly dated an insurance adjuster named Clay, or maybe it was Ken? Whichever. He was a huge fan of British comedy and acted like she'd told him she didn't bathe regularly when she'd confessed to having never seen any of the Monty Python skits. So, of course, he showed up at her condo with a stack of videos. The only part that had stuck with her had been the Killer Rabbit of Caerbannog skit, where the knights were terrified of a vicious monster that guarded a cave—she'd dozed off during the DVD and had awoken to see the knights dismissing the creature as a threat because it turned out to be a rabbit. The rabbit then attacked and decapitated one of them, then killed two other knights. She still didn't understand how the skits were even remotely funny, and the Anglophile insurance adjuster was barely even a memory. But, every once in a while, either in court or during a Krav Maga session, she thought of herself as that bunny. A ferocious, killer bunny.

Out in the hallway, Braeburn led her over to the far wall and leaned against a large rectangular window with an arched top. The sill looked grimy, but the window itself was solid. Sasha would've wagered it was original to the building.

Braeburn ducked his head and spoke in a soft voice, just above a whisper. "I'm not sure how these hearings are handled down in Allegheny County, but your role here is more or less a formality, for appearance's sake."

Sasha raised a brow. "Oh, really?"

He rushed to add, "You see, Judge Paulson just likes to be squeaky clean. You may not realize this, but the statute doesn't mandate the appointment of counsel for the incapacitated person. That's left to the court's discretion. And, really, it isn't usually necessary."

"Allegedly incapacitated person."

"Pardon?"

"You just referred to my client as the incapacitated person. That's not been determined. You've alleged it."

She smiled up at him and wondered if he saw her sharp bunny fangs for what they were. Probably not yet. But he would.

Braeburn started to frown, then caught himself and smoothed his expression into something neutral, if not exactly pleasant.

"See now, that's what I'm saying. It is not customary in this county for an incapacitation hearing to be adversarial, Ms. McCandless. Our court-appointed attorneys generally understand that the Department of Aging Services always has the best interests of the *allegedly* incapacitated person firmly in mind. They recognize that these people are the experts. If you oppose this petition, you won't be doing Mr. Craybill any favors. He's a sick old man who needs help."

Sasha considered her response. Braeburn was letting her know the local attorneys—and there couldn't be many of them—rolled over for one another at these hearings. She could see how that kind of back-scratching might take hold in a community with a small bar.

Pittsburgh, in contrast, had a large and active bar. In fact, Allegheny County had one of the highest concentrations of attorneys per capita in the nation; the bar approached ten thousand practicing attorneys. Mainly, because Pittsburgh was the kind of city newcomers moved into gladly but natives had to be dragged kicking and screaming to leave. She was a case in point.

No lawyer in Pittsburgh would dare do what Braeburn was proposing, unless he or she was a fool. Even if a lawyer was inclined to do it, the competition for clients was so fierce and the risk that another lawyer would get wind of the situation and make a bar complaint was too great.

Braeburn may not have known it, but Judge Paulson had to have realized that Sasha wouldn't be inclined to play ball when he appointed her. Yes, she'd been in the wrong place at the wrong time. But, Sasha was certain a call from the county's only judge would have sent any one of the local lawyers flying over to the courthouse to take Jed's case. She had to believe the judge had appointed her counsel precisely because she was an outsider.

Braeburn stared at her, waiting.

Sasha sighed. In the end, it didn't matter what Judge Paulson knew or thought he knew about her when he ordered her to represent the angry old man storming his courtroom. She was who she was. She hadn't changed that for one of the largest, most prestigious law firms in Pittsburgh and she sure wasn't about to change it for some part-time county solicitor.

"If, in fact, it is in Mr. Craybill's best interests to have a guardian appointed, then I'm sure you'll have no problem meeting the burden of proof on that issue. If the experts at the Department of Aging Services can satisfy the court that Jed Craybill is incapacitated, it won't much matter if I oppose your petition, now will it?" she said.

"But . . . you aren't going to consent?" Braeburn's voice cracked.

"No, Mr. Braeburn," she said as evenly as she could manage, "you're going to have to make your case."

She stepped past him and walked back into the courtroom.

The sleepy-eyed deputy had resumed his post alongside the flag, so she knew Judge Paulson would be making his entrance soon.

She hurried to the table and gave Jed's arm a reassuring squeeze as she took her seat. Once she was settled, she leaned over and whispered, "He wanted us to consent to the appointment of a guardian so they wouldn't have to present their case. Either there are a lot of backroom deals around here or he's worried he can't meet his burden."

Jed nodded. "Probably both."

The door from the hallway swung open and Braeburn trotted down the aisle. Sasha was delighted to notice that his cheeks were flushed with either anger or embarrassment. She hoped both.

Braeburn looked over at her. She could tell he was weighing whether to force the issue and make her switch tables. She half hoped he'd do it, but he stood there for a minute and then dropped his files on the defendant's table. He took his seat just in time to pop out of it when the door from chambers opened and Judge Paulson swept into his courtroom.

"All rise. The Honorable Harrison W. Paulson presiding."

Usually, a courtroom became a stage after the deputy opened court. In most courtrooms, in most cases, the judge and the attorneys were actors. Everyone knew both their lines and everybody else's lines, and there were no surprises. Unless someone deviated from the script. Even then, though—say, a witness got rattled and started babbling something other than the answers the attorney had rehearsed with her or an expert suddenly backed away from his opinion right there in open court—a decent lawyer could do damage control. Ask a gentle leading question to get the witness back on track or introduce a document to shore up the opinion. Whatever. This hearing, however, was going to be more like a night of improv than a well-rehearsed show.

Braeburn wasted no time derailing the proceedings. As soon as the judge read the caption into the record, before he could even ask Braeburn to present his case, the county attorney leaned forward, his hand holding his tie flat against his chest, and cleared his throat.

"If I may, your honor? The Department of Aging Services has just learned that Mr. Craybill is not going to consent. In light of this eleventh-hour ambush. . . ." He paused here to shoot Sasha a look, then he continued, "The County respectfully requests a continuance to prepare its case."

The judge frowned down at Braeburn. He turned to Sasha but kept the frown in place.

"Ms. McCandless, what do you have to say for yourself?"

Sasha blinked. Was this guy for real?

The judge moved his chin, just the barest bob, motioning toward the court reporter, as if to say, come on, now, play along for the record.

She searched her brain for a non-sarcastic response.

"Well, your honor, it's true that Mr. Craybill does not consent to having a guardian appointed. As for counsel's dramatic claims of ambush, I don't know what to say. It's his petition. He shouldn't have filed it until he was ready to have it heard."

She decided not to mention that she had been representing her client for all of one morning, as the court well knew, and couldn't have provided notice any sooner. Judges tended not to like it when you sullied the record with facts that made them look bad.

Judge Paulson looked at her with no expression. "Anything else?"

Sasha thought.

And then it hit her. "Actually, yes, your honor. Even if Mr. Craybill were to consent, which, again, to be clear, he does not—but if he did, that consent could not be valid. If he is incompetent in the eyes of the law, then, without question, he's not competent to consent."

The judge smiled and said, "That's an interesting point, Ms. McCandless. I have to agree. It makes one pause and wonder what the attorneys who ask their clients to consent to a finding of incompetence are thinking, doesn't it, Mr. Braeburn?"

Braeburn's face tensed. Sasha watched his pulse throb in his neck. Judge Paulson's eyebrows crept up his forehead as he waited.

Braeburn smoothed his tie. Picked up his pen. Put down his pen. Finally, he said, "Your honor, I am not aware of any case law holding that a consented-to guardianship is prima facie invalid."

Weak sauce, Sasha thought. Judging by the snort Jed let out and the expression on the judge's face, she was not alone.

Judge Paulson shook his head. "That's not particularly responsive, Mr. Braeburn; nor is it particularly persuasive. Regardless, your request is denied. Let's get started, shall we?"

Braeburn looked around the courtroom but found no help in the empty gallery. He squared his shoulders and said, "Respectfully, your honor, the Department of Aging Services believes its petition sets out the grounds for declaring Mr. Craybill incapacitated and appointing a guardian."

Braeburn looked up at the judge, expectant and eager. The judge looked back at him for a long moment.

"And?"

"Your honor?" Braeburn asked, blinking.

Judge Paulson sighed. "Marty, obviously the county thinks Mr. Craybill needs to have a guardian appointed. How about telling me the basis for that opinion?"

Braeburn stammered. "Respectfully, judge, the petition . . . well, it speaks for itself."

Sasha rolled her eyes. Lawyers loved to say that documents spoke for themselves. It was a meaningless, nonsensical statement. What they meant was a written document was the best evidence of its own contents, but that, too, was a pretty meaningless point to make.

Judge Paulson's brows came together in an angry vee. "Counselor, are you telling me you aren't prepared to introduce anything into evidence? You want to rely solely on the contents of your petition to make your case? No witnesses?"

Braeburn failed to keep his own irritation out of his voice in his response. "Your honor, you know the folks over at the Department of Aging Services are really busy these days. I couldn't in good conscience ask a social worker to burn an afternoon sitting in court when it is so patently clear that Mr. Craybill needs to have a guardian appointed."

Jed started to rise from his seat. Sasha pushed him down firmly with one hand and stood herself.

"Your honor, Mr. Craybill requests that this petition be denied with prejudice. This is an outrage. This court cannot grant the petition without giving Mr. Craybill the opportunity to question a representative of the county agency. And where is the proposed guardian?" Sasha checked her papers for the name. "Was Dr. Spangler also too busy to waste her time in court?"

"Good question, counselor," said the judge, nodding. "Mr. Braeburn?"

Braeburn stammered. "Your honor, please. We anticipated that Mr. Craybill would consent . . ."

Judge Paulson chuckled. "Come now, Marty. If you really believed that old Jed here would consent to this, we need to have a guardian appointed for you."

His smile faded, and he leaned forward to catch the court reporter's eye. He didn't need to say anything; she nodded to let him know she'd edit the remark out of the record.

Sasha had lost count of how many times she'd ordered a transcript in state court only to find that the official record of the proceedings bore nothing more than a passing resemblance to what had actually transpired.

Braeburn straightened his sagging shoulders and tried one more angle. "The county calls Jed Craybill."

Sasha shot out of her seat. "Objection. The county can't compel my client to testify."

The judge raised one eyebrow as if he was asking her if she was sure. Of course, she wasn't sure. She had no earthly idea what she was doing. But, she did know she wasn't going to put her client on the stand to be questioned by opposing counsel. Especially not this client. She had no idea what on earth Jed would say, other than it would contain a lot of profanity. There was just no way she could allow it.

As she gathered her thoughts, Braeburn pressed on. "Your honor," he said, "that's a baseless objection. This isn't a criminal matter. Mr. Craybill has no Fifth Amendment right against self-incrimination here."

The judge nodded.

Sasha saw her opening and seized it, imaging she had Braeburn's neck in her bunny mouth and was shaking him back and forth like a ragdoll.

"First of all, Mr. Craybill hasn't invoked the Fifth Amendment. But, I note that he likely could. There is ample Pennsylvania precedent for invoking in a civil case when the witness is facing criminal charges. For example, in *McManion's Gemtique v. Diamond Dealers, Inc.*, a jewelry wholesaler was sued by a retailer for selling counterfeit rubies. An employee of the wholesaler who had participated in the criminal conspiracy invoked his Fifth Amendment privilege against self-incrimination in a civil suit brought by the jewelry store."

Even now, four years later, it burned Sasha that the court had agreed the dirty employee did not have to testify, which had made her client, the jewelry store, accept a lowball settlement offer, because the owner was afraid he wouldn't be able to prove his case without the testimony. But, the rights of the accused had trumped the right of a small business owner to be compensated for the hundreds of thousands of dollars he'd spent on red paste rubies.

Braeburn shot back.

"That is both true and irrelevant, your honor. Mr. Craybill is not—at least to my knowledge—facing criminal charges. Is there something Ms. McCandless would like to share with us?"

Braeburn glanced over at her and smirked.

"No, your honor, as far as I know, Mr. Craybill is not facing criminal charges. He is facing something much worse. Here we have an upstanding, law-abiding citizen who has worked hard his whole life. And now, simply because he is older, the county is threatening to take away his freedom for the crime of what exactly? Aging?"

Judge Paulson gave a half-nod. Sasha imagined he was thinking that Jed Craybill had, at best, five or so years on him.

Braeburn opened his mouth, but Sasha rolled right over him.

"And," she continued, "if I don't call Mr. Craybill, which I do not intend to do, the county has no right to cross-examine him. They need to be able to make their case without him. If they can't, the court should dismiss the petition."

Braeburn's mouth flew open again.

This time, the judge silenced him with his palm.

"I am inclined to agree with Ms. McCandless. However, before ruling, I would like to see briefs on the issue, as well as on the issue of whether an allegedly incapacitated person could be deemed competent to consent to the appointment of a guardian."

The judge produced an iPhone from a pocket in his robe and swiped the screen.

"Let's see. We'll want to get this resolved before trout season is in full swing, eh, Mr. Craybill?" He glanced at Sasha's client with the hint of a smile. "So, let's have the briefs contemporaneously in two weeks. No replies. Argument one month from today at 10:00 a.m. Mr. Braeburn, you're on notice that you need to show up prepared to present your case."

"Yes, judge," Braeburn said, his head down while he scribbled the dates in his datebook.

Sasha pulled out her Blackberry and thumbed in the deadlines. Then she wrote them on her legal pad. Her belt and suspenders calendaring system gave both her and her malpractice carrier a degree of comfort.

The judge stood. "On your way out, Ms. McCandless, stop by the court administrator's office on the first floor. You'll want to the get the paperwork so you can bill the county for your time. Twenty dollars an hour, by the way. Don't spend it all in one place." He chuckled and swept out of the courtroom.

Sasha packed up her bag while Jed yammered at her.

"I'll take the stand. I'm not afraid of Marty Brae-burn. He's a pencil-necked twerp if I ever saw one. I have the right to tell . . ."

Sasha shushed him as the pencil-necked lawyer approached. "We'll talk about it later, Mr. Craybill."

Braeburn looked down at her with a frown. "What a waste of resources you've caused, Ms. McCandless. Perhaps you'll take this time to recon-sider."

Jed started to push himself out of his seat. Sasha put a hand on his arm.

"Perhaps, but I wouldn't count on it." She gave the county's attorney her sunniest smile to let him know his scolding had no effect on her and went back to packing up her bag until he took the hint and walked off.

~ ~ ~ ~ ~ ~ ~ ~ ~ ~

Harry stood at his window and watched the feisty little attorney from Pittsburgh cross the square. She was moving at a good clip, he thought. Probably wanted to make it back to the city before the rush hour traffic started to clog up the roads.

He congratulated himself on his cleverness as he shed his black judicial robe, shook the wrinkles out, and hung it on the coat tree in the corner of his chambers. He loved it when a plan came together.

And this one had gone off without a hitch. As soon as the motion to compel discovery had crossed his desk, Harry had sprung into action. He'd called and checked out Sasha with some judges and lawyers he knew in Allegheny County and had gotten a unanimous report: she was a straight shooter and sharp, too. He told himself she'd be able to piece the thing together and would do the right thing.

Then, it had just been a matter of scheduling the discovery motion for the same day as old Jed's competency hearing and praying that Showalter's moronic client didn't do the right thing and turn over the e-mails before the hearing date.

Jed showing up, foaming at the mouth, had been a stroke of luck. It had saved Harry the trouble of calling Sasha in to chambers and concocting an excuse to appoint her as Jed's counsel after the discovery motion had been heard.

Her back disappeared around the corner.

She must've followed the signs to the municipal parking lot when she'd come into town, Harry thought. The municipal parking lot, with its two-dollar a day parking seemed like a bargain to out-of-towners. In reality, it was just a money grab. A relic from the past, from before Springport had re-alized its rivers ran with gold. The city council had erected the parking lot in an effort to bleed some money out of strangers who didn't realize there was ample free parking day and night in the center of the small town.

When the lot had been erected, it had seemed to epitomize cynicism and greed to Harry. Now it seemed downright quaint and innocent, given the changes in town.

The changes. Thinking about the changes in town made Harry's stomach roil. Or he was just hungry.

He took his fedora from the hat rack and shrugged into his tweed jacket. He'd step out and have a slice of pecan pie at the diner, homemade by Bob's wife. He might as well enjoy it while he could. He reflected that the money-hungry leeches who had backed Bob up against the wall and then bought him out of the diner would likely replace the pie with salted caramel gelato or some such nonsense.

He turned off his desk lamp and passed through the door to his secretary's office. Gloria looked up from her crossword puzzle.

"Judge," she nodded.

"I'm going over to Bob's," he told her. "Can I bring you back a slice of pie? Or a gob?" Gloria's sweet tooth was an open secret.

Her eyes widened, but she resisted. "No, thanks, your honor. Oh, um . . . he called again."

Harry watched as visions of sugar plum, or more accurately two chocolate cakes with vanilla filling, faded from her mind, replaced by ugly worry.

He patted her arm. "Now, don't you worry about them, Gloria. I've got it covered."

She murmured something encouraging, but he could feel her eyes, uncertain and anxious, following him as he headed out for his pie.

4.

SASHA HURRIED TO HER CAR, fueled by equal parts frustration and anxiety.

Frustrated because she'd burned the better part of the day representing a cranky old man. And instead of it being a one-time appointment, it now appeared she had an ongoing relationship with her newest client. She'd given Jed a business card and tried to get a telephone number in return. He'd claimed not to have a phone. No land line, no cell phone, no e-mail address for old Jed. So, not only would she have to come back for yet another hearing, she'd have to drive back up here to meet with Jed if she wanted to do any kind of preparation.

Anxious because she had only just gotten up to full speed. The first several months after leaving

Prescott & Talbott, she'd done all the things she'd sacrificed in her pursuit of partnership. She'd slept in, taken long weekends, and had left her office at midday to go skiing at Seven Springs. She'd helped out with the Valentine's Day party in her youngest niece's preschool class. Caught up with girlfriends she had literally not seen in years. And had thrown herself headlong into her new relationship with Leo Connelly. It had been a glorious break. But it was over.

She now had an active caseload of matters that required her attention. As a one-woman shop she couldn't afford to divert her time from her corporate clients to research esoteric points of elder law just to satisfy some judge's curiosity. Especially not at the princely sum of twenty bucks an hour—not while clients like VitaMight were paying her three fifty an hour.

What she needed was a bright-eyed, eager-to-please young associate. Someone who would view a trip to Springport as an adventure, not a giant time suck. Someone she could turn to and say, "I need you to find a case that holds an allegedly incapacitated person is not capable of providing informed consent to the appointment of a guardian." But, what she had was Winston, a virtual assistant who compiled her invoices and sent them out to clients from somewhere in Nepal while she was sleeping. It seemed unlikely he would be much help in this situation.

She would love to hand the case over to someone local, like Drew Showalter. She'd run into Showalter at the court administrator's office, while she was being instructed to fill out the form in triplicate and not to bill for travel time.

He'd been openly interested in the incapacitation proceeding, asking her how she'd been appointed, when the next hearing was, and whether she'd be back in town before then. She hadn't gotten a vibe that he'd been hitting on her, so she assumed he wanted to know how to expand his practice in Orphan's Court. She'd told him to try walking out of court more slowly, but she wished she could have just handed him the file.

She sighed and reached into her bag to pull out her parking ticket as she neared the municipal lot. The sun had disappeared behind a clot of heavy clouds and the air had gotten cool. It wasn't the kind of day that lent itself to loitering outdoors; so, the cluster of people near her car, parked at the edge of the lot adjacent to a small park, caught her eye.

Drawing closer, she realized they weren't hanging out without a purpose; they were up to something. A tight knot of two sign-waving, long-haired guys and two women with braids hanging down their backs and flowing skirts was skirting the edge of the adjacent park and chanting something about gas. Two more men were crouched beside the front of her car. She saw a flash of silver in the smaller man's hand.

"Hey!" she yelled, walking faster. "Get away from my car!"

The smaller one started and turned toward her.

"Corporate whore!" one of the women shouted from the fringe of the park.

She didn't turn toward the voice; she kept her eyes on the two men who were closer.

The taller one stood and yanked his friend to his feet. The shorter guy folded his blade and slipped it into his pocket.

The group was breaking up. The women and two of the men were drifting off to the right, headed into the park. Apparently, they weren't interested in joining their friends.

Two was better than six.

Krav Maga taught the best response to a threatened attack was prevention or avoidance. Too late for that. The next best response was escape or evasion. Only if that failed would she stay and fight. And if she fought, she'd fight to win—not something she relished. Especially not in fitted dress and heels, in a strange small town, against six people. Two guys were more manageable.

But the better course would be to get in her car and drive the hell out of town.

She aimed her remote key at the door and jabbed the button. The car beeped. And then she froze.

Flapping rubber by her left front wheel caught her eye.

She hurried to the front of the car and stooped beside the door to inspect her tire. Slashed. She turned and looked over her shoulder. The rear tire was in the same condition.

"Now what, bitch?" The taller guy laughed and whaled a handful of gravel at her as she stood. It hit the hood of the car and fell to the ground in a shower. His friend stood, frozen, arms at his side.

Sasha waited until the tall guy bent down for another fistful of rocks and made her move. She pulled the driver's door open, threw herself into the seat, slammed the door shut, and hit the lock.

She had no idea if Springport had a 9-1-1 dispatch but she took out her cell phone and keyed in the numbers anyway, tilting her rearview mirror so she could keep her eyes on the protesters or whatever they were.

"Nine-one-one. What's your emergency?"   A male voice, crisp and alert filled her ear.

"I'm in Springport. At the municipal parking lot. A group of—uh, I don't know—activists is here.

They slashed my tires. Most of them have run off, but there are two men. One is throwing rocks."

"Ma'am, Springport Township does not have a local police department. That area is served by the State Police out of Dogwood. I need to contact their dispatch. Please hold." The phone clicked in her ear as he placed her on hold.

Sasha gritted her teeth. The Commonwealth of Pennsylvania's patchwork of home-rule counties, townships, and municipalities was many things. Efficient was not one of them.

Hurry, she thought, as the phone rang. Once. Twice.

The hippies had come around to the front of her car and were staring at her through the windshield.

She stared back.

Two white males, early twenties, maybe mid-twenties at the oldest. The tall one was on the left. He was well over six feet but rail thin. Light brown hair, long, pulled back in a low ponytail. Those giant earrings that looked like black plugs in both ears. His feet were planted in a wide stance, and he'd acquired a thick tree branch from the park.

His friend was shorter, stockier, and antsier. His dark hair frizzed out around his head in a cloud and his brown eyes darted from the branch in his companion's hand to Sasha and back. He jittered from side to side in a little hop step.

Three rings. Four.

The tall guy smacked the branch against his hand.

"Come on," Sasha said aloud. "Answer the phone."

Five.

"Dogwood Station." A woman's voice this time, overworked, not interested.

"Yes. I'm being attacked in the municipal parking lot in Springport. Please send someone. I'm in the dark gray Passat in the far corner of the lot. My tires are slashed. Two men are—"

"Ma'am. Ma'am," the woman interrupted her, no longer bored, her voice full of concern. Sasha heard the clatter of keys. "The nearest unit is currently outside Firetown, approximately 25 minutes from your location. I need to put you on hold now and radio the car." The line went silent.

Within a minute, the dispatcher was back. "Officer Maxwell is en route. What's your name, ma'am?"

"Sasha McCandless. I'm . . . not local."

She'd been about to identify herself as an officer of the court but thought the better of it. She never knew how someone would react to a lawyer. A person who'd had a nasty divorce or been ordered to pay damages after a car crash could carry a grudge against the whole profession. After hearing her primary care doctor's rant against medical malpractice lawyers during her annual exam one year, Sasha had made a point of always mentioning to Dr. Alexander that she didn't do any med mal work.

"Okay, now, Sasha, you hold tight until the officer gets there. Do not exit your vehicle."

"Don't worry," Sasha said. She had no plans to get out of the car.

As the call ended, the tree branch smashed into her windshield.

Sasha flinched and braced herself, but the glass held.

The tall guy pulled back to take another swing. His friend caught his arm mid-swing.

"Jay, c'mon, let's get out of here. This is not peaceful." He was still hopping from one foot to the other, but he hung on to the tall guy's arm. His voice was strained and loud enough to hear from inside the car.

Jay tried to shake him off.

"Dude," Jay shouted at the smaller guy, "we need to stand up for Mother Earth."

His friend shook his head. "No, man, I'm out." He dropped Jay's arm and took off toward the park, kicking up gravel in his wake.

Jay watched him go and then turned back to Sasha.

He hefted the tree branch and crashed it into the windshield again. His lips were pulled back, like a wolf's, and his eyes never left Sasha's.

The stick bounced off the glass, and a web of cracks spread out in front of Sasha. The next hit would finish the job.

Sasha checked the rearview mirror. No one else in sight.

She stared at Jay through the pattern of cracks and calculated her options, ignoring the ache in the back of her head. She could turn on the ignition, gun the engine, and see how far she got on two—probably four—flat tires. But he might get the last swing in first.

Sasha sighed.

She placed her phone in the center console, unlocked the door, and stepped out.

Maintaining eye contact, she stepped around in front of the car and stood right in front of Jay, planting her feet wide and bending her knees slightly. Looked up at him and hoped his fleeing friend had the only knife.

"You want to mix it up?" He laughed. But she could hear the uncertainty behind it. This wasn't part of his plan.

She waited a beat while he tried to decide: attack a five-foot-tall, one hundred-pound woman or walk away.

"Here's what you're going to do," she told the wild-eyed man in front of her. "You're going to toss the stick at my feet and then back away slowly."

"Or what?"

She kept her voice soft and even. "Or, Jay, I am going to beat you to a bloody pulp. Then, after you've crawled away to lick your wounds, I'm going to track you down and press criminal charges against you and your friend. And, then, I'm going to file a civil lawsuit against you and beat you to a bloody pulp again in the courtroom."

He smirked at her, then feinted like he was going to drop the stick. Instead, he lunged at her, swinging it fast and wild over his head toward her.

Instinct told her to lurch back, but training told her lean forward fast. Training won out.

Block. She burst toward him, moving in close and hit his upper arm with both hands while driving a knee into his groin. A hard block. Sometimes that was all it took to disarm a person; the force from the block would drive the stick from his hands.

Not Jay. He hung on tight to the stick.

Lock. Sasha slid her left arm over his bare, hairy arm and right under his elbow, rotating his elbow up. With her left hand, she clasped her right forearm and squeezed his shoulder with her right hand. He tried to squirm free, but she pushed down firm on his shoulder as her left wrist came up under his elbow, creating a lock and immobilizing the stick.

Control. From there, she stepped forward, her legs behind his and took him down. He landed heavily on the gravel, his legs splayed out and his arm twisted up. He clawed at her with his free hand.

Strike. She grabbed the stick and wrenched it free of his hands. She popped his knee with it and then brought it up and hit him three times in rapid succession in the head. She swung in fast, short bursts.

He threw his hands over his head to shield his face.

"Had enough?" she asked, stepping back, but keeping the stick raised, ready to strike if he moved toward her.

He struggled to get up, first to his knees and then, unsteadily, to his feet. He stared at her and crabbed backward for several paces before turning and running hard toward the park.

She waited until his back had disappeared into the trees and tossed the branch to the ground. Then, she leaned against the hood of her car and waited for Officer Maxwell to show up.

~ ~ ~ ~ ~ ~ ~ ~ ~ ~

Sasha rolled her neck to the left, then to the right. She was right back in the same courthouse where she'd wasted her morning. After hearing she was an attorney returning to her car from a court appearance, Officer Maxwell had driven her straight to the sheriff's office and made her the deputy on duty's problem.

Maxwell had scanned the deputy's badge, which identified him as G. Russell, and given him an overly hearty greeting.

"Deputy Russell," he'd said, overly familiar. "Good to see you."

The deputy had eyed him from behind his desk. Finally, he'd risen from his seat and held out a reluctant hand. "Maxwell, how you doing?"

With the pleasantries out of the way, the state trooper had gotten down to business. He'd explained an officer of the court had been attacked and the sheriff's office was responsible for the primary investigation. Russell had tried to refuse her. Like she was a package he hadn't ordered. He'd claimed the sheriff's office didn't have jurisdiction. The two officers had argued back in forth in hushed tones, but in the end Maxwell had prevailed.

Deputy Russell, resigned but polite, took a long look at her and then disappeared in search of coffee. She sat back in the deputy's creaking guest chair and looked around the office. It had none of the aged glamour and charm of the county's only courtroom. Instead of burnished hardwoods and brass, the office was awash in fluorescent lights and seventies-era carpet. Russell's metal desk had seen better days. It was scratched all over and had what appeared to be a dent in the top left drawer. She leaned forward to get a closer look. It was big enough and deep enough that she wondered if it had been created by a head.

She straightened as Russell walked back into the office with two ceramic mugs and placed one on the desk in front of her.

"Sorry it took a bit," he said, pointing with his free hand at the coffee mug in front of her. "You look like you could use a fresh cup, so I made a new pot."

He raised his mug and inhaled before taking a sip. "Fair trade, shade-grown organic Cubano," he told her.

Sasha raised a brow along with her mug. She had always thought law enforcement outfits specialized in barely drinkable, burnt Folgers.

Her first swallow corrected that notion. The coffee was hot, robust, and strong. She thought she might cry from joy. As the adrenaline had drained from her body, she'd started to drag. It had been a long day. She could use a decent cup of coffee.

"Wow. Thanks."

He shrugged but couldn't hide a smile. "Coffee is sort of a hobby of mine."

She smiled back at him. "It's sort of a requirement of mine."

He cleared his throat and lowered himself into his desk chair. They drank their coffee in silence for several minutes. Russell seemed to be in no hurry to take her statement.

"Did you use tap water to make this?" Sasha wondered if the waitress at the diner had blamed the water for the coffee's taste when the culprit was more likely cheap, stale beans.

Russell knitted his eyebrows together at the question but answered it. "As a matter of fact, I didn't. The oil and gas people swear the water is fine, but I notice they all carry around bottled water. They even pitched in and got one of those water coolers and set up delivery of water for the Recorder of Deeds office since they spend so much time there. If they aren't gonna drink it, I'm not gonna drink it."

"The oil and gas people?"

Russell gestured toward the window. "You know, the Shale."

The Marcellus Shale was the thick layer of gas-rich rock running deep under most of the state—in some places, nine thousand feet below the ground. For ages, everyone had believed there was no cost-effective way to get to it, but in recent years, the oil and gas industry had begun to bore wells and pump them full of sand and water mixed with a chemical cocktail. The pressure would fracture the shale and gas would be released. And so hydrofracking was born.

In just a few years, the oil and gas companies had entered into mineral rights leases with thousands of landowners and entire swaths of Pennsylvania were dotted with wells, drilling rigs, and equipment. At first, everyone had been a fan of fracking. Environmentalists, farmers, corporations, and local politicians all gushed about the cleaner fuel, the jobs, and the money that it would pump into the towns and rural areas that dotted the state. Sasha knew several attorneys who had focused their practices entirely on oil and gas rights; they couldn't work fast enough to satisfy the demand for their services.

Fast forward four years, and the cheerleading had been replaced by yelling, finger-pointing, and lawsuits from all parties concerned. Possibly toxic wastewater was being sent to water treatment plants that weren't sure what they were getting, let alone how to handle it; gas and radioactive material had seeped into the drinking water; and homeowners were posting videos of brown water pouring from their kitchen faucets. And hydrofracking was being blamed for everything from anemic children and cancer-stricken adults to polluted fish and earthquakes.

Politicians were arguing over taxing and regulating the gas companies, and neighbors were arguing over whether hydrofracking was saving or destroying their towns. All the while, more wells were being drilled.

It had become a loud, ugly, stinking mess—literally and figuratively—as far as Sasha could tell.

"Fracking's big around here?" she asked. She'd done most of her driving before the sun had risen that morning and hadn't noticed the dark shapes of derricks looming over the farmlands that lined the highway.

Russell laughed. "I'd say so. In fact the guys who attacked you probably thought you were one of the suits."

"Suits?"

"You kind of have to see it to believe it. Come with me."

Russell drained his mug and stood. Sasha followed him through the glass door stenciled with gold lettering that read Sheriff and out into the hallway. As they followed the corridor around the corner to the left, the clacking of their shoes striking marble was drowned out by the sudden clamor of dozens of conversations drifting down the hall.

At the far end there was a door identical to the one they'd just come through, except its gold letters spelled out Recorder of Deeds. But that wasn't what Russell wanted her to see. It was the suits.

Long wooden benches flanked the door for twenty feet on each side of the hallway. The benches were packed with men, interspersed with women here and there, sitting elbow to elbow, knee to knee. They were all wearing suits, mainly black pinstripes, but there were some navy blue renegades in the mix. Rows of briefcases lined the floor at their feet. Overflow suits who couldn't find seats milled around, crowding the hallway.

From the too-hearty laugher and shouted conversations, Sasha could tell the suits weren't strangers. They also weren't friends. But it was clear they'd whiled away long hours sitting on those hard benches together. She recognized the signs of enforced camaraderie. She'd lived it, in long-running, multi-party cases where, for the first months or years, the defense group clustered together on one side of the room and the plaintiffs' attorneys kept to themselves on the other. But after the first year or two of circling around each other at depositions, hearings, and status conferences, they'd lean across the aisle and ask after one another's families. They'd share the big news—a daughter's marriage or a parent's cancer diagnosis—and the mundane news—an alma mater winning a championship or someone getting a new car—before standing up in front of the judge and accusing one another of being, at best, misguided buffoons, or, at worst, scum-sucking subhumans. Then it would be back into the hall for some more backslapping and chitchat.

As Sasha and the deputy drew closer to the office door, Sasha noticed a deli counter ticket machine resting on a table next to a water cooler.

"Is that for real?"

Russell nodded. "Yep. The oil and gas suits installed that, too. After the fire chief told them the fire code limited occupancy in the office to thirty people, it got hairy. People started camping out on the courthouse steps to be the first ones here when the doors opened. That violated the vagrancy code. Then I had to break up a fistfight when one of the gals saved another one's place in line while she used the facilities. The Recorder tried an appointment system, but these jackals kept canceling each other's appointments and signing up for seven, eight blocks of time at once. All sorts of dirty tricks.

Finally, Big Sky Energy showed up with the ticket machine. Runs a lot smoother now."

"What are they all doing here? Filing mineral rights leases?"

"This is where they file them, yeah. But the frenzy is over researching new ones. They go in there and pull old deeds from the archives to find the landowners who haven't yet signed away their mineral rights."

"At this rate, there can't be many left, can there?"

Russell gave her a resigned look. "Clear Brook County spans approximately five thousand square miles. They've barely scratched the surface."

He nodded to a few of the waiting researchers then turned to leave. "Let's call Bricker's Auto and see how they're making out on your car. Then I guess I'd better get your statement."

5.

CROSS THE STREET, DR. SHELLY Spangler walked Miriam King to the door. As she reminded the woman to check her blood sugar more frequently, she saw her sister approaching.

Shelly pasted on a smile and said goodbye to her patient.

"Oh, hi, Commissioner Price," Miriam said, excited by her brush with minor celebrity, as Heather rushed past her.

Shelly watched as her sister's political instinct kicked in, compelling her to stop and shake Miriam's hand with that two-handed clasp that all elected officials seemed to use.

She had taught her old spaniel, Corky, that trick. "Shake like a politician," she'd say, and Corky would offer up a paw, wait for Shelly to take it, then put his other paw down on top of her hand. Now, every time she saw Heather do it, she had to resist the urge to toss her a treat.

"Is my sister taking good care of you, Mrs. King?" Heather asked, radiating concern.

"Oh my goodness, yes," Miriam burbled, "I just need to lay off the pastries, I guess, right, doc?"

Shelly nodded. "You've got it," she agreed. "Now, you give Ken my regards."

As Miriam stepped out onto the sidewalk from the doctor's office, Heather swept inside, rolling her eyes.

"Perhaps a glimpse in the mirror should have clued her in to the need to lay off the pastries," she cracked, dropping the politician act to ridicule the woman waddling away.

Shelly ignored it. The easiest way to deal with Heather's mean streak was just not to feed it.

"What's the occasion?" she asked instead.

Heather rarely stopped by unannounced.

"Oh, I just wanted to check on the preparations for the grand opening. Aren't you going to be excited when I turn that dump next door into a decent restaurant?"

Shelly shrugged. Bob's served perfectly good food, as far as she was concerned, but Heather was dead set on bringing organic, locally-sourced, farm-fresh cuisine to town. It wasn't a bad idea, as many of Shelly's patients could stand to eat a healthier diet. Of course, the café wasn't for *them,* it was going to be geared to the oil and gas crowd, with their ample per diem stipends, so people like Miriam King probably wouldn't be able to afford the beet and goat cheese salad or whatever Heather was planning to serve.

Heather was waiting for an answer, her eyes narrowed to slits.

"Oh, uh, yeah, I can't wait!" Shelly enthused.

Satisfied, Heather draped herself over a waiting room chair and crossed her legs, letting her high heel shoe dangle off one foot.

Shelly sat across from her and waited. Apparently, Heather was in the mood to chat.

Heather cut her eyes to the empty reception desk. "Where's Becky?"

"I sent her out to the store. We're getting low on some office supplies."

"Did you hear about the attack?"

"What attack?"

Heather's eyes, so blue they were purple, sparked with excitement.

"Apparently, one of Danny Trees's idiot followers attacked an out-of-town lawyer with a stick in the municipal lot this morning."

"Was he badly hurt?"

"First of all, it was a she, and she wasn't, but I guess *he* was," Heather said with a laugh. "She grabbed the stick off him and beat him with it."

"Good for her!"

"Yeah," Heather agreed, "good for her. But not for you."

"What?"

Shelly's heart dropped because she had no idea where this was going, but most surprises from Heather weren't the nice kind.

"Well, Shelly, it seems Judge Paulson appointed the stick-wielding lawyer from Pittsburgh to represent Jed Craybill at his incapacitation hearing. Didn't Marty Braeburn call you?"

"No, he didn't say anything. Now, why would Judge Paulson go and do something like that?"

Shelly was annoyed, but she didn't think it was a big deal.

Her sister, however, was working herself up over it.

"I don't know, Shelly, maybe that old fool finally caught on to us. We can't afford this, you know that, right? We need that land, and we need it now."

"Calm down, Heather. Just because Jed has an attorney doesn't mean anything. Paulson will declare him incapacitated, I'll take control of the property, and we'll move forward. At most, it's a tiny delay."

"You better hope so, Shelly. That parcel is the key to the rest of our plans. Not just the wells, you know, but the hotel and all of the rest of the development. His lot abuts Keystone Property's land. His house is going to have to go; I don't want tourists to have to drive by that old shack on their approach to the resort."

Heather and her flipping hotel resort were driving Shelly crazy. Her job was to get the leases. Period. But, Heather was always yapping about building the next Nemacolin Woodlands right here in Clear Brook County. For one thing, Shelly thought Nemacolin was bizarre. There you are, just driving through Uniontown, as rural as could be, and some giant building modeled after a French castle pops up over the hill. It was off-putting if you asked her. But, of course, Heather hadn't asked her, and, as long as the money flowed in the way Heather said it would, Shelly didn't much care about the aesthetics.

"Anyway," she said, "even if the judge denies the petition, we can just appeal."

Heather shook her head so hard the Prada sunglasses perched on top wobbled.

"No, Shelly, we don't have time for appeals. Not for this, not for the declaratory judgments. Time is money. Haven't you learned that by now? I told you all along you should have gotten the county to use Drew instead of Marty for this work."

Shelly didn't want to get into it.

Drew Showalter was the county solicitor; he advised the commissioners. Heather firmly believed she controlled him through a combination of desire and fear. Shelly had no doubt Drew both wanted and feared her sister, but every once in a while she thought she saw something like regret or conscience spark in the man. Anyway, it wasn't her call. The Department of Aging Services used Marty because he was cheaper than Drew.

"Well, what does Drew say?" she asked.

"I don't know, he's always yammering about evidentiary standards and elements, four-pronged tests, yada yada. It's like he's getting paid by the word."

"He is, isn't he?"

The sisters shared a good laugh over that. Shelly was glad to have distracted her from this latest issue. Keeping Heather happy was becoming a fulltime job.

6.

BACK IN RUSSELL'S UNCOMFORTABLE CHAIR, Sasha was heartened to find her coffee still warm. She wrapped her hand around the mug while the deputy called Bricker's to see if her tires had been replaced yet. After reporting that the mechanic had replaced her windshield but had had to send someone out to Hickory to get the replacement tires, he told her it would be at least a few more hours.

"Sorry you're stuck here for a while," he said, untangling the cord to his tape recorder. He bent down and worked the plug behind his desk, feeling around for the outlet. Then he ejected the tape from the recorder, wrote her name and the date on it with his pen, and returned it to the deck. He depressed the "record" button and waited for the reel to start turning. He cleared his throat and set the recorder on the desk equidistant between them. He announced the date and her name, then gave her a smile.

"Let's do this thing," he said. "Ms. McCandless, what were you doing in town today?"

It looked like Russell was going to skip all the formalities about name, address, occupation. Sasha recognized the approach. She used it herself in depositions of fact witnesses from time to time. By adopting a conversational tone, you could make the witness forget she was being recorded. The result was more fully developed answers, because she wasn't choosing each word with care. For the first time, she got the sense that the coffee-loving deputy might actually be a skilled investigator.

"Well, I was in town for a discovery motion before Judge Paulson this morning."

"So, you're an attorney?"

"Yes. I practice in Pittsburgh."

"What firm?"

"Presc.. .," she caught herself, "The Law Offices of Sasha McCandless." The habit of identifying herself as a Prescott & Talbott attorney was dying hard.

"So, who's your client up here? And what was the hearing about?"

She hesitated then decided to answer. It was a matter of public record. "VitaMight, Inc."

He waited.

"VitaMight has a distribution center outside town. The commercial landlord, Keystone Properties, terminated the long-term lease on the property with no notice. It's a breach of the lease agreement, so we sued. The landlord has refused to turn over e-mail messages related to the lease termination, so we filed a motion to compel. The judge granted it."

She was pretty sure the attack hadn't had anything to do with the interpretation of clause 14(G)(iii)(c) of the lease, but she knew Russell had to cover all the bases.

"Why'd Keystone break the lease?"

"I honestly don't know. That's why we want the discovery—they haven't shared the basis with us."

He was silent for a minute. She watched him try to decide if there was anything more to the discovery dispute.

He looked down at his notebook, scribbled a sentence, and moved on.

"After the hearing, did you go straight to your car?"

From his tone, she knew he already knew the answer, but she hadn't told him. Probably the other deputy—the one assigned to the courtroom—had already filled him in on Jed Craybill's outburst.

"No. As I was packing up to leave, Jed Craybill burst in yelling at Judge Paulson. Somehow, when the dust settled, I'd been appointed to represent Mr. Craybill at an incapacitation hearing that was scheduled for this morning. Mr. Craybill and I went to Bob's Diner to get a bite and prepare for the hearing. At the hearing, I argued that the county failed to meet its burden to show that Mr. Craybill needed to have a guardian appointed to manage his affairs, and Judge Paulson scheduled a hearing and ordered us to brief the issue."

Russell reached out with his index finger and paused the recording. "Do you think old Jed's incompetent?"

She shrugged. "I only met him this morning. What do you think?"

He considered the question. "I think he's a cranky old coot."

He nodded and started the recording again. Sasha walked him through her visit to the court administrator's office, her conversation with Showalter, and her uneventful walk to the parking lot. Then, she gave him a blow-by-blow of the attack and described the two men to the best of her ability. Russell let her go without interruption and stopped her after she recounted Maxwell's arrival at the scene and before she could describe the jurisdictional pissing match.

"Thank you, Ms. McCandless."

He turned off the tape recorder, popped out the tape, and reached under the desk to unplug the recorder.

After depositing it back into his drawer, he leaned back, tipping his chair on two legs and regarded her.

"I don't know anyone by the name Jay or anyone who matches that description. But the guy who got cold feet, that sounds like Danny. Little guy, wild black curly hair. He's pretty much the leader of PORE."

"PORE?"

"Protecting Our Resources and the Earth," Russell said. He suppressed a chuckle. "Gotta be Danny Trees."

"His real name is Danny Trees?"

"No, his real name is Daniel J. McAllister, III. Heir to the McAllister timber fortune. But after all that timber money sent young Danny to college at Antioch, he grew quite the conscience and has devoted himself to environmental activism. He finances PORE with his trust fund."

Sasha raised an eyebrow. "What kind of organization is it?"

Russell pursed his lips and considered his answer. Finally, he said, "A disorganized organization. For a long time, PORE was just Danny and a few of his college friends wandering around, passing out flyers about reducing, reusing, and recycling. The irony of wasting paper on those flyers, which just ended up in the trash bins all over town, seemed to escape them. But once the drilling started up in earnest, Danny gained a focus. He's got a core of, oh, I'd say, twenty, protesters who were showing up at the courthouse fairly regularly to heckle the suits, until Big Sky got the county council to tell Danny his permit applications were faulty. That's when they moved down to the public park near the municipal lot. Danny's folks have also chained themselves to a derrick here or there on occasion. Nothing violent, though. Until today. Danny's no dummy, though. He reached out to some of the local fishermen, who are unhappy about what all the fracking's supposedly done to the fish. They teamed up and got a petition going. They've been going to all the county council meetings, too. It's not going to do them any good, though. Most of the commissioners own local businesses, which have seen a huge boom from the suits. The only hotel in town is booked solid through 2014. Folks are renting out their spare rooms. It's like the Olympics are in town or something."

Russell clamped his mouth shut all of the sudden, like he realized he'd been rambling. He looked up at the metal clock on the wall. "Well, you got some time to kill. Want to pay Danny Trees a visit?"

~ ~ ~ ~ ~ ~ ~ ~ ~ ~ ~

Russell brought his Crown Vic to a stop in front of an old Victorian mansion on the edge of town. The house had once been gorgeous, but its grandeur was faded. Paint peeled down from the outside walls in long, limp curls. Several ornate, hand-turned wooden spindles on the curved porch were either broken or missing entirely. And where Sasha imagined starched white lace curtains had once hung, grungy woven blankets now served as window dressing.

"This is it," Russell said, killing the engine. "The McAllister mansion. Now home to Danny Trees and PORE's headquarters. This place is on the National Registry of Historic Places."

As they stepped out of the car, Russell holstered his service weapon and radio. Sasha stared up at the blighted house.

"It's a shame."

"It is, and it isn't," Russell answered, as they picked their way across the cracked walkway, dotted with weeds. "It's a big, expensive house. To restore and maintain it would cost more than anyone around here is willing to pay. Danny may not be keeping up appearances, but he pays the taxes and hasn't let the place crumble to the ground just yet. He says it would be wasteful not to use the house, given how many trees were massacred—his word—to create it." He shrugged and pointed over his shoulder to a house directly across the street. "It's better than what happened to the old Wilson place."

Sasha turned to look. It was another Victorian, this one with a turret and wide wraparound porch. A dilapidated gazebo peeked out from the backyard, mimicking both the architecture and the current state of the home. Judging by the plywood nailed over the front entryway, and the missing glass in the front upstairs windows, it was abandoned.

"What's the story?"

Russell rested his arm against a stone lion guarding the steps from the street to the front yard. "Clyde Wilson had a prosperous home heating business in the 1950s and '60s. He installed oil-fired furnaces in a territory that covered the entire county. That's a lot of homes. But when the oil crisis hit in the '70s, he missed the handwriting on the wall. Instead of branching out into electric heat, he just clung to the idea that his market would rebound. Instead of cutting back, he continued to spend money like he had an endless supply. Anything his girls wanted, they got. His wife had family money, and they ran through it pretty quick. So, old Clyde went and got a high-interest loan and pledged everything, and I do mean everything, they owned as collateral. The bank called the loan and they lost their house, their furniture, you name it. The house was sold at auction to a developer who cut it up into apartments and rented it out. Over time, the caliber of tenants he could attract declined and it ended up, well, a flophouse. It's condemned now."

Sasha stared at the sad house. "What happened to the family?"

"They moved to the wrong side of the tracks. Clyde committed suicide and left his wife and two daughters destitute. They squeaked by, barely. The girls have done well for themselves. Their mom died a few years back."

They started up the stairs to the porch. The wood boards creaked under their feet, effectively announcing their arrival, if the presence of the sheriff's car hadn't. The wide double doors swung open, and a woman stepped out to greet them. She wore her long hair in a braid and her peasant skirt billowed out above her bare feet. Sasha recognized her from the parking lot. Judging by the spark of fear in the woman's blue eyes, she recognized Sasha, too.

"Melanie," Russell greeted her, with a tip of his deputy's hat. "Is Danny around?"

Melanie blinked and looked over her shoulder. She swallowed.

"Uh, he's in the community lounge. You wait here, okay? I'll get him." She disappeared back into the dimly lit hall, pulling the door most of the way shut, but not closing it entirely.

Sasha glanced at Russell to see if he'd follow the woman inside, but he just grinned and deposited himself into a long wooden glider by the door.

After several minutes, during which they could hear the murmur of voices floating out through the open window just behind the glider, the door reopened.

The shorter man from the parking lot came out onto the porch and pulled the door shut firmly behind him.

Russell stood. "Afternoon, Danny."

"Deputy," Danny said with a nod. He turned his attention to Sasha, "We haven't been formally introduced. Daniel J. McAllister, III." He stepped forward with an outstretched hand and a wide smile.

Sasha took his hand but didn't return the smile. "Sasha McCandless. Esquire," she added as an afterthought.

The grin faded.

"So, Danny," Russell said, "I guess you know why we're here."

"Let me start by saying I don't condone violence in our movement." His eyes darted between the two of them. He was nervous and trying to hide it.

"What do you call attacking an unarmed woman, Danny?"

He flinched. "That got out of hand, and I'm truly sorry. But, don't forget, I did try to stop Jay."

Sasha raised a brow.

"What about the vandalism, Danny? Slashing tires? Doesn't that create waste? Now four perfectly good tires are ruined." There was a hint of mockery in Russell's voice, but Danny either missed it or chose to ignore it.

"We have some new members," he told them. "Some of them don't yet understand our philosophy fully."

"That'd be this Jay character?" Russell rested a hand on the butt of his weapon.

"For one," Danny agreed.

"Who else?"

"Well, he's the main one, I guess. We have had several people join recently. None of them local. They responded to our web posting."

"Jay was one of them?"

"Yes."

"What's his last name?"

"I don't know it."

"Where's he from?"

Danny shrugged.

"Where's he staying?"

Another shrug. Russell stepped close to the smaller man and stared down at him. Waited.

"Uh, he was staying here," Danny admitted. "But, he didn't come back after the . . . uh, incident at the lot. To be honest, I figured the state police had probably picked him up and I'd be bailing him out later. What happened after I left?" He directed this last part to Sasha.

"After you fled," she said, "your new friend took another swing at my windshield, cracking it. I couldn't wait for the police any longer, so I disarmed him and beat him with his branch."

Danny swung around to Russell. "Is she serious?"

"She seems to be. Turns out Ms. McCandless here has some self-defense training. Your buddy probably has a hell of a headache right about now."

He was silent.

Russell pointed over Danny's shoulder into the house. "You know, I don't ordinarily try to enter your premises. I have no interest in harassing you and your merry band of tree huggers. However, I want to satisfy myself that you're not harboring a fugitive, which is what this Jay character is now, just so we're clear. Plus, you're going to need to get your checkbook, Danny. Ms. McCandless will take a check to cover the cost of her car repairs."

Danny opened his mouth to protest then thought the better of it. "Okay. She waits out here, though."

"Fine by me," Sasha told him, sinking into the glider. "The smell of patchouli gives me a headache."

Russell smirked at the comment and followed Danny into the house.

Sasha passed the time on her Blackberry. She texted Connelly explaining why she'd been delayed in Springport and composed an e-mail to the General Counsel and the Vice President of Operations at VitaMight to let them know they'd won the motion to compel. She was just about to call her mother to get some ideas for a birthday present for her dad, when Russell reappeared.

He was alone and holding a blank, signed check, which he folded in half and handed to her. "With Danny's sincere apologies."

She stuck it in her jacket pocket. "No sign of Jay, I take it?"

They stepped off the porch together.

"Nope. He did leave behind a duffel bag in the room he was using, but it had no identification or other items of interest. Just a tie dye t-shirt and a pair of jeans that probably could have stood up by themselves they were so dirty."

"No one else knows anything about him?"

Russell shook his head. "Danny's the only one who has any kind of focus. I don't know if the rest of them are high or lazy or what, but they couldn't agree on where this guy was from, how long he'd been here, nothing. They did say he didn't have a car. He claimed to have hitched his way in from somewhere. They were hazy as to where that was. I find that hard to believe. Not too many folks around here would stop and give a ride to a stranger. Not these days. But, if he doesn't have a ride, he won't get too far."

Russell held the passenger door open for her. "Speaking of rides, let's go see if Bricker's has yours ready yet."

7.

CARL STICKLEY WAS IRRITATED. He was the *sheriff,* dammit. *He* didn't need to be running all over the county serving eviction notices and warrants. For one thing, it was beneath him. For another, his knees were bad.

But of his two useless deputies, one had gone missing. Russell had better have a watertight excuse for this nonsense, he thought.

He'd just returned from serving a domestic relations warrant on a dirtball out in Copper Bend, and the squalor of the man's shack still clung to him. He was going to ream Russell but good when he turned up.

A light rapping at his door interrupted his musing about what he'd say to his errant deputy.

The door swung open, and Russell's flushed face peered in at him.

"Claudine said you wanted to see me, sir?"

Stickley waved a hand. "Get in here."

The deputy hurried around the door and pulled it shut behind him. He hung there, right by the door. Everyone on Stickley's staff did that: they'd just barely creep into the office and then hang back by the door. He liked it. Figured it meant they were intimidated.

He narrowed his eyes and glared at the deputy. "Where you been, son?"

Russell cleared his throat. "There was an attack on a lawyer, sir."

Stickley leaned forward. "In the courtroom? Why wasn't I notified, deputy?"

"No sir. A female attorney who parked in the municipal lot interrupted some vandals who were slashing her tires. Most of them ran off, but one of them stayed and attacked her with a tree branch. She called the state police and Maxwell dumped her in our lap. You were at lunch when he brought her in."

Stickley shook his head and gave a low whistle. "She hurt bad?"

Russell chuckled. "No sir, she gave the guy a whooping, to hear her tell it. She's just a tiny thing, but she knows some kinda self-defense that the Israeli Army uses."

"Krav Maga?"

"Yeah, that's it."

Stickley nodded. "Good on her. Any id on the attacker?"

"One of Danny Trees's people. Goes by the name of Jay. He's not local. The attorney and I took a drive over to Danny's place while Bricker's Auto worked on her car. Danny claims not to have seen him since the attack. I took a look around. He left a duffel bag there, so maybe he'll be back."

Russell finished his report and stood there at attention, waiting for Stickley to dismiss him.

Stickley waved his hand again. "Go on, get out. Make sure you write it up and send a copy to Dogwood Station. I swear those troopers get lazier by the day."

Russell grabbed the doorknob and raced out of the room. Stickley watched him go and grinned at his eagerness to escape. Then, he swiveled his chair around and thought. A violent environmental protester. Seemed like there should be a way to use that to his advantage. He turned the piece of information over in his mind, examining it from all angles. He'd come up with something.

8.

Pittsburgh, Pennsylvania
Monday evening

IXTEEN HOURS AND TWENTY
MINUTES after she'd left Pittsburgh for a
twenty-minute discovery hearing, Sasha
pulled back in to her reserved parking spot at her
condo. The sun, which had not yet risen when
she'd set out in the morning, had long since set.
She was tired, hungry, and cold.

She trudged through the parking lot and into
the warm lobby. She was tempted to take the elevator instead of the stairs, just this once. But that

was how it started. Take the elevator tonight because she was tired and her feet hurt from having been trapped in three-inch stilettos all day, and then tomorrow she'd want to take it because she was running late. Then, the next thing she knew she'd be taking elevators all over the place because she got winded climbing stairs. Besides, stairways gave more options in the event of an assault. Get attacked in an elevator and you were a sitting duck.

She straightened her back and adjusted the weight of her bag over her shoulder. Then she pushed through the metal door to the stairwell. To make up for her moment of weakness, she took the stairs two at a time.

That small burst of activity improved her mood slightly. The smell of spices and roasting meat that emanated from her unit put a smile on her face. By the time she opened the door to see Connelly waiting for her with a glass of red wine in his hand, she'd forgotten to be miserable.

It had been six months since Leo Connelly had entered her life in the oddest way imaginable. Sasha never would have guessed that her longest relationship to date would be with a federal air marshal whose nose and finger she broke while disarming him in the apartment of a murdered stranger. But, as her nana used to say, there's a lid for every pot. So here he was, Agent Leo Connelly. Her lid. At least for the present.

"How are you doing?" The corners of his eyes crinkled with concern as he handed off the wine glass and leaned in to kiss her.

She gave herself a minute to relax in his arms before pulling back.

"Better now. Dinner smells amazing."

She raised her glass in tribute to his cooking skills before heading up the stairs to her loft bedroom to get out of the high heels and change into a sweater and jeans.

Over a second glass of syrah and between mouthfuls of Connelly's lamb tagine, she filled him in on the goings on in Springport. He listened without interrupting, nodding along as he processed the information. She could see him mentally sorting and cataloging it between bites of food for later analysis.

He put down his fork and raised a hand to stop her when she got to the part about Danny Trees's blank check.

"Do you still have it? You haven't deposited it yet, have you?"

"No, I just wanted to get home. I'm not sure I'm going to anyway. It could be viewed as settling any claim I might have against Danny and PORE for the cost of the repairs. I think I'll give it a day to make sure they didn't mess with anything else."

For all she knew, there was sugar in her gas tank.

He cracked a grin. "Spoken like a true lawyer. If you give me the check, I can run his bank account through the database and see what pops."

The database was Guardian, into which law enforcement agencies from around the country fed suspicious activity reports, called SARs. Six months earlier, while investigating a plane crash, Connelly had accessed the classified database to make a connection between a dead city laborer and a psychotic technology developer, leading him to the apartment where they'd met. But that had been official business. This was . . . not.

She looked at him closely. "Are you sure that's a good idea?"

He looked away, but not before she saw in his eyes that he wasn't sure at all.

"I'm sure," he said.

9.

ASHA'S EYES BURNED AND THE characters on her computer screen swam together in a blur. She checked the time. No wonder. She'd been staring at the monitor for nearly five hours. She'd even eaten her lunch at the computer. It was well past time for a break.

She unrolled the purple yoga mat that she'd stowed under her desk. She worked through the three Warrior Poses, holding each for several minutes. She willed her mind to be still and focused only on her lengthening muscles and her slow breathing. She stayed there until the chimes from a nearby church drifted through the window as the bells struck three. Then she sank into Child's Pose.

Connelly had brought yoga practice—along with home-cooked meals—into her life. Despite his high-risk, stressful work, he was uniformly placid. He didn't overreact. He didn't worry.

She'd noticed that, no matter the demands on his time, he always managed to fit in a quick yoga session. So she had decided to find a way to squeeze yoga in between her Krav Maga training and her running schedule.

The fifteen minutes she spent on the asanas each afternoon rejuvenated her. She wished she could return the favor and give Connelly a tool to deal with his borderline obsessive compulsive need for order.

After rolling up her mat, she walked over to the coffee station she'd set up in the corner of her rented office and poured an oversized mug of fresh black coffee. The one-room Law Offices of Sasha McCandless, P.C., located on the second floor of a storefront in her neighborhood, were a far cry from the opulent, Class A downtown real estate her former law firm called home, but she had taken one play from Prescott & Talbott's play book. Fresh coffee was always available. Only hers was stronger. And no longer free.

Break over, she returned to her desk, sipping the coffee and turning the information on her computer over in her head. Early that morning, not long after Sasha had unlocked the door to the building and gone upstairs to turn on the heat in her office, she'd heard the tinkle of bells that announced a visitor downstairs. The retail space below was vacant, so she hurried down the staircase to greet whomever had wandered in.

She'd come face to face with a UPS guy on his way up the stairs with a delivery for her. It was a slim letter envelope. Inside she found a CD and a cover letter from Drew Showalter, which said the CD contained all the documents Judge Paulson had ordered Keystone Properties to produce. The letter went on to ask VitaMight to agree to an early close of discovery, since it now had all the documents.

The package was remarkable for two reasons.

First, it was almost a certainty that the CD had been prepared in advance of the previous day's hearing. Sasha thought it extremely unlikely that Showalter would have rushed back to his office and spent his afternoon compiling the e-mails to get the CD burned and out for delivery by the UPS deadline. Given the lack of spark Showalter had shown at the hearing, she'd go so far as to call it impossible.

Either way, the e-mails were either already ready to be produced when they argued the issue or were so few in number that they could be prepared by a lazy man in less than a day. This raised the obvious question of why Keystone Properties hadn't simply turned over the e-mails before the hearing. Showalter had to have known he would lose his opposition. There was no good reason to keep the e-mails from VitaMight. So, Sasha surmised, there must have been a bad reason: there was something in those e-mails that Keystone Properties had wanted to hold back from VitaMight for some period of time.

Which led to the second reason the package was remarkable. There was no need to overnight the documents. Judge Paulson had given Keystone until the end of the week to turn them over. Today was Tuesday. Showalter could have saved his client some money and put them in the regular mail or sent them ground. But, instead, he'd paid extra for early morning delivery. After dragging its heels for months, suddenly, Keystone was in a big hurry for her to get the documents. Baffling. That was the only way to describe Showalter's behavior.

The games Keystone was playing around the timing of the document production seemed senseless. And, thus far, her review of the e-mails hadn't shed any light on the issue. She'd seen nothing but e-mails that set forth the mundane minutiae of a typical commercial landlord-tenant relationship: the activation procedure for VitaMight new hires' access badges; the after-hours heating and cooling policy; a request from the landlord that no one park under a diseased oak tree so it could be removed from the lot; an invitation to a pizza lunch Keystone had sponsored for one of the candidates for county council; the e-mails scrolled across her screen in a seemingly endless parade of irrelevant information. Whatever was there, she wasn't seeing it.

She finished her coffee and stood looking at the computer screen. Then, she put down the mug and powered off the screen. Noah used to say when you can't see the forest for the trees, get out of the blasted forest.

~ ~ ~ ~ ~ ~ ~ ~ ~ ~

Sasha sat in the gerontologist's waiting room and tried to make sense of the magazine selection. Doctors' offices, perhaps the last refuge of the magazine industry. She understood the presence of *Reader's Digest,* of course, and *AARP Magazine.* She had to wonder, though, how many of Dr. Kayser's patients were fans of *Wired* and *Bride*. Unless those were aimed at adult children shuttling their parents to appointments.

The door from the outside corridor opened and an elderly woman shuffled in. She nodded a greeting to Sasha, then eased herself into the chair nearest the door and placed her large pocketbook near her feet. She unwound her scarf and folded it into a neat rectangle but did not remove her jacket. Sasha watched the woman get comfortable and made a silent bet as to which magazine she'd choose.

The woman ignored the magazines. She reached into her bag and took out a glasses case and an iPad. She snapped the case open, put on her glasses, and powered up her tablet. Sasha smiled to herself. Maybe magazines' days were numbered here, too.

Sasha checked the time. The receptionist on the phone had told her Dr. Kayser's last appointment was at 3:30 and that he'd give her a half an hour after that. It was now close to four o'clock. If he was running late, she'd come back. Sitting and waiting wasn't her strong suit.

"Ma'am, are you here to see Dr. Kayser?"

The woman looked up from her device. "No, honey, Dr. Jenner." She smiled and then bent her head back over the screen.

Intrigued, Sasha craned her neck subtly to see the screen. The old lady was updating her Facebook status.

The interior door swung open into the waiting room and an elderly man came through the doorway followed by a nurse wearing Scottie dog-patterned scrubs.

"You have a nice evening, Mr. Chatsworth," she called to the man's back in a loud, singsong voice.

She turned to Sasha and spoke in a normal tone. "Ms. McCandless? Dr. Kayser asked me to have you join him in his office."

Then, her voice rose again and she addressed the old woman. "Dr. Jenner will be right with you, ma'am."

"Okay, dearie," the woman responded without looking up from her Facebook wall.

"Kids today and their electronics," Sasha cracked as she followed the nurse through the doorway and past two exam rooms. At the end of the short hallway, the nurse delivered her to the doctor's office without so much as a fake chuckle at the joke.

Dr. Alvin Kayser set aside his paperwork and rose to greet her.

"It's good to see you, Sasha," he said, shaking her hand. His eyes were magnified by his round, rimless glasses. He looked kind, almost jolly, like a balding, beardless Santa Claus.

"I really appreciate your taking the time to see me today," she told him.

He waved her into a chair and shrugged off her thanks.

"It's my pleasure. Your late grandmother was very fond of you. And proud of you, I should add. She said for a tiny thing you really held your own with your strapping brothers from the time you were a child. And, look where it got you, she used to say."

Sasha smiled. Her maternal grandmother had always seemed mildly horrified by Sasha's tomboy adventures as a child and her unladylike pursuits as an adult, but Nana Alexandrov was never shy about bragging about her grandchildren. She'd seen Dr. Kayser for the last several years of her life—with increasing frequency, as her frail body deteriorated over time—so, the doctor had probably learned more than he ever needed to know about the McCandless clan. Especially toward the end, when their doctor-patient relationship had deepened into a true friendship. For over a year, the doctor had brought her grandmother a burnt almond torte from Prantl's Bakery every Sunday, and the two of them had worked on the crossword puzzle between bites.

He reclaimed his leather desk chair and leaned back, folding his hands over his belly. "Now, what can I do for you?"

"As I told your receptionist when I called, I've been appointed to represent a gentleman at an incapacitation hearing up in Clear Brook County. Elder law isn't an area I'm familiar with, so I'm starting from scratch here. Anything you can tell me will be a help."

The doctor nodded. He had testified in more incapacitation hearings than he could count.

"Okay, now, understand, I am most familiar with Allegheny County, but the general process should be the same. Typically, the issue will arise when a family member or friend of the elderly person raises a concern or if a physician thinks there's a problem. So, how did your client come to the attention of the court?"

"It's not clear. The county Department of Aging Services is the petitioner. The petition just says they received a report. My guess—and it's only a guess—is that a local doctor made a report after my client consulted her informally about a fall."

Dr. Kayser nodded. "That'd be Dr. Spangler, I take it?"

Sasha blinked. "Well, yes. But, surely, she's not really the only doctor in town?" She'd assumed Jed had been exaggerating.

"There are others in the general area, but I do believe she has the only office in the town itself. In any case, she seems to be, by far, the busiest general practitioner up there. There aren't any geriatric specialists in that county, at least not to my knowledge, and the handful of other G.P.s up that way are always griping about the stranglehold she has on the client base at conferences and meetings. I assume the locals are loyal to her out of a sense of sympathy."

Sasha stopped him. "Sympathy?"

He sighed, then said, "Dr. Shelly Spangler is a Spangler by marriage but a Wilson by birth."

"A Wilson?"

"Yes. Clyde Wilson was a well-respected businessman in the area until the mid-70s. All before your time, of course. But, his business failed in spectacular fashion and it destroyed his family. Shelly is his daughter. From what I understand, after Clyde killed himself, his wife scraped out an existence. Shelly buried herself in her studies, and won a scholarship from the local Lions Club to college. She continued to apply herself and was accepted to medical school. People who know her story wouldn't dream of changing doctors. She's the hometown girl who made good."

Sasha thought about Dr. Spangler's childhood home, condemned and bleak, standing across the street from Danny Trees's place and could understand why the townspeople would support her.

"Okay, the county's petition failed to provide any concrete evidence of incapacity. What should it have included? I mean, what would you have done?"

On comfortable ground, his answer came quickly and with authority. "Before I would presume to classify one of my patients as incapacitated, I would do a thorough evaluation, starting with a complete physical examination. I'd also do a psychosocial information intake."

Sasha jotted his answer on her notepad. "Let's take those one at a time. What would you be looking for in the physical?"

"Signs of dementia, primarily. Any changes in existing conditions that might be caused by a patient's failure to comply, for example, a diabetic who stops following an appropriate diet or someone who stops taking prescribed meds."

"Okay, say, the patient hasn't come in for a physical for years," Sasha said. "So you have no baseline."

He nodded. "I'd still do a workup. But, you're right. It would be hard to draw any conclusions from the results. In that case, the psychosocial information might carry more weight." He waited until she stopped scribbling. "Ready to discuss that?"

"Yes. Thanks."

"Of course. At a minimum, I'd perform a MMSE—that's a mini mental state examination. It takes about ten minutes. I'd ask the patient a series of questions intended to screen for cognitive impairment: what time it is; the date; who the president is, that sort of thing. Also some simple calculations. I'd ask the patient to repeat a list of words to test for recall. The highest possible score is 30 points. A score of 25 or higher would indicate no impairment. Between 21 and 24 would suggest a mild impairment. I'd be most concerned about a score of 10 to 20 points, which correlates to moderate impairment. Anything under 10 indicates severe impairment and, for a patient at that level, it would be fairly obvious that there was some age-related dementia or other problem."

"That's the standard accepted test?"

"Yes. There are others, of course, but most gerontologists will use the MMSE. Sometimes a social worker or other non-doctor will use an abbreviated MMSE. Some doctors will create their own unique tests. Pulling from the various accepted tests." He paused here and pursed his lips to show his displeasure. "That's not a best practice and it can skew results dramatically."

Sasha wondered if anyone had performed a diagnostic battery of any kind on Jed Craybill and wrote herself a note to find out.

"Since Dr. Spangler isn't a geriatric specialist, would it be appropriate for her to administer and score a test like this?"

Dr. Kayser sighed and pushed his chair back from his desk. He steepled his fingers together and looked up at the ceiling tiles before answering. "As I'm sure you can appreciate, that's a difficult judgment to make. Is it appropriate for a general practitioner to administer the test and interpret the results? Certainly, just as it would be appropriate for a family doctor to perform a pregnancy test or to screen a patient for hearing loss. In my view, however, the next step, if any of those diagnostic tools indicated further care was warranted, would be to refer the patient to a specialist. There are physicians who are board certified in obstetrics, audiology, and, of course, geriatric medicine for a reason." He drew his lips into a firm, thin line when he finished speaking.

"Of course."

"Now, if I had a patient whose score on the MMSE concerned me, I would gather additional psychosocial information, such as the presence of formal and informal support systems, including membership in a church or club, relationships with neighbors, relatives, or friends; whether the patient already received any services; and if any recent psychological stressors were in play."

"Like the death of a spouse?"

"Absolutely."

"After gathering all this information, you would be comfortable making a diagnosis?"

Dr. Kayser straightened his back. "Some would. And, a diagnosis based on that information would be defensible. I, however, would not. We're talking about wresting control of a person's life."

"What other steps would you take?"

"For one, I would have a social worker perform a safety assessment of the living environment. Does the patient's home have fire alarms, adequate lighting, sturdy stairs, or grab bars in the bathroom? Is the home clean and uncluttered? That sort of information."

He stood and paced behind his desk, his hands clasped together behind his back. "Then, I would consider what services might be appropriate to provide support to enable the patient to continue to function independently. Would a walker be helpful? A medical alert necklace? Would an alarmed pill box that dispenses the patient's medication in the correct dosage and provides reminders be useful? Could Meals on Wheels deliver food to the patient? Could the patient's banking be automated, both for deposits and bill payment?"

He turned and faced her. "There is a wealth of services and products intended to help people age in place with dignity. In my view, these should be exhausted first. If, after all that, it is clear the patient cannot function safely without a guardian, then and only then would I get on the stand and testify that this patient is incapacitated."

He sat back down, with a sheepish smile, like he realized he'd been up on a soapbox.

"This is very helpful background," Sasha reassured him, then asked, "How often in your practice do you ultimately conclude that a patient needs a guardian? I mean, out of the times that someone files a petition?"

He rubbed his belly while he considered the question. "More than half the time. Sometimes, it's just clear as day. The patient is in full-blown dementia, say. Sometimes, we can put off the determination of incapacitation for months or years by devising an appropriate care plan, but ultimately, independent daily living becomes too much for the patient. And, sometimes, a patient like your grandmother will function independently until she dies in her sleep. Of course, in her case, your mother was there to help her, if needed."

He smiled at the memory of her grandmother, who read *The New York Times* every day, up to and including the day she died, and was always ready to talk politics.

Sasha smiled back, then asked the money question. "Have you ever testified in opposition to an incapacitation petition?"

He cocked his head and thought. "No. I don't believe I have."

"Will you?"

10.

DREW SHOWALTER CHECKED THE NOTES on the podium in front of him. Speaking at these commissioners' meetings could be more nerve-wracking than arguing in front of an appellate panel. At least with judges, he could predict the questions and issues with some accuracy. But the county commissioners were a retired banker, a minister, and the owner of a trucking company. He never had any idea what they were going to ask him.

He snuck a look behind him. The audience was thin, at least. He saw the politics editor of the paper, the hapless Danny Trees and a handful of his people, and a cluster of retirees with nothing better to do on a Tuesday night. Maybe they'd get out of here at a decent hour for once.

Lately, the monthly meetings had been running on for hours, what with every red-faced homeowner in the county wanting to yell about too much fracking, not enough fracking, chemicals in their water, the noise, the smell, the too-lax regulations, the too-strict regulations. It was worse than the year they'd done real estate reassessments.

The acid started to rise in his throat just thinking about it. He popped an antacid and told himself to put it out of his mind. Being county solicitor was a civic duty. And a guaranteed forty grand a year.

The commissioners filed in together, whispering and gossiping. They took their seats behind the long table.

After the Pledge of Allegiance, they got down to business. It was clear sailing until they got to the declaratory judgment actions that Big Sky had filed.

Big Sky. Those guys didn't mess around. A day didn't go by that they weren't suing somebody over something or other. And, of course, they used big law firms to do all the work and just hired someone in town as local counsel to shepherd the cases through the court. So, it was motion after motion, preliminary objections, and endless discovery requests. It was like their strategy was to bury the town under paper.

Cort Garland, the retired banker, started with the questions right away.

"How can they keep filing these frivolous lawsuits? Don't they understand we don't have the resources to respond to all these cases?"

The business owner, Heather Price, snapped at him. "Don't be naive, Cort. Of course they understand that. That's *why* they're filing all these lawsuits. Right, Drew?"

Heather could be a real ball buster, but he imagined being a woman in the trucking industry was no picnic. Especially a woman as drop-dead gorgeous as she was.

He cleared his throat. "I tend to agree. They're trying to keep us on the defensive. It's only going to get worse, I'm afraid, now that you've voted to consider the drilling moratorium."

Cort jumped in, "I want the minutes to reflect that I was the lone dissent on that vote."

Heather rolled her eyes.

Troy Benjamin, the minister, spoke up in the rich baritone that made him so popular behind the pulpit. "Now, let's not revisit settled issues. We agreed that we need to examine whether we're being good stewards of the bounty of resources the Lord gave us. Let's be at peace with that decision."

Heather rewarded Troy with one of her dazzling smiles, and he ducked his head in embarrassment.

Drew had once remarked to his wife how Heather sure could wrap her fellow commissioners around her fingers when it suited her. Betty had roared with laughter and said, "Counselor, your house is made of glass."

Ever since then, he was self-conscious around Heather, worried that he came across like a love-struck schoolboy. It made these meetings even more trying.

Heather turned her violet eyes his way. "Counselor, what's the process for these declaratory judgments? Are they fast-tracked or what?"

He peeked at his notes even though he knew the procedure cold. "Well, Judge Paulson has both sides' briefs. On the moratorium issue, he also has the amicus brief filed by PORE."

Behind him, he heard the PORE members whispering in excitement. It had been a bit of a surprise to everyone that they'd spent the money to file an *amicus curiae,* or friend of the court, brief on the issue.

He continued, "Now, Judge Paulson has set a hearing for early May on the moratorium issue. Because the council didn't vote to actually ban drilling but just voted to consider the issue, he ruled there was no need for expedited review."

A smattering of boos and hisses erupted from the PORE contingent.

Cort put a hand up. "Please control yourselves."

The noise died down, and Drew picked up where he'd left off. "On the other issue, Judge Paulson said he didn't need to have a hearing. He's going to decide it on the papers."

"What's the timing on that then?" Heather pressed him.

"Harry Paulson's a creature of habit, you know. He hasn't had a law clerk in years, so he writes all his own opinions, and he does them in order. First in, first out. Every afternoon, after a slice of pie, he stands at that window of his and dictates his opinions. Fridays, he reviews the drafts. That week's batch goes out the following Monday, and the whole process starts over. Based on when the briefing was completed, he won't get to our case this week, but he'll decide it one day next week. So, we should have the opinion two weeks from today."

Drew looked at the three commissioners, trying to gauge a reaction. Cort was nodding; he couldn't tell whether it was in approval or just understanding. Troy had adopted the peaceful martyred expression he wore whenever council business held no interest for him. And Heather was staring right back at him, giving him a heavy-lidded look that sent a thrill of imagination up his spine.

He reached into his jacket pocket as inconspicuously as he could and unwrapped another antacid.

11.

Thursday morning
Pittsburgh, PA

"**N**ICE WORK TODAY," DANIEL SAID, pounding Sasha on her shoulder with a fist.

She smiled at her instructor, lapping up his rare praise. She could tell she'd done well during the exercises. Her encounter with Jay earlier in the week had reminded her she couldn't afford to get lazy.

One of Krav Maga's tenets was that repeated, progressive drills under stressful conditions would develop muscle memory in the student, enabling her to react automatically instead of freezing. Because human instinct when under attack isn't fight or flight: it's fight or flight or freeze. And while fighting and fleeing were both acceptable responses, freezing was a good way to get a girl killed.

The way to avoid the freeze response was consistent, faithful training. But, lately, Sasha had been slacking off from her early morning training sessions in favor of spending extra time in bed curled against Connelly's broad, warm back, listening to his even breathing, too comfortable to get up.

No more.

She said her goodbyes to the other students and grabbed her backpack from her locker. Before slipping it on for the three-mile run home, she took her Blackberry out of the side pocket and checked for messages. She hadn't really expected to have a message at seven in the morning on a Thursday, but she had two. She could tell they'd both been forwarded from her work line, because no caller identification information was available.

The first call was from Dr. Kayser:

Sasha, hi, it's Al Kayser. Sorry to call so early, but I wanted to let you know I had a meeting on my calendar for most of the day that's been canceled suddenly. I'm going to take advantage of the block of free time to take a drive and visit with Mr. Craybill. I should have a written report of my observations to you before the weekend's out. Take good care."

Great news. When Dr. Kayser had agreed to examine Jed and perhaps testify, his one caveat had been that his schedule was jam packed. She had been worried she might have to ask Braeburn to agree to an extension of the briefing schedule. Now, that worry was behind her.

Her next message made clear that someone else's worries were eating away at him:

Hi, Sasha. This is Drew Showalter, calling on the Vit-aMight matter. I, uh, just wanted to see if you'd gotten the discovery I overnighted? I was hoping you'd had a chance to review it by now. Maybe you could give me a call, so we could talk about any questions it raised? Or if you're planning to be in Springport on your Orphans' Court matter, let me know. We could get lunch. Thanks. Bye.

Call him to discuss any questions his discovery responses had raised? No one did that. What was going on with Showalter?

She shrugged. The man was a mystery to her, but it didn't matter. She'd resolved not to work on her Springport cases for the rest of the week. She was going to dig out from under the work that had piled up while she was out on Monday.

Then, she was going to spend whatever was left of the weekend with Connelly. Her brothers had invited them to the hockey game on Saturday night, but Sasha didn't know how to break it to them: Not only was Connelly *not* a Pens fan, he was a Rangers fan.

She laughed at the image of the family drama that confession would create and snapped her backpack straps across her chest. Then she pushed through the door out to the street and started her run.

~ ~ ~ ~ ~ ~ ~ ~ ~ ~

Thursday afternoon
Springport, Pennsylvania

Drew was trying to focus on his objections to the interrogatories the insurance company had served on his client. His attention kept wandering to the desk phone.

Was she going to call him back? It had been several hours since he'd left his message.

You should have waited until nine o'clock, like a normal person, he chided himself. Who's in the office at six forty-five in the morning? Besides him, of course.

But, Sasha had struck him, for no good reason, as a morning person. He liked to think he could sense his fellow early risers. Maybe she did get up early, he theorized, but she had to get her kids to school or walk her dog.

It doesn't matter, he told himself. Who cares if she wakes up at six a.m. or noon? She just needs to call me back.

She was going to be his way out of this . . . morass. Mess didn't do the situation justice. Predicament sounded too permanent. No, this was a morass.

He tapped his highlighter on the desk and tried to ignore the gnawing pain.

It was no use. He pulled open his top desk drawer and took out the jumbo-sized container of antacids Betty bought for him in three packs. He jammed a red one into his mouth and waited for its chalky magic to ease his stomach ulcer.

She'd call. She had to call.

12.

HARRY STOOD AT HIS WINDOW. Usually he liked to watch the shoppers and errand runners traipsing across the square. When school let out, he watched the children skip and squeal and laugh their way home. But, today, he looked out toward the rolling hills in the distance, covered with trees still bare from the winter.

In a few months, they'd be verdant and full of life. And in several months more, they'd be a fiery display of gold and red. Those mountains, massive and far off, were in *his* county. Just as the streams, creeks, and lakes cutting through the mountains were. They were his responsibility as much as the men and women, the business owners, and the careless drivers. As much as the children, and the uninsured, the abused, and the abusers.

This was his county and he was its judge.

What was he going to do? How could he fairly decide this growing mountain of cases brought by and against the oil and gas companies? All the ancillary cases that somehow, some way, managed to relate to hydrofracking?

Forget legal precedent, he thought. What kind of moral precedent would he be setting?

Come off it, Harry. Your job, your duty, is to follow legal precedent. Do your job and the rest will sort itself out. It had to.

He didn't know how much longer he could ignore the phone calls. The visits. The looking up from his newspaper in his booth at Bob's to see an uninvited guest in the booth across from him, smiling too wide.

His imagination was working overtime. He'd begun to think he was being followed. As if there was any need to follow him. He went to work, Bob's, work, home. On Saturdays, he hiked around Patterson's Lake. Sundays, he went to church. A person could set his watch by it.

He turned from the window and walked to his desk. His hand hovered over his phone. He should call his son. He hadn't spoken to Shane in over a month. He was somewhere in the Middle East, deployed for yet another six months. He'd want to hear from his father; after all, that was why Harry had given him that fancy GPS satellite phone.

No. He should do what he was supposed to be doing. Methodically work through the printouts of the draft opinions he'd dictated and make the corrections so Gloria could finalize them on Monday. After all, that was what he did on Fridays.

13.

XACTLY ONE WEEK AFTER SHE'D left the Springport municipal parking lot, Sasha eased her Passat in to a spot in the lot. This time, however, out of prudence, she parked right next to the attendant's shack. Despite the unusually sunny April day, Danny Trees and his friends were nowhere to be seen. Instead, a tired-eyed mother rested on the bench in the adjacent park and watched her toddler chase a yellow rubber ball around the grass at what appeared to be warp speed.

Sasha smiled at them as she lifted her briefcase from the front seat. Inside, a copy of Dr. Kayser's report from his visit with Jed last week rested in a manila folder. As far as she was concerned it should have been wrapped in Christmas paper. The geron-tologist had evidently caught her client on a good day. Jed had scored 29 out of 30 on his MMSE, had shown the doctor around his place, and had taught him how to de-bone a trout. The doctor had agreed to testify on Jed's behalf.

Now, all she had to do was work with Jed on his own testimony. He still had a tendency to curse a blue streak and she was determined to get him to tone it down before the hearing. She figured she might be able to bribe some good behavior out of him with a pie from Bob's Diner. She'd seen him looking at them longingly as they'd passed the glass case on their way out.

As she walked from the lot to the square, she found herself daydreaming about Deputy Russell's coffee with equal longing. So, when she ducked into Bob's, she had Marie wrap up a gob for Russell along with the pecan pie—authoritatively identi-fied as Jed's favorite by the waitress.

"You enjoy that gob now, honey. Diner's closing Saturday. When it reopens, who knows what kind of frou frou desserts we'll be serving," she called to Sasha's back.

As she cut across the square in the middle of the block, the late afternoon sun was in her eyes. She almost ran into a tall, thin man. She side-stepped at the last minute to avoid him, shielding her face from the glare with one hand and holding the pastries with the other.

"Excuse me," she muttered.

"Good afternoon, Ms. McCandless," he said. "I see you've discovered the desserts at Bob's. Lydia makes them from scratch."

She squinted. It was Judge Paulson.

"Hi, your honor. I didn't know that. Is Lydia his wife?"

"She is indeed," the judge said, taking Sasha's elbow lightly in his hand and moving her backward and onto the sidewalk as an oversized Ford pickup roared past. "It's not advisable to jaywalk around here, Counselor. Pedestrians may have the right of way in downtown Pittsburgh, but you're a long way from Pittsburgh."

"I've noticed, your honor. Thanks for the hand."

The judge released her elbow and came around to stand beside her. "Yes," he said, "Springport is a different place entirely."

He pointed across the square to the clock tower on the courthouse. "Do you see the statue atop the clock tower?"

Sasha looked hard at the statue of a woman in flowing robes. She could make out the scales of justice held aloft in her left hand and a double-edged sword in her right.

"It's Lady Justice, isn't it?"

"Very good, Ms. McCandless. But, did you know that sculpture of Lady Justice is one of only five in the entire country that doesn't depict her as blindfolded?"

"No, I can't say I did."

"Yes. The blindfold, of course, represents blind justice and impartiality. But, the elder statesmen who commissioned our statue seemed to think that justice in Clear Brook County has its eyes wide open."

He waited for her to say something.

"Maybe that's a good thing?"

"Perhaps," he said. "But, I doubt it." He touched the tip of his hat and continued on his way, headed toward Bob's and his own slice of Lydia's home-baked goodness.

~ ~ ~ ~ ~ ~ ~ ~ ~ ~

Deputy Russell had been happy to fill Sasha's stainless steel travel mug with some of his robust coffee in exchange for a gooey gob. He'd been somewhat less happy to report that he'd made no progress on identifying Jay and that Danny Trees had neither seen nor heard from the man.

Sasha savored the hot coffee as she drove out of town toward Jed Craybill's home. Tall trees, just starting to bud, dotted the ribbon of highway between Springport and Firetown. Behind the trees loomed even taller oil derricks. Through the closed car windows, she heard the constant hum of the compressor stations bringing up the pressure of the gas released from the shale into the gathering lines, so it could feed into the large pipelines.

Twenty minutes outside town, she pulled off the highway, turned right, and bounced along a partially paved unmarked road. The car rose and fell, following the natural peaks and valleys of the field.

Sasha held her mug out from her body as coffee sloshed over the lip of the purportedly leak-proof lid. Steering one-handed, she swerved to miss a large bird walking along the path.

She turned her head to get a better look. It was some kind of waterfowl. A duck, maybe, or a goose. She craned her neck but saw no water. Nothing but rows of long, wavy grass, still bleached tan from the winter. Lonely green shoots peeked out here and there.

A weathered ranch-style house came into view at the end of the lane. No other houses were in sight. Sasha slowed the car as she neared the house and parked in front of the attached carport, which listed slightly to the right, leaning into the house.

Jed stood near his front door. He was holding a bag of bread. He sneezed loudly and pulled a handkerchief from his pants pocket.

"Damn allergies."

He nodded a greeting as she got out of the car, pecan pie in hand.

"Hi, Jed. How are you this afternoon?"

"Can't complain," he said, the fact that he just had apparently lost on him. "Just got back from feeding the ducks. That a pie from Bob's?"

"Yes it is. Pecan. Marie tells me it's your favorite."

"That's right. Well, come on in," he said, turning toward the door.

He braced himself against the door frame, jammed a key into the lock, and turned it fiercely. The door flew open.

"It sticks," he explained unnecessarily.

Sasha followed him into a small entryway. She wiped her feet on a colorful rag rug that sat just inside the door and pulled the warped door shut behind her.

He shuffled through the living room without stopping and went straight to the kitchen in the back of the house. It was painted yellow. Red and white checked curtains framed the window over the sink. The appliances were old and scratched but clean. A clock shaped like an apple missing a bite hung over a square table shoehorned into the far corner.

Dr. Kayser had described Jed's home as spare and worn, but tidy and clean. Looking around, Sasha concurred with his assessment.

Jed stopped beside the refrigerator and opened a rectangular metal box that sat on the counter. He placed the loaf of bread inside and pulled the cover back down.

Sasha tried to recall the last time she'd seen a breadbox and came up empty.

"Do you always feed the ducks?" she asked.

Jed answered her without turning around. "Lately. The creek runs through the yard out back." He paused and nodded toward the window. "But they won't eat from that anymore."

"Why not?"

He pulled two white dessert plates, rimmed with blue, from the cabinet and took two forks from the silverware drawer beneath it.

Then he turned around and said, "I suspect they know it's poisoned."

"Poisoned?"

"Poisoned, polluted, what the hell's the difference? God knows what chemicals are running through that water from all the fracking."

He gestured with a pie cutter at the window, making a jabbing motion in the air.

"You leased your mineral rights? A gas and oil company is fracking on your land?" Sasha asked him.

Jed wheeled around. "Are you out of your mind? I won't let those bastards rape my land. Chased them off the front lawn with my hatchet when they came sniffing around. That contaminated water's coming from upstream."

The pie cutter clattered to the counter. The old man's face was red and his arms shook.

"Okay, I'm sorry. I didn't mean to upset you."

Sasha walked over to him and touched his arm. "Why don't you sit down and I'll dish us up some pie?"

He let her lead him to the table and sat muttering while she cut two slices of pie.

They ate in silence for several minutes. Sasha stared at the apple clock and tried to think of a topic that wouldn't set off the old man.

"You know they sued the county commissioners?" he demanded out of the blue.

"Who sued the county commissioners?"

He threw her a look of disgust. "The oil and gas dirtbags. Who else?"

"What's the basis of the suit?"

Jed snickered around a mouthful of pie. "Those other dirtbags—the commissioners—are holding up the oil and gas people who are so desperate to get their precious gas out. Take Heather Price. She runs her husband's trucking company. Heather opposed some of their permits. Then, suddenly Big Sky has an exclusive contract with her company to truck out the gas. Guess who gets their permits all of a sudden? That sort of thing. I guess the drillers figure since they're scratching everyone's back, they should get a scratch once in a while, too. But, last month, at the meeting, the commissioners accepted a petition from that McAllister kid and a bunch of hunters and fishers to consider a ban on drilling. They didn't vote to ban it, mind you, they just voted to vote on it. The oil and gas people got their panties in a twist and ran over to the courthouse to file some kinda petition that the vote would be invalid if they held it. Seems like they're right about that. The commissioners shouldn't be able to interfere with any business they want. They're worse than gangsters."

"So, you're anti-fracking and anti-banning fracking?"

Jed let out a genuine laugh. "Marla used to say I'm anti-everybody and anti-everything. I suspect she was right about that, except for this here pie."

~ ~ ~ ~ ~ ~ ~ ~ ~ ~ ~

Sasha left her misanthropic client's home feeling good about her case. She thought she'd made it clear to Jed that he'd have to tone down the swearing and the anger some at his upcoming hearing if he wanted to testify. Truth be told, though, she thought a little righteous indignation would be fitting the circumstances. She'd just have to keep him on a tight leash.

April in Pennsylvania is rarely balmy, but the afternoon sun was warm enough that she cracked the windows and let the air in as she drove back toward Springport. She even hummed along to the radio, which seemed to be limited to country music at the moment. Country singers told the best stories, she thought, as she listened to the Dixie Chicks sing about a traveling soldier.

As she hummed, a name popped into her head: Heather Price. The commissioner Jed had mentioned. She'd encountered that name before. But where? She searched her memory but before she could make a connection, her cell phone rang. She glanced down at the display. It was Connelly.

She turned down the volume on the radio and activated the hands-free setup through the car. She hated the delay that the Bluetooth caused but not as much as she would have hated running over someone because she was on her phone.

"Hey."

"Hi, beautiful. How'd your meeting go with your new boyfriend?"

She laughed. "As well as could be expected, I think. I just left. Should be back home by seven or so."

"Excellent. Do you want fish tacos or my Thai chicken and noodles for dinner?"

"The chicken and noodles with the peanut sauce?"

"That's the one."

It was too hard to pick, what with the belly full of pie.

"Chef's choice," she told him.

He groaned, as she knew he would. Connelly didn't like it when she punted on the decision making.

"Listen," she cut him off. "Does the name Heather Price mean anything to you?"

There was a pause while he considered it. "No. Should it?"

"I don't know."

A beeping sound filled the car through the speakers.

"Shoot," Sasha said, "I have another call. I'll call you back."

"Okay. I love you."

"Bye!"

She depressed the button to switch over to the other call and hoped he'd think she hadn't heard the profession of love.

Recently, Connelly had started randomly telling her he loved her. She wasn't sure what to do about it. For now, it was another decision to punt on.

Because she had swapped calls, her phone didn't display the caller.

"Sasha McCandless."

"Ms. McCandless, this is Gavin Russell."

"What can I do for you, Deputy Russell?"

She wondered if he had located Jay.

He cleared his throat. "Are you still out at Jed's?"

"No, I just left."

"Could you stop by the courthouse on your way through town? It's important."

"Is this about Jay and Danny Trees?"

"No, ma'am, it's not."

She worked to keep the irritation out of her voice. "Well, I'm fresh out of gobs, deputy, so—"

"Judge Paulson's been shot."

"Shot? Is he okay?"

"No, ma'am. He's dead."

14.

USSELL WAS WAITING FOR HER on the sidewalk in front of the courthouse. When she pulled up, he waved her into an official parking space. She parked the car and sat there for a minute before getting out. It seemed impossible to her that the judge was dead. It hadn't been three hours since their encounter in the street.

She stepped out of the car into the fading light of the late afternoon and her eyes were drawn to the clock tower and its all-seeing Lady Justice.

The deputy hustled over to her. It was the fastest she'd seen him move.

"Thanks for coming," he said in a strained voice.

"Of course. But, like I said on the phone, I don't see how I can be of any help. We exchanged pleasantries about the desserts at the diner. That was about it." She left out the mention of Lady Justice because it seemed somehow private in retrospect.

"I understand. But the sheriff heard that the two of you had a chat this afternoon and he asked me to have you come in."

"The sheriff? Surely the state police aren't trying to push a murder investigation off on your office?"

Russell gave a dry laugh. "Oh, no, you can be sure the Dogwood Station will be swarming all over this. That's why Sheriff Stickley wanted me to talk to you before we inform them."

"You haven't reported the judge's death to the police yet?"

"No, ma'am. Sheriff Stickley has been specifically instructed not to do so until the AG and Justice Bermann have given him the go-ahead. They should be here soon. Another twenty minutes, maybe."

"The Pennsylvania Attorney General and the Chief Justice of the Pennsylvania Supreme Court are coming here personally?"

"A sitting judge has been murdered, Ms. McCandless. Of course they are. Do you really think that pair would pass up all the media coverage this will generate—in an election year, no less?" His voice was thick with sarcasm, but he kept his expression neutral.

He led her up the stairs and through the lobby, bypassing the metal detector.

"Stairs okay with you?" he asked.

"They're preferable, actually," she answered.

They didn't speak as they climbed the stairs and walked through the too-quiet hallway to the sheriff's office.

Not until they were at Russell's desk, with the office door closed, did he say, "Sheriff's in the judge's chambers now. You feel up to going over there after you walk me through your conversation with the judge?"

"That's where it happened? In chambers?"

"Yep. Judge Paulson was a creature of habit. Every afternoon, he walked over to Bob's for a slice of pie. Then, he walked around the square—he called it his daily constitutional. Then, if he wasn't on the bench, he stood at his big window overlooking the square and dictated opinions and orders into a handheld dictaphone until the sun set. After he watched the sunset, he put the dictaphone tapes on his secretary's desk, locked up the office, and walked home."

"He was the only judge in the county. Wasn't he on the bench most days?"

Russell shook his head. "Most mornings. He never scheduled arguments or sentencing in the afternoons. So he was only in court in the afternoons if he had a jury trial. And we don't have any scheduled this week."

"Okay, so he was looking out his window?"

"Right. Judging by where we found him, he was looking out toward the park. We found one 120-grain Nosler Partition bullet in chambers. He took a clean hit, through and through."

Russell caught her blank look. "That's a bullet for a hunting rifle. A really heavy bullet."

"Okay, the judge was shot through his second-story window with a hunting rifle?"

"That's how it appears."

"How far away could the shooter have been?"

"Depends on the gun and the trajectory. We'll need to get a firearms forensics expert, but take the 257 Weatherby Magnum, for example. With the factory loads using that bullet, a decent shot—not a great shot, mind you—would be accurate from about 100 yards."

Sasha's ignorance about guns was rivaled only by her lack of spatial ability. "Uh, so three hundred feet. Where would that put the shooter?"

"Can't say until we talk to someone with ballistics expertise."

"But you think it was a hunter?"

Russell passed a hand through his hair in frustration. "I guess so. I also think that the list of hunters in the county pretty much overlaps almost one hundred percent with the list of able-bodied people in the county. Only exceptions being Danny Trees and his group."

Sasha watched him work through it.

He chewed on the inside of his cheek, then said, "Course, if it was PORE, then they'd sure want us to think it was a hunter, wouldn't they?"

Sasha shrugged. She was a commercial litigator not a homicide detective.

"I still don't understand why the court wouldn't just turn this over to the state police. No offense."

"He shrugged back at her. "None taken. I'd love to, personally. But, I have my orders."

"Who found the judge?"

"His secretary, Gloria Burke. She thought she heard a thump from inside around 2:15 and knocked on the door to make sure the judge was okay. He didn't answer. She gave it a minute and knocked again. When he still didn't answer, she opened the door. And there he was, sprawled on the carpet with a hole in his head and most of his face missing. Glass shards from the window were all over the place. Between the solid door and thick carpet, it's a surprise she heard anything."

Sasha closed her eyes. It had been six months since she'd seen a murder victim. The owner of the apartment where she'd met Connelly—a guy in his twenties—had been beaten until his head was bashed in and then tossed in a dumpster by two Russian thugs. She and Connelly had found him. Days later, she had watched as her mentor's widow stabbed one of her clients, puncturing her lung. The client had died at Sasha's feet with frothy blood bubbling from her lips. That had been an unusually bad week.

But the image of the kid in the dumpster, wrapped in a blood-soaked sheet, that's what was imprinted on her brain. He was who she saw sometimes as she was falling asleep. She hoped the judge's secretary wouldn't have a similarly gruesome bedtime image.

When she opened them, Russell was staring at her, worried. "You okay?"

"Sure." She smiled. She hoped it didn't look as forced as it felt.

"Why don't I get us some coffee and you can tell me about your chat with Judge Paulson."

"Fine."

~ ~ ~ ~ ~ ~ ~ ~ ~ ~ ~

Before Russell could make good on his promise of coffee, the sheriff called and ordered his deputy to meet him in the judge's chambers and to bring Sasha along.

They walked over slowly. On the way, Sasha relayed her conversation with the judge. When she mentioned the speeding pickup truck that had nearly hit them, Russell perked up.

"Did you get a look at the driver?"

"No. The truck was going too fast."

"Did Judge Paulson do or say anything that indicated he thought the truck might have been gunning for him?"

Sasha thought a minute. "No."

She decided not to hold anything back from the deputy. "But, he did say something strange. After the truck went by, he pointed out the statue of Lady Justice on the clock tower and said it wasn't blindfolded."

"So?"

"So, Lady Justice is usually depicted wearing a blindfold. It signifies that justice is blind. Everyone's on equal footing before the law."

"Okay?" Russell was looking at her with a harassed expression, like she needed to get to her point.

"The Judge seemed to suggest that wasn't the case locally. Or maybe that's what he was suggesting. I'm not sure."

Russell dismissed the idea with a small frown. "Let's get back to the truck. Did you see the license plate? Maybe get a partial?"

Sasha shook her head. "No, sorry." She pictured the truck. "It did have a gun rack in the back, though."

"Like a hunter would have?"

"Just like that," she said as they approached the door to the late judge's chambers.

The door was ajar. Russell nudged it inward and then stood back to let her go through first. Inside was a reception area. A middle-aged woman with tight cropped curly hair sat miserably at the desk. Her eyes were rimmed with red and she clutched a twisted tissue in one hand. She looked up when Russell passed through the doorway.

"Gloria," he said, touching the brim of his hat. "How are you holding up?"

"Oh, Gavin. This is so horrible. I can't even believe it. They just took his body out." Her voice broke, but she didn't seem to have any tears left.

"Me neither. Gloria, this is Sasha McCandless, she's an—"

The woman cut him off and addressed Sasha. "You're the attorney from Pittsburgh who was up here on the discovery motion last week. Judge Paulson appointed you to represent Mr. Craybill, too. I recognize the name."

Sasha was impressed the secretary hadn't shut down after the shock of finding her murdered boss.

Russell inclined his head toward the inner door, leading to the judge's private office. "Is Stinky still back there?"

The secretary choked out a laugh. "He's there."

Sasha arched a brow at the nickname, and Gloria came to Russell's defense.

"You'll understand when you meet him."

As if he'd been summoned by the mention of his name, just then a perfectly nondescript man poked his head through the door. He was neither young nor old; fat nor thin; tall nor short; handsome nor ugly. He just was.

"Russell, get in here. Gloria, don't go anywhere."

The sheriff disappeared back into the interior office. Russell swallowed a sigh and gestured for Sasha to follow him. He patted the secretary's shoulder as he walked by her.

Sasha stopped beside her and said, "I'm so sorry about Judge Paulson, Mrs. Burke. And I'm so sorry for what you must be going through.

Gloria gave her a wobbly smile. "Thank you."

As soon as Sasha stepped into the judge's office she realized she'd been wrong. Sheriff Stickley wasn't completely nondescript. He had one characteristic that stood out: he exuded horrific body odor. For a split second she thought it might have been the scent of death lingering at the scene, but when the sheriff pumped her hand in greeting, it disturbed the air around him, leaving no question that he was the source of the smell.

Sasha's nose burned but she managed not to recoil.

"Attorney McCandless," he said in a too-hearty, politician's voice, "it's a pleasure to meet you, although I wish the circumstances were different. Carl Stickley."

Sasha freed her hand. "Nice to meet you, Sheriff. Although I was just telling Deputy Russell, I don't think I can add anything to your investigation, so I'll just get out of your way and . . ."

He cut her off. "I'm afraid I can't let you leave."

"Can't *let* me? Am I being detained?"

His smile didn't reach his eyes. "No, no, of course not. It's nothing like that. No, Attorney General Griggs and Chief Justice Bermann are on their way. They'd just like to talk to you."

Sasha'd had enough. "With all due respect, Sheriff, I can't wait for them. I have a law practice to get back to. I'm terribly sorry about Judge Paulson. He seemed like a man of great integrity, and I certainly hope you catch whomever shot him. But, this tragedy has nothing to do with me. I'm just passing through your lovely town. And now it's time for me to go."

Stickley motioned with his head, and Russell moved to stand between Sasha and the door.

Russell made a pained face at her.

She ignored him and focused on the sheriff. "So, I am being detained, then? Fine. I want an attorney."

Stickley's nostrils flared, but before he could answer, Sasha heard a commotion in the reception area.

It was the fuss that attended the arrival of two powerful men. Gloria's chair scraping across the floor as she hopped up to greet them. The murmur of excited voices floating in from the hallway. And the soft thud of expensive dress shoes crossing the office floor.

She turned around and came face to face with the most senior judge and the highest-ranking law enforcement officer in the commonwealth.

The supreme court justice spoke first. "So, you've invoked your right to counsel, eh, Ms. McCandless? Will a doddering old fool like me do?"

Unlike Stickley, Justice Bermann gave her a smile that lit up his entire face. His eyes crinkled and he chuckled at his own self-deprecating joke.

"Justice Bermann, it's truly an honor to meet you, sir. And, you, as well, Mr. Griggs. I just heard you speak at the civil RICO CLE in Pittsburgh. Fascinating."

If Sasha's time working at Prescott & Talbott had taught her anything it was how to handle a roomful of titans. During high-level meetings of the powerful business executives who were their clients, the attorneys at Prescott & Talbott took great pains to ensure that each CEO left thinking that he or she had been the most important of the VIPs present. The fact that she'd recently suffered through a mind-numbing CLE at which the attorney general had delivered a droning keynote was a stroke of luck.

Both men beamed.

Russell caught her eye and raised his brow to let her know he was on to her.

Stickley looked like he smelled something bad. Maybe himself, she thought.

She went on, "I was just explaining to the sheriff that, despite the terrible news of Judge Paulson's death, I need to be getting back to Pittsburgh."

Griggs frowned. "I'm sorry, Ms. McCandless, but we really do need to speak with you. You aren't being detained, of course. But, the Chief Justice and I would like to impose on just a few more minutes of your time. Consider it a personal favor."

Justice Bermann nodded along like a metronome to the flat voice.

She didn't have a choice, of course. Not unless she wanted to set her bar license on fire and find a new line of work. And everyone in the room knew it, but at least the two power hitters had the decency to give it the appearance of free will. Not like old Stinky, she thought.

"Of course."

Griggs rewarded her with a bright white smile. "Thank you."

He turned to the sheriff and tilted his head in the direction of the door. "Carl, we need to speak to Ms. McCandless in private."

Stickley's face clouded. His started to speak, then his mouth clamped shut. Open. Shut. Like a fish.

After he'd swallowed whatever he'd been planning to say, he managed a strangled, "Yes sir," and headed for the door, motioning Russell to follow him. "C'mon, Russell."

Justice Bermann stopped him with a raised hand. "Actually, Sheriff, we'd like you to post your deputy at the door. To secure the scene, you know. Deputy, if you'll just stand guard outside."

"Yes, sir," Russell said, trailing his boss out of the room with a grin he couldn't quite hide.

The chief justice claimed the seat behind Judge Paulson's desk and the attorney general perched on a straight-backed chair tucked into the corner behind the desk and a bookcase lining the far wall. That left a choice between two leather guest chairs in front of the desk for Sasha. She sat in the closer of the two and watched as the two men passed a series of meaningful looks back and forth.

They put her in mind of her older brothers trying to decide who was going to tell their mother the details of one of their childhood misdeeds. *You tell her. No, you tell her. It was your baseball. You're the one who threw it.* Sasha just waited. It was what her mother had always done. Sasha saw no reason why the tactic wouldn't work on senior public officials just as it did on a pack of unruly Irish-Russian-American troublemakers.

Justice Bermann weakened first. He leaned forward, elbows on Judge Paulson's polished desk, and said, "We'd like your help, Ms. McCandless."

"My help?" she repeated, cringing at how stupid she sounded. "Please, your honor, call me Sasha."

"Yes. We'd like you to help out with the investigation into Judge Paulson's horrific murder."

"Help out?"

"We understand you had a case pending in front of Judge Paulson." Griggs horned in.

"Yes. Well, actually, two. I was here arguing a motion last week for a client and the judge ap-

pointed me to represent a gentleman at his incapacitation hearing, which is also pending. That's
why I'm in town today, to meet with the allegedly
incapacitated man."

She didn't care if they were the chief justice and
the attorney general—her clients' identities were
confidential unless they chose to reveal that she
represented them. She realized, of course, that
both men could access the identity of each client
she'd ever represented in less time than she could
order a pizza, but she saw no upside in volunteer-
ing the information.

What Griggs said next made her wonder if
they'd done just that.

"No good deed goes unpunished, eh? I'm sure
when you were at Prescott & Talbott you never imagined you'd be representing someone like Mr.
Craybill."

Justice Bermann got out in front of her next
question.

"We called some of our friends at your former
firm when we learned that you had spoken to the
judge this morning. I must say, they spoke quite
highly of you," he said, then nodded to Griggs.

Griggs added, "So highly, in fact, that we would
like to appoint you special prosecutor to oversee
the investigation into Judge Paulson's murder."

Sasha would have been set back on her heels if she weren't sitting.

"I have no prosecutorial experience, sir. I have, at best, a glancing understanding of how things work in the county. I don't know anything about Judge Paulson, other than he liked pie."

"All true," the justice agreed. "But, you're obviously bright and not easily intimidated, as evidenced by that mess with Hemisphere Air last year. We need someone who's not going to be cowed. Someone who isn't tied in to the local scene. The handful of attorneys who practice up here have dozens of cases on the judge's docket. And, you may not know this, but Judge Paulson was being threatened. That's not to say that the threats were coming from a local lawyer, but they did relate to his docket. The attorneys who practice here have their own agendas. You have no agenda."

Everyone has an agenda, she thought. Hers was to grow her fledgling solo practice. Would devoting the time and resources required to serve as special prosecutor in a county four hours away further that agenda?

She wasn't sure. She started to ask for some time to think about it, but she caught herself before the words were out.

An opportunity like this could make her career. Why was she even entertaining the idea of passing it by?

While the judge and the attorney general waited for her answer, she examined her reaction. To her disgust and surprise, she realized she was afraid. Afraid she'd fail.

Fear could be an important survival mechanism. It alerted a person to danger. Fear of failure was just an unproductive emotion, an excuse for the weak.

"I'd be honored," she said.

15.

ASHA COULD HEAR GLORIA'S STOM-ACH growling. It was well past quitting time, but the secretary refused to leave.

After Chief Justice Bermann and Attorney General Griggs had gone off in search of the sheriff, she joined Sasha in the judge's chambers.

"I'm told you'll be working out of the judge's office?" she said.

Sasha searched the woman's tone to get a sense of how she felt about that development, but found nothing.

"Only for a day or two. My understanding is the chief justice will be appointing one of the retired judges to finish out Judge Paulson's term. Once those arrangements have been made, I'll be kicked out. I guess they'll find me a desk somewhere."

"There are plenty of empty offices in this building. Where are you planning to stay?"

Sasha hadn't thought about it. "Can you recommend a nearby hotel?"

Gloria chuckled. "No chance. The oil and gas people have booked every room within one hundred and twenty miles of the courthouse through next year and then some. We're talking every hotel, motel, bed and breakfast, and inn. Big Sky even brought in some trailer homes and set people up in the motor court out on past Herr's run. There's no room at the inn, honey."

It figured.

The thought of driving home to sleep and then turning around to drive back before the sun rose in the morning did not appeal to her. She contemplated sleeping in her car.

"You can stay in the judge's apartment, I guess."

"Oh, I don't think . . ."

"No, it's okay. I'm his landlord."

"You are?"

"I was. He's been renting the top floor of our home since 1994, when his wife died. It has its own entrance, a kitchen, and a private bath. Really, it'll be fine. We won't even know you're there."

Sasha was about to decline but, considering her options, simply said, "I appreciate that. Thank you."

"You're welcome." The secretary smiled. "You don't mind cats, do you?"

"The judge had cats?"

"Two of them. Poor things, they're not going to understand what happened."

Tears filled Gloria's eyes. Sasha could see her mind racing—who was going to pack up the judge's things, take care of the cats, cancel his appointments? Her days were going to be filled with the sad business of wrapping up a life.

Sasha asked, more to distract the woman than anything, "Did you know the judge was being threatened?"

Gloria swallowed hard but answered the question. "Of course. I'm the one who told the sheriff. Judge Paulson kept saying he could handle it, but it was weighing on him, I could tell."

"What kind of threats?"

"Someone, a man, kept calling. He wouldn't give his name but he his voice sounded familiar, I just couldn't place it. Anyhow, he'd ask for the judge and, of course, I'd say he wasn't available. Then, every time, he'd say the same thing. 'Give the judge this message: A lawyer with his briefcase can steal more than a hundred men with guns.'"

Sasha looked at her closely. "That was the threat?" It sounded more like a warning to her.

She nodded. "It's from *The Godfather*. The judge just laughed it off, but it was creepy. He'd call once a week, like clockwork."

"Did Judge Paulson know what it was a reference to? Aside from the movie, I mean. Was there a particular case or litigant?"

"No. But, almost his entire docket is somehow related to the Marcellus Shale now. Except for criminal stuff, but the criminal matters are always drunk driving or petty theft. Once in a blue moon, there's a domestic matter or a small drug bust. Nothing that anyone would get worked up over."

"Oh. Well, there were also cases like Mr. Craybill's incapacitation hearing. That has nothing to do with the shale."

"That's what you think."

Sasha arched a brow. "Pardon?"

The older woman sighed, like she wished she hadn't said anything, but now that she had, she plowed ahead.

"Jed Craybill is sitting on 160 acres of land. All of his neighbors have signed leases with the oil and gas people. All of them. He's an island in a sea of drilling and he refuses to sign. He's been fighting with his neighbors over it since before Marla died."

"But, what difference does it make to them what he does with his land?"

The secretary shook her head. "I'm not sure. We live here in town, so there's no drilling near us. But, as I understand it, they—the oil and gas people—can't really use all the mineral rights on the adjacent property because they can't do anything that impacts Jed's land. And, even if they are toeing the line, they have to deal with old Jed out there, shaking his shotgun at them and cursing a blue streak. Big Sky already told him if he doesn't knock it off, they're going to get a restraining order."

Clients, Sasha thought. It didn't matter if the client was the CEO of a publicly traded company or an angry old man trying to stay in his home; they never told you the whole story.

"I see. Listen, why don't you head on home? I'm just going to make a few calls and check my e-mail. I'll lock up."

Sheriff Stickley had sent Russell on his way hours ago.

"Are you sure?"

"I'm positive. You have to be exhausted. If you'll just give me directions, I'll come over to your house when I've finished up here."

Gloria leaned across the judge's desk and scrawled her address on the notepad by the phone. She handed it to Sasha along with two brass keys that she removed from a key ring. "This key with the red fingernail polish dot locks his office. The other one is to the door to my office. My house is literally around the corner. You can walk there. Turn right at the light on the corner. That's Primrose Street. My house is on the left, four houses in—it's the red brick house. I'll leave the porch light on for you. When you get there, I'll show you around the judge's apartment and introduce you to Atticus Finch and Sir Thomas More."

Sasha stared at her for a moment before it dawned on her.

"The cats?"

"The cats," she confirmed.

After Gloria put on her coat and fetched her handbag from her desk drawer, Sasha closed the exterior door and called Connelly to let him know that she wouldn't be coming back to Pittsburgh after all.

16.

Pittsburgh, Pennsylvania
Monday evening

EO HELD THE PHONE AWAY from his ear with one hand and carefully slid the chicken and noodles into a storage container with the other. On the other end of the phone, Sasha was rattling off a list of instructions that she'd started in on as soon as he'd offered to drive up to Springport.

She was talking much too fast for him to actually follow what she was saying, so he put the phone down on the counter to have both hands available to pour the spicy peanut sauce into a separate container. When he picked it back up, she hadn't yet taken a breath, but from her cadence, he thought she'd need to pause soon.

She did, and he jumped in. "So, you need me to bring your laptop, your VitaMight files, and an overnight bag. Got it. Does the judge's apartment have a microwave?"

"I don't know, Connelly. I haven't been there yet. Probably? Call me when you're fifteen minutes away and I'll meet you there."

"Okay. Hang in there, Mac. I'll be there as fast as I can."

His eyes fell on the coffeemaker sitting in the exact middle of the recycled glass countertop. "Oh, should I bring the coffeemaker along?"

It would be one thing if Judge Paulson's bachelor pad lacked a microwave. It would be quite another if there was no caffeine-delivery device. Leo'd learned that during a romantic weekend at a secluded bed and breakfast that turned out to serve herbal tea with breakfast. Deprived of her coffee, Sasha had been drowsy and slow all morning. And maybe just the tiniest bit irritable.

"Oh, good idea."

A hint of a smile slipped into her voice and Leo smiled himself. She claimed to be high maintenance, but it was just a matter of paying attention to the details, which was a skill Leo had in spades.

"Done. See you—," he paused to check the time, "—probably around nine thirty, maybe a little after."

"Thanks." She hung up in a hurry. Before he had a chance to tell her he loved her.

He unplugged the coffeemaker and its matching grinder and found a reusable cloth grocery bag in the pantry. Before putting them in the bag, he wiped the appliances with a dish towel. Then he took the container of coffee beans from the freezer, wrapped it in the towel, and added that to the bag. He stacked the food containers holding dinner in the bag and tested the handle to confirm the load wasn't too heavy. The bag was plenty strong.

That task completed, he left the bag at the bottom of the steps leading to the loft bedroom and methodically searched through Sasha's closet to find her a comfortable outfit to change into for the rest of the evening, pajamas, a suit for the next day, and all the attendant accessories. He gathered up her bathroom supplies and quickly, but neatly, packed everything away in her small red roller board bag, taking care not to wrinkle the clothes.

At the bottom of the stairs, he bent to retrieve the kitchen bag, slung the strap of his own overnight bag over his chest like a messenger bag, wheeling the red bag behind him.

At the door, he checked the time. Three minutes from the end of the call to completion of his first task. An acceptable pace, he thought.

He stepped out into the hallway and locked the condo door behind him. Next stop, Sasha's office to retrieve her computer and files.

~ ~ ~ ~ ~ ~ ~ ~ ~ ~

He found a spot on the street just two doors down from the office and eased the car in to the snug parking space. It was that limbo time between evening and night; the storefronts were closed for the day and the restaurants had emptied of their dinner rushes, but it was too early for the bar scene to be in full swing.

Leo punched Sasha's code into the keyless lock at the entrance to the tall, narrow building where she had a second floor office. The vacant retail space on the first floor was illuminated only by the red glow of an emergency exit light and the streetlights that filtered through the front window. He took the stairs by twos. The building was on a busy commercial strip in an upscale neighborhood, but the lack of a ground floor tenant gave it a desolate air.

At the door to the office, he keyed a second code into a second keypad and swung the door open. He flipped the switch on the wall near the door and blinked as the overhead lights came to life. The desk was piled with papers, but they had been separated into neat stacks. He swept the stack nearest the computer into a redweld labeled "VitaMight."

Sasha had left her laptop running when she'd left the office that morning. He brought the screen to life and typed in her password so he could shut it down properly.

It occurred to him he might not have e-mail access in Springport. He pulled out the desk chair and opened his account to send a message to the Field Office that he'd be working remotely for a few days. Although he worked out of the Pittsburgh Field Office, it was just a place with a desk. He was part of the Internal Affairs Department and, at least for now, they seemed happy to let him set up shop wherever he wanted.

His inbox was brimming with messages. He scanned them and stopped on an automated message from the Guardian database. His search request on Daniel McAlister's bank account had been completed. He opened the attachment and stared at the words: *The information you have requested has been designated SECRET and poses a grave danger to national security if disseminated. Demonstrate need to know.*

Leo massaged his forehead. That message could mean one of a handful of things: Not one of them was good.

He deleted the e-mail and powered down the computer.

17.

Springport, Pennsylvania

KNOWING LEO WAS ON HIS way helped Sasha quiet her mind, which had been firing off in about a dozen directions. She found a fresh legal pad and shut herself up in Judge Paulson's office to write up some notes and see what the process of reviewing the day would yield. She hesitated for a minute before deciding to sit in the leather chair behind his desk, but it was the best spot to spread out her papers.

From behind his desk, she switched on Judge Paulson's green-shaded banker's lamp and surveyed the room by its soft light. The furniture was masculine and well made. The colors were all dark purples and reds. It was dignified but understated, like the judge.

Someone, probably Russell, had covered the bullet hole in the window behind with a square of cardboard secured by a silver X of duct tape and had removed the oval rug where the judge had fallen along with his body. Those were the only two discordant notes in the room. She never would have guessed the judge had been murdered right there just hours earlier.

Why Stickley hadn't sealed chambers as a crime scene was beyond her.

Sasha shook thoughts of the judge's death from her mind and picked up her pen. She started to free write, as quickly as she could, jotting down her impressions from the day first, and then worked backward to create a history of all of her interactions with anyone in Springport from the time of the discovery hearing.

She would label the notes "privileged and confidential attorney work product" on each page, so she scrawled everything that came to mind onto the paper. In the past, through this exercise, her subconscious mind had given her the tools to solve more legal problems than she could count. Now, she hoped it could solve a murder.

She'd written more than a dozen pages when a muffled thud interrupted her train of thought. She stopped writing and sat motionless. She listened hard for a minute. Heard nothing but the hum of an old building after hours.

She resumed her writing. Then she heard the jangle of a brass handle being jiggled and a desk drawer rolling smoothly on its track.

Someone was in the outside office opening one of Gloria's desk drawers.

If it had been the secretary coming back for something she'd forgotten, she'd have called out to Sasha. This was someone else. Someone who didn't know Sasha was behind the door in the judge's chambers.

She silently laid the pen on the pad. Then she reached over and slowly turned the knob on the lamp to shut out the light, cringing when it gave an audible click.

She waited.

Outside a drawer bumped shut and a second one rolled open. She had to decide. Stick it out in chambers and hope whoever was outside left without checking the interior office or open the door and confront the intruder.

Krav Maga theory said never go to the fight. But she wasn't interested in being the second person to die in Judge Paulson's chambers. If the intruder opened the door, she'd have nowhere to go. If she opened the door, she'd have options. And the element of surprise.

Her heart thrummed in her ears.

Another drawer banged closed in Gloria's desk.

She stood and kicked off her heels. She prowled the room. Her bare toes sunk into the thick, plush carpet, which swallowed any noise her footsteps might have made.

She scanned all visible surfaces for an improvised weapon. The best option would have been the coat rack if she were taller, but it would be too unwieldy for someone her height. She didn't want to risk the noise of opening the judge's desk drawers to search for a letter opener or a pair of scissors. Her eyes fell on the bookcase. On a shelf three-quarters of the way up, nestled between a leather-bound law copy of Black's Law Dictionary and a set of law review journals sat a ceremonial gavel.

She crept over and stretched to reach it. Couldn't. She swore under her breath. Stretched again, straining to gain an eighth of an inch more height, but it was still out of reach.

She couldn't drag a chair over. Too noisy. She eyed the bookcase again and considered climbing up on the shelves. The problem was she had no idea how sturdy they were. If she pulled the whole thing down on herself it would make a racket and she'd be trapped underneath when the intruder came to investigate. No good.

Outside, on the other side of the substantial walnut door, the person had moved from Gloria's desk to the row of filing cabinets that lined the wall beside the door to chambers. When she opened the door, he might have his head down looking through the drawers, but he'd be facing her. It was always better to assume one's opponent was a male when gender was unknown. That way you wouldn't underestimate your foe's strength.

If she could just reach that gavel. She walked through it in her mind. She could pull the door open and swing the gavel all in one motion. She'd have an excellent shot at the top of his head.

Let it go. You can't reach the gavel.

Time for a plan B. If he was bent over the filing cabinet, he'd be low enough: she could burst through the door, rear back, and smash him with a head butt. The human forehead made an excellent blunt weapon, if a person could force herself to literally rush headlong into a collision with someone else's head.

Her mind made up, she moved toward the door.

As she put her hand on the knob, she heard the outside door ease open and shut softly. Whoever had been out there had left.

She ran back to the desk and scooped up her notes with shaking hands. It was time to go.

18.

SASHA WALKED THE BLOCK AND a half to the Burkes' home at a good clip. She didn't run, but she moved with purpose and paid close attention to her surroundings. She passed one couple walking a puppy that hadn't yet grown into its paws, and, at the traffic light, Sheriff Stickley rolled through the intersection in his black and white and gave her a half wave.

That was it. No one else was out and about in Springport.

She reached the red brick house. Low hedges edged the walkway to the porch. They were too short to provide cover to an assailant, but Sasha remained alert anyway. A man had died today. It was no time to be complacent about personal safety.

With that thought front and center, Sasha darted up the stairs to the porch and rang the bell. Then she turned around and faced the street while she waited for Gloria to answer the door. As the sound of footsteps grew louder inside the house, Sasha turned around to see a heavyset man peering through the glass at the top of the door. He smiled at her as he opened it.

"Well," he said, "Gloria said you were a wee thing. You must be Sasha. I'm Jonas Burke. C'mon in."

He reached out to shake her hand and led her into the foyer. While he shut and locked the door, an antique gun cabinet in the front room caught her eye. One door hung open, and there was an empty space in the collection. Her gaze fell to Jonas's waistband. A telltale lump poked out from under his sweater.

He followed her gaze and gave her a sheepish smile; then he hurried over and closed the display cabinet door, checking to confirm it had locked.

"Jonas," Gloria called from the back of the house, "you bring Sasha in here, now."

"Oh, boy," he chuckled. "Gloria's been cooking up a storm ever since she got home. Since our kids flew the coop for college, she hasn't had anyone to mother. Consider yourself warned."

"How many children do you have?" Sasha asked as she trailed him along a hallway. She figured the answer was two, judging by the portraits that lined the hall on both walls, tracing the growth of a tow-headed boy and a serious-looking, freckled girl, but it was easy conversation.

"Two. Our Linnea is at Bucknell, studying history. Her older brother, Luke, graduated last year. Got his degree in geoengineering. Didn't know what the devil he'd do with that, but it turns out all those oil and gas companies were knocking on his door before the ink on his diploma was dry."

Even without being able to see his face, Sasha could tell the proud father was beaming.

"Does he work here in town, then?"

"Nope, afraid not. Much to Gloria's eternal dismay, he's at the corporate headquarters in Texas, rotating through some management training program they've got. Right now, he's attached to the public relations department but he's itching to finish that up and get some mud on his boots. I keep tellin' him, management is the way to go. Especially at a place like Big Sky. But, you know kids, he just wants to be out in the field."

Sasha was surprised Gloria hadn't mentioned that her son worked at Big Sky earlier.

They entered the brightly lit kitchen. Gloria was standing at the stove, stirring something in a copper pot. A loaf pan was cooling on the counter and the smell of freshly baked bread met Sasha at the doorway.

"I'm just finishing this up. It seemed like the sort of day that called for stew. Jonas'll show you the judge's apartment. I already fed the cats. Why don't you settle in and then come down and eat?"

"That's really too kind of you. It smells wonderful."

Ordinarily, Sasha would've begged off, but she wanted to talk to the woman about the intruder in the office.

"Oh, my, uh, friend from Pittsburgh is driving up with some things I need. My computer, a change of clothes. Is it okay if he stays the night?" Her cheeks burned.

She was a grown woman, but here she was, asking someone else's mother for permission to have her boyfriend sleep over. And, to top it off, she couldn't even bring herself to call Connelly her boyfriend. It sounded ridiculous to her; she was in her thirties, after all.

Gloria just chuckled. "I never inquired about the judge's overnight guests. I don't suppose I'll be inquiring about yours. Will your friend be joining us for supper?"

"Oh, he's going to be awhile."

"That's no problem. This'll keep just fine. We'll hold dinner until your friend gets here." She said it in a tone that didn't invite discussion.

Jonas motioned for Sasha to follow him.

At the other end of the kitchen, a door led to a narrow stairway. As they mounted the stairs, he explained the layout of the house.

"So, this house is very old. It was built in the 1920s or so. There's this back stairway. I guess the staff used this back in the day. Then, there's the formal stairs in the front. Now, we'll give you the key to the judge's private outside entrance, though truth be told, he quit using that a few years back. It's a metal staircase attached to the side of the house. I think the climb, especially in the dark, was getting to be a bit much for him. He mainly used this staircase instead."

On the second floor, the stairway ended, and they turned a tight corner in the hallway and ended up in another stairway to the third floor.

As they wound their way up, Jonas continued, "Our bedroom's in the front of the house on the second floor. There's a guest room up front, too, but Gloria uses that for her scrapbooking. Down that hallway we just went through, in the back, are the kids' old rooms and their shared bathroom."

At the top of the stairs, the doorway opened up to a small square space, lit by a dim ceiling light. "Now, this light's on a timer. It'll come on at sunset and go off at eleven. That's when the judge retired for the night. If you want to override it, go right ahead."

"Great. Thanks."

He took a key ring with a green rubberized tag advertising a locksmith's service from his shirt pocket, eased a key into the lock on the white wooden door, and jangled it until it turned.

"Here you go." He handed the keys to Sasha and flipped on the lights. Two calico cats—one fat, one thin—darted into the entryway from somewhere in the apartment and wrapped themselves around his legs, mewling and purring. He bent to pet them.

"Poor things," he said, looking at the cats, not at her. "I guess we'll keep them. The judge's son is active duty military. He can't take 'em."

The fat cat collapsed on its side and rolled over to show its belly. Jonas rubbed it and the cat arched in joy. Its thinner friend pranced over to Sasha and sniffed her outstretched hand.

"Who are you?" Sasha asked, "Atticus Finch or Sir Thomas More?"

The cat butted against her hand with its head.

"That there's Atticus Finch. This plump fella is Sir Thomas More." Jonas gave the cat a scratch under its chin and stood.

He walked into a spotless galley kitchen to the right of the door and flicked the light on. The cats trailed behind.

"Help yourself to any food or anything, I guess." He gestured toward the refrigerator and the cabinets beside it.

Sasha saw a small countertop microwave. No dishwasher, so Connelly would have to show some restraint. His cooking was the stuff of her dreams, but it apparently required him to dirty every pot, pan, and utensil she owned. There was a tea kettle on the stovetop but no coffeemaker on the counter. She mentally awarded Connelly a gold star for thinking to bring hers.

Jonas turned and walked out of the kitchen.

"Bath's over there," he said, pointing to a short hallway on the left. "Bedroom is behind it. Gloria stripped the bed and put on a set of our guest sheets. Towels are in the bathroom."

He stood in the middle of the main living space and turned in a slow circle. "So, uh, I guess that's it."

"I really can't thank you and Gloria enough."

He waved off her gratitude. "We're glad someone from outside is going to be looking into the judge's death. He was a good man," he said with a catch in his voice. "He didn't deserve . . . this."

He cleared his throat. "You go ahead and get settled. Come on down whenever you're ready. Like Gloria said, the stew'll keep till your friend arrives."

He bent to pet Atticus Finch and then walked through the door, closing it behind him.

Sasha walked through the tidy apartment. It was decorated in the same spare style as the judge's chambers. The living area housed a chocolate brown leather loveseat and a matching oversized chair and ottoman. A red and blue area rug anchored the room. One wall was lined with books. A low sofa table held framed pictures of a serious-looking man in a military dress uniform, a yellowing black and white wedding portrait of a much younger Judge Paulson and his bride, and a recent color photograph of the judge with Chief Justice Bermann. They were both in suits, sitting at a table covered with a white tablecloth, smiling up at the photographer. They appeared to be at some kind of reception or benefit dinner judging by the uninspired centerpiece and uneaten chicken dinners on the table.

She poked her head into the narrow bathroom. A clawfoot tub with a shower head hanging from a bar above it took up most of the floor space.

She continued down the hallway to the bedroom. A king bed with a dark wood headboard faced a matching dresser. Gloria must have used her daughter's bedding to make up the bed, because the pale yellow and pink striped sheets and white eyelet blanket looked wildly out of place in the masculine room. In the corner, a tan armchair sat next to a small table piled high with a neat stack of papers and legal journals.

Burgundy drapes covered most of the far wall. She tugged on the rope to pull them back, revealing a large square window. It looked out over the Burkes' backyard and the alley running behind their wooden fence. Next to the window was a glass door. She peered out through the glass. Metal steps led from a cement pad in the backyard, up the side of the house, and stopped at the door. She could see why Judge Paulson had abandoned his private entrance.

She twisted the knob to confirm the door was locked. There was no deadbolt. She stood with her hand pressed against the cold glass and stared out into the yard, unseeing and lost in thought, until an insistent meowing shook her out of her musing.

Sir Thomas More took a running start and hefted himself up onto the judge's bed. Atticus Finch followed close behind and with a good deal more grace.

"You guys are looking for the judge, aren't you?" Sasha said, going over to sit on the edge of the bed beside them. "He's not going to be coming back."

Atticus Finch meowed at her.

She stroked his back.

"The Burkes are going to take good care of you," she told them.

Sir Thomas More purred his agreement and rolled himself into a ball. She sat there, petting the cats, while she pulled out her phone to call Connelly.

He answered on the second ring. "Hey, I'm still about a half hour away. Are you at the judge's?"

"I am. When you get to town, drive straight through on Main, turn right at the light at Primrose Street. The Burkes live in the fourth house down on the left. I guess you can just park on the street."

"Great. Have you had dinner? I have the Thai chicken. I can assemble it there."

"I haven't eaten and that sounds divine, but we'll have to save it for tomorrow. The Burkes are holding dinner for us. Or supper, they call it. Stew and homemade bread. It'd be rude not to eat with them. Plus . . .." She trailed off and rubbed Sir Thomas More's head.

"Plus?"

"Plus, I need to talk to them. Someone was rifling around in Gloria's desk and filing cabinets after she left the courthouse. Someone's looking for something. If they think she has it . . .." Her voice trailed off again, but this time Connelly didn't need to ask.

"Understood."

"Hey," she said, just remembering. "Did anything pop in the Guardian database when you ran Danny Trees's account number?"

There was silence on the line.

For a minute she thought she'd lost the call, but then he said, "Not exactly. Let's talk about it later."

~ ~ ~ ~ ~ ~ ~ ~ ~ ~

After a rib-sticking dinner with the Burkes, Sasha and Connelly returned to Judge Paulson's apartment and opened a bottle of his wine. It was strange and awkward to sit in a dead man's apartment, drinking his pinot noir out of his wine glasses, but Jonas and Gloria had repeatedly urged them to make themselves at home.

They sat sideways on the judge's loveseat, facing each other, with their backs against the armrests and their knees bent. It was a cozy arrangement, but one that was sure to become uncomfortable halfway through the first glass of wine.

Connelly said it. "You know she's lying, right?"

Sasha sighed and wrapped her arms around her knees. She knew.

Over dinner, she had gently probed to see if Gloria had any idea why someone would have come into her office and gone through her drawers after hours. The secretary claimed to have no idea what the searcher could have been looking for. She also had no thoughts as to who would have known when she left for the evening and said she hadn't seen anyone on her way out.

Her purported ignorance might have been believable, if she hadn't stared unblinkingly at the table the entire time she spoke. And, if her hands hadn't been shaking so hard that her china teacup clattered against the saucer when she reached for her after dinner coffee.

Even her husband had noticed. While Connelly was helping Gloria clear the table, Jonas had pulled Sasha into the doorway near the servants' stairs and whispered, "I'll talk to her about the break in. She's just scared. Maybe in shock."

Sasha had just nodded. She didn't doubt that he was right, but she was going to need the woman to come clean. And soon.

Now, she looked at Connelly. "Oh, she's definitely holding something back," she agreed. "Of course," she added, sipping her wine, "she's not the only one."

Connelly held her gaze but his right cheek twitched, just barely, under his eye. He was quiet for a long moment.

Then he said, "You mean about Danny Trees, I take it?"

She arched a brow in response.

Connelly rested his glass on the side table and interlaced his fingers. "All I can tell you is . . . I can't tell you anything."

Sasha put down her glass, too. "You can't tell me what? Whether there was a hit in the database or what it said?"

"Either."

She rubbed her temple with both handed. "Can you tell me that there wasn't a hit?"

"I cannot. The information came back with a classification level that requires me to demonstrate my need to know it. I don't have a legitimate need to know. And you don't have a security clearance. I'm sorry, Sasha, but you need to consider it a dead end." His voice was firm.

She felt her temper rising but exhaled and tamped it down. After all, he had taken a risk even running the account. She couldn't ask him to divulge something the government had decided was top secret.

"Okay, fine. I'm just going to say something, and you should feel free to comment on the wisdom of my plan, okay? My current operating theory is that either Jay, acting alone, or PORE is behind Judge Paulson's murder."

If Danny Trees was involved in something bad enough that Connelly couldn't even give her a hint, well, then, she'd make his organization her number one suspect until someone better came along.

Connelly smiled. "Nice try. I have no views about your plan, Madam Special Prosecutor."

He said the title with deliberate emphasis, and she couldn't help giggle.

As much as she wanted to be back in Pittsburgh, back in her comfort zone, the Chief Justice of the Pennsylvania Supreme Court and the Attorney General had dropped an amazing opportunity in her lap. She had no intention of squandering it.

19.

BOB GRIGGS GULPED HIS DRAFT beer. He wanted to get this over with and get the hell out of town before any of the yokels lining the bar recognized him from television. For now, he'd settle for staying upwind of Stickley. Next to him, the sheriff was nursing his sweating bottle of Bud.

"What were you thinking, Bob, appointing that girl as Special Prosecutor?"

They'd been over this. He wasn't any happier about the appointment of a special prosecutor than the sheriff, but he had decided to look on the bright side. Bob believed in the power of positive thinking.

"It was out of my hands. That old coot Bermann wasn't going to sit by and do nothing in the face of a murdered judge, much less one who was his friend. Look at it this way, that girl, as you call her, doesn't know the local ropes. She's not going to be able to identify the players, let alone piece together the action. If you're smart, you'll drop a few hints and lead her down a garden path."

Stickley chewed the inside of his cheek and thought it over. He reminded Bob of a cow working on some cud.

Bob shook his head at himself for the image. He needed to start thinking in a more sophisticated manner, like an urbanite. That farmer shit might play around here, but he needed to move beyond the local voters and set his sights on the urban voters in Philly and Pittsburgh, who probably couldn't tell a cow from a horse. After all, he had plans beyond the AG's office. And, with enough money and well-placed friends, maybe even beyond the commonwealth.

Finally, Stickley nodded, "I have an idea."

Bob cut him off before he could share his brilliant insight. "Great. Take care of it. After a respectable amount of time, I'll shut down her investigation for lack of results. Bermann won't dare interfere. He wouldn't want to be accused of overstepping and meddling with an issue that's solidly in the purview of the Attorney General's Office."

"What about the other thing?"

Bob resisted the urge to strangle the putrid law enforcement officer beside him. He counted to ten silently, then pasted on his politician smile.

"You're the sheriff, Carl. Surely you can take care of it."

Stickley stared at him. Bob stared back.

He wasn't about to explicitly tell the idiot to break the law. For all he knew, Stickley was playing both sides of this thing. Lord knew Shelly and Heather were working multiple angles.

If those two airheaded bimbos had just listened to him and kept it simple, they wouldn't have all these problems. There was plenty of money in shaking down the oil and gas companies. More than enough, as far as he was concerned. But, not for those two. No, they had to have a piece of all the action. And a brain-dead sheriff on the payroll.

He drained his mug and slammed it down on the bar. He peeled a twenty off the roll in his money clip and tossed it down beside the mug.

"I've got to get back to Harrisburg. Have another one on me."

He slapped the sheriff on the shoulder and hurried to the door.

~ ~ ~ ~ ~ ~ ~ ~ ~ ~

Carl watched the door swing shut behind Griggs. He was a piece of work, Carl thought. Typical politician; all he wanted to do was glad hand everyone and take all the credit. The actual work? That all fell to Carl.

What had he been thinking, getting in bed with, not one, but two pols?

The bartender came over to scoop up the twenty and wipe down the bar with his dirty rag. He gave a nod to the door, "That who I think it was, Sheriff?"

"I dunno, Mikey. Do you think it was a dumbshit politician?"

Mikey roared with laughter, then motioned toward the Bud. "You want another?"

Carl nodded. Might as well.

As he twisted off the cap, the bartender commented, "It's a shame about Judge Paulson, huh?"

"Sure is. God rest his soul."

They fell silent for a minute.

Then, Mikey asked, "Got any leads? I heard it looked like a hunter picked him off. Maybe somebody riled up about the Shale?"

Carl took his time answering. "Not exactly sure. But Danny Trees and his hippies have been getting violent lately. They attacked some lawyer lady last week. Might have a talk with them in the morning."

Mikey cocked his head, "That so? Doesn't sound like Danny. He's a squirrelly kid, but a lot of the guys think he's right on about the drilling."

Carl nodded. Hunters didn't much like running across the tanks and capped wells on their favorite spots. And fishermen swore the trout tasted off now. Danny had been smart to get them on his side.

"Like I said, I'm not sure what's going on. Now listen, that was just between us, right?"

Mikey agreed right away.

They both knew Mikey wouldn't keep his trap shut. He manned a bar. He offered cold drinks and fresh gossip. That was fine by Carl. All part of the plan.

20.

ASHA STARTED AWAKE.

Her arm jerked out to her side and into a pile of warm fur. Sir Thomas More was curled into a ball next to her. He didn't move.

She lay still, listening to her heart pound. She turned her head to the side and saw Connelly, splayed across the bed on his stomach, with Atticus Finch perched on his back. Connelly breathed deeply, and the cat rose and fell in a hump with each breath.

She squinted into the dark. Without her contact lenses, the numbers on Judge Paulson's alarm clock on the dresser across the room were just a luminescent blur.

She rolled on to her side and resettled into a comfortable position. Just as she was drifting off to sleep again, she heard the clang of metal hitting metal.

That was the noise that had awakened her, she realized. She raised herself on her elbows and scanned the room. She couldn't remember anything in the apartment that would make that sound.

Clang.

It was outside. Maybe a wind chime or a metal trash can banging around.

Clang. Louder this time.

Disoriented from sleep and wine and unfamiliar with her surroundings, it took another minute before she realized what she was hearing. The sound of shoes scraping across the metal stairs outside. Someone was coming.

She reached over and shook Connelly. He moaned but didn't wake. She shook him harder, dislodging the cat, who rewarded her with a hiss before settling in where he landed.

"Connelly," she whispered, "there's someone outside on the stairs."

He was wide awake in an instant. He sat upright and reached for the lamp on the bedside table.

"Wait," Sasha said, putting a hand on his arm to stop him. "If you turn it on, we're on display. We won't be able to see out."

Connelly nodded. "Okay. I stowed my gun in the bathroom closet. You cover the door. I'll be right back."

He swung his legs around and silently rose from the bed in boxers and a t-shirt. He stepped into the sweatpants lying on the floor and made his way down the darkened hallway.

Sasha threw off the blanket and crept toward the door.

Judging by the clanging, their visitor had neared the top of the stairs. Sasha pressed herself against the wall and peeked through heavy drapes that covered the window beside the door. She couldn't see a thing.

Her glasses were on the dresser, next to the alarm clock. Presumably, whoever was coming would break the glass in the door, which would slow him down for a minute or two.

She raced over, grabbed the glasses, and jammed them onto her face. She blinked as her eyes adjusted and took up a position behind the door.

But, she'd been wrong. The dark shape now stood on the other side of the door wasn't intent on breaking the glass. He was jiggling a key in the doorknob.

Connelly returned, his Glock in his hand.

"Wait!" she hissed. "He has a key. What if it's the judge's son?"

She had no idea how long it would it take for the military to notify him or if he would have been given leave to attend his father's funeral. But if it was the son, shooting him seemed like a spectacularly bad idea.

"What if it's not?" Connelly whispered back, but he lowered the gun to his side.

Sasha shrugged.

The key turned in the lock.

Curious about all the activity, Sir Thomas More picked that moment to lunge at the windowsill. He missed and hit the floor with a loud thump. His tail smacked against the cord to the drapes and the round plastic end piece swung wildly against the window, hammering out a loud rapping noise.

The figure in the doorway had just twisted the knob to open the door. At the sound, he backed out and pulled the door shut.

"Go!" Connelly yelled, but she was already going.

She yanked the door open and raced out into the chilly night air.

The man was already more than a third of the way down the stairs, not worrying about the noise, clattering in a hurry.

She took off after him, the metal cold on her bare feet. She could hear Connelly running hard right behind her.

At about the halfway point, the shadowy figure turned to see how close she was. Then he jumped to the bottom, landed in a heap on the concrete pad, and rolled. He got to his feet and took off into the alley.

Sasha flew down the remaining stairs and through the yard. She lost sight of him as he passed through the high bushes that lined the alley, but she kept running. When she reached the end of the crushed stone alley, she stopped. He was gone.

Leo came up behind her, gun drawn.

"Did you see his face?"

She shook her head. Then, she reached out and held his forearm to steady herself, while she picked the sharp stones out of first one bare foot and then the other. She shivered in her thin shirt and yoga pants.

"We lost him. Let's go back."

~ ~ ~ ~ ~ ~ ~ ~ ~ ~ ~

It was two in the morning, but trying to get back to sleep would be futile. Adrenaline rushed through both their bodies. Sasha made a pot of coffee, while Connelly rummaged around in the judge's refrigerator.

"I could do omelets," he said over his shoulder.

"I'm not really hungry, but feel free if you want one."

He closed the refrigerator and joined her at the counter. "No, I guess I'm just looking for something to do."

They spoke in low whispers.

No lights had come on in the house below during the commotion. The Burkes, in their bedroom in the front of the house, had managed to sleep through the racket. There was no point in waking them now.

They toyed with the idea of calling 911, but given that the Sheriff's Office hadn't turned over the investigation into the judge's death, Sasha was pretty sure the state trooper on duty would take a report of an attempted break in at the judge's residence and dump it right back on the Sheriff's Office.

They'd just end up with Stickley—or more likely, Russell—showing up and waking the Burkes.

No, they agreed, it was better to just hold tight and deal with it in the morning. Whoever he was, he wouldn't be coming back tonight.

While the coffeemaker hissed and steamed and worked its magic, Sasha examined the set of keys that Connelly had taken from the doorknob. Their visitor had left them dangling from the lock in his hurry.

There were five brass keys on the chain. No tag or charm. One key obviously fit the outside door. She tested them and found that another worked the lock on the door leading from the apartment to the third floor of the house. They agreed a third probably worked the front door of the house.

Sasha retrieved from her bag the keys that Gloria had lent her. The two remaining keys matched the keys to Gloria's office and to Judge Paulson's chambers.

"So, these have to be Judge Paulson's keys, right?" she said, more to herself than to Connelly.

"I don't know who else's they could be," he agreed.

He reached over her head and brought down two ceramic mugs from the cabinet. They drank their coffee in silence.

~ ~ ~ ~ ~ ~ ~ ~ ~ ~ ~

Five hours later, after Sasha and Connelly had done a little sparring and had worked through Connelly's morning asanas, they went out and stood on the small metal balcony to watch the sun rise.

Sasha rested her head against Connelly's chest and willed herself to focus on the moment: the pale orange sun, the pink streaks in the gray sky, the call of a bird. But her mind refused to be still.

Not long after the sky lightened, the Burke household hummed to life. Doors banged shut and water burbled through the pipes.

They hurried down to the kitchen, where they found Gloria making oatmeal. The running shower meant Jonas would be unavailable for at least several minutes.

As Gloria turned from the stove to greet them and offer them breakfast, Sasha dangled the keychain directly in front of her surprised face. "Do you recognize this?"

She recoiled but took the key ring from Sasha's hand and held it between two fingers, keeping her arm rigid and away from her body, like she had a dead mouse by the tail. "Yes, this is the judge's. It used to have a silver doodad on the end, but it fell off and rolled under his desk over a month ago, way back by the wall where he couldn't reach it. Where did you get this?"

Her back was pressed against her kitchen counter, and Sasha could see her leaning into it. Maybe to keep her knees from buckling. Sasha glanced over at Connelly to try to read his face; as usual, it was impassive.

"In the lock on Judge's Paulson's outside door," she said. "Someone tried to get in last night, after one a.m."

She was watching Gloria's face, so she didn't see her sway.

Connelly did, though, and he eased the woman into a kitchen chair before she could fall.

"Are you okay? Can I get you a glass of water?" Connelly asked in a gentle voice.

"Yes, please." She adjusted the collar of her blouse with trembling hands.

Sasha walked over and crouched beside the chair. She looked up at the secretary for a minute before speaking.

"I need you to tell me what you know."

Gloria took the glass of water from Connelly without breaking eye contact with Sasha.

She took a long, slow sip, then said, "Okay. Deputy Russell took the keys from the judge's office yesterday. I guess they were in the judge's pocket and when he . . . his body . . . they must have tumbled out. They were on the floor beside him. How? Why would . . ." Her voice trailed off.

Sasha's stomach seized. Russell? She had him pegged as an ally.

"Gloria," she said, careful about how she phrased the question. "Who knew I'd be staying at the judge's apartment?"

Gloria thought about it. "Well, there was no one else around when I told you about the apartment. We were in chambers, right?"

"Right," Sasha agreed. "And Deputy Russell had already left for the day."

Gloria nodded. "That's right, Stinky—er, Sheriff Stickley—came by and sent him home not long after the bigwigs left the courthouse."

Connelly met Sasha's eyes over the secretary's shoulder and jerked his thumb toward the door, then pantomimed talking into a cell phone. Sasha gave him a curt nod, and he made his way out of the kitchen silently. She turned her attention back to Gloria.

"Did you tell anyone?"

She started to shake her head, then stopped and said, "Well, I called Jonas, of course, to let him know."

"Anyone else?"

"I had called the kids earlier in the day, to let them know about the judge. He was like a grandfather to them—he'd lived upstairs ever since they were wee little ones. I caught Linnea in her dorm room between classes, but I had to leave a message for Luke. He was in a meeting, so he called back here at the house while you were still finishing up at the courthouse yesterday evening. I believe I mentioned it to him."

"Did he happen to mention if anyone at Big Sky had already heard the news?"

Tears threatened to spill over Gloria's eyes. "No. You don't think Big Sky was involved, do you?" Her voice quavered.

"I don't know what to think, I was just wondering. Even if they did know, it might not mean anything. They have cases on his docket; their attorney could have called and told them."

Sasha felt guilty about pushing her. She seemed to be veering toward a breakdown.

~ ~ ~ ~ ~ ~ ~ ~ ~ ~

Leo sat on the Burkes' porch swing and swayed back and forth, waiting for Sasha to finish interrogating Gloria. His eyes burned from lack of sleep and his throat was tight with worry. He considered his next step.

His policy was to always, if possible, grant favors or requests for information, without regard to which part of the governmental alphabet soup they'd come from. Such generosity was rare in the federal agencies, where territorial directors vied with one another for power and budget dollars. As a result, everyone owed Leo one. He had chits spread throughout the federal government that he could call in when it was time.

It was time. He thumbed through his contacts list and highlighted Molly Dougherty's name. He selected her number at the Bureau and waited for the call to connect.

"Dougherty. Anti-terrorism."

"Molly, it's Leo."

"Leo Connelly," she said, drawing out his name the way she always did. "Are you calling for business or pleasure?"

"A favor."

"Hit me. Heaven knows I owe you."

"Can you tell me anything about a Daniel J. McAllister, III, or an outfit that goes by PORE? Stands for Protecting Our Resources and the Earth."

"Cute," she remarked.

He could hear her fingers flying over her keyboard, calling up the information while they chatted.

"How've you been, Molls? Still a fan of red wine?"

"Our weekend in Napa got me hooked, Leo. I'm thinking about investing in a vineyard in Virginia."

He ignored the purr that had crept into her voice.

"That seems like a lifetime ago."

"Mmm-hmm. Oh, wait." She snapped out of her reminiscing and was all business when she said, "Sorry, Leo. No can do."

"Pardon?"

"I can't tell you anything about that particular case."

"So there is a case?"

"Knock it off, Leo. If I could help you, I would, but I can't. I'm sorry."

She'd already told him all he was going to get: there was an active file on either McAllister or PORE and the domestic anti-terrorism unit could access it.

"I got it. Thanks anyway, Molly. Send me a bottle of your first vintage when you become a vintner, okay?"

She laughed. "Sure, so you can share it with your little attorney, huh?"

He blushed. News of his relationship was making the rounds.

When she spoke again, her tone was serious.

"And, Leo, whatever you're involved in, be careful."

21.

SASHA AND DEPUTY RUSSELL PEERED into the open evidence locker, which to Sasha's disappointment looked to be no different than a wall locker at any gym, skating rink, or day spa.

She checked the Sheriff's Office inventory sheet that detailed Judge Paulson's personal effects. *Set of keys* was on the list as item number 3, right between number 2, *men's watch, silver*, and number 4, *dictaphone*.

"Gloria's sure this is the judge's set and not a copy?" Russell asked, waving the keys in the air.

"She's sure."

"No one could have taken them from this evidence locker. Sheriff Stickley and I are the only ones with access."

"And yet, here they are."

Sasha and Gloria had agreed in the kitchen that it was almost impossible Deputy Russell was dirty. Gloria based her view on having known "young Gavin" nearly his entire life; Sasha based hers on the belief that anyone who could create such a heavenly cup of coffee had to have a good soul.

They'd further agreed that someone in the sheriff's office had to have been the intruder. That left the stout female receptionist or the odoriferous sheriff himself. Unless Claudine had a partner, it had to be Stickley, because the shadowy figure trying to gain entry to the apartment had been a man.

Neither Sasha nor Gloria had found it too much of a stretch to believe the sheriff had stopped by chambers to rummage through Gloria's desk and the filing cabinets and then taken a run at sneaking into what he'd thought would be an empty apartment.

Russell seemed to be having a harder time accepting it.

He threw her a skeptical look.

"You don't really think Stinky stole the keys. Why would he? He's the sheriff. If he wanted to search Gloria's office or the judge's apartment as part of his investigation, he could just do it. In the light of day. It doesn't make any sense."

He rejected the idea with a sharp shake of his head.

"It does if he's looking for something he doesn't want anyone to know about."

"Like what?"

She had no idea.

She stared into the evidence locker. There were no keys inside, of course, but the other items on the list all seemed to be there: the watch; an iPhone; a wallet; and the dictaphone.

The voice-activated dictaphone was a tiny handheld recorder. She could picture Judge Paulson at his window with the slim rectangle in his hand, surveying his town in the late afternoon light while he handed down orders and set forth his opinions in a measured, solemn tone.

She squinted and leaned into the locker to get a closer look.

"Like the mini-cassette that should be in the dictaphone."

Russell snaked his hand into the locker and pulled out the recorder. He popped the cassette deck. No tape.

"What the devil?"

Sasha asked, "You're sure you got to his body first yesterday? Before anyone else?"

Russell nodded, still staring at the empty tape recorder.

"Yeah, I'm sure. Gloria called from his chambers phone when she saw him sprawled on the floor. I ran right over. She was still there, no one else was in the room. His keys were on the rug beside him and this--," he waved the dictaphone, "was still in his hand."

"I don't suppose you noticed if it was empty?"

He looked down at the floor, embarrassed probably, and said in a thin voice, "No. I assume it had a tape in it. I mean, he was dictating when he was shot. Gloria said he stood at the window and dictated every afternoon. Why else would he be holding it? I just never thought to check. It was so . . . surreal, I guess. I mean, there was Judge Paulson with a huge chunk of his face blown off, right there in front of me."

"I understand."

He looked up at her. "I'm a deputy sheriff in Springport, Pennsylvania. I serve eviction notices and bench warrants. I don't investigate assassinations."

She kept her voice gentle. "I'm not suggesting you screwed up, deputy," she said, although they both knew he had. "I just wonder if the sheriff might be looking for a tape that went missing after you took possession of the judge's corpse."

It made sense, she thought. Stickley had no more experience securing a homicide scene than

Russell. If he noticed the tape was missing, he might have panicked. Incompetence wouldn't win him reelection, So, maybe he hung around until Gloria left, checked her work area and found nothing, then decided to take the keys and give the judge's apartment a look.

As a theory, it hung together okay. It was far from airtight, but it was a start.

~ ~ ~ ~ ~ ~ ~ ~ ~ ~

Sasha had talked Russell out of formally interviewing Gloria again, but he'd insisted on sitting in on her chat with the secretary.

So the three of them arranged themselves in Judge Paulson's chambers: Sasha behind the desk; Gloria in the guest chair Sasha had occupied the previous afternoon; and Russell in its mate.

Connelly, who had completed his walking tour of town in all of ten minutes, had been chatting with Gloria at her desk and had trailed into chambers behind them. He took up the post the Attorney General had taken day before, sitting in the chair in the corner.

Russell tried to catch her eye. He tilted his head toward Connelly to indicate he wanted her to ask him to leave.

She ignored it. This was her investigation. Connelly had extensive training in detecting deception during interviews. Besides, his interrogation techniques and her witness examination style made for some lively personal discussions between the two of them; she might as well get the benefit of his training.

"Do you remember seeing the judge's dictaphone when you found his body?" Sasha leaned forward over the massive desk to get a closer look at Gloria.

The secretary's eyes flicked toward the ceiling and then to her right.

"Yes, it was still in his hand." She closed her eyes briefly at the memory.

Sasha nodded to Russell. Gloria's statement squared with his recollection, and her behavior was consistent with the pointers Connelly had given Sasha about eye direction. She was telling the truth.

"Did you happen to notice if the tape was still in the recorder?"

The eyes went back to the ceiling, but this time they flitted to the left.

"No, I'm sorry, I don't remember."

Sasha's chest tightened. Gloria was lying.

She pressed on. "Did you touch the recorder?"

"Why would I?"

"I don't know. Did you?"

Gloria looked straight at her.

"Actually, no."

"Okay, more generally, what's the system with the tapes. The judge would leave a tape on your desk for you at the end of the evening?"

"That's right."

"After you transcribed it, then what? Did you keep them? Reuse them?"

Russell shifted in his chair. She could tell he was itching to butt in.

"We had eight tapes—numbered 1 through 8— two weeks' worth. On Fridays, the judge didn't dictate; he reviewed the drafts from the week. After I drafted an opinion or order or whatever was on the tape, I'd set that tape aside until the judge had reviewed and signed off on the document, just in case I needed to go back to the recording during the edits."

Sasha nodded. "Makes sense."

Comfortable now, explaining the minutiae of their routine, Gloria kept going.

"We really only needed four tapes, but it just seemed more prudent to have a week in reserve. On Mondays while he was on the bench, I would input his edits and finalize the documents. He'd sign them before he went over to Bob's for his pie. Then, I'd give him four tapes for the week. The four we had just used would stay in my desk drawer until the following Monday."

"Where'd the judge keep his four?"

"Well, one in the dictaphone, of course. The others . . . I'm not sure. Maybe in his top desk drawer?"

Sasha rolled it open. It was empty, except for a paper clip and a roll of stamps.

Connelly and Russell looked at her expectantly. She shook her head.

"Huh. I don't know, then. That's where he stored the dictaphone. I'd have thought he'd keep them together."

"Okay, have you checked your drawer? Are the four most recently used ones still in there?"

"I'm not sure, but I imagine they are."

"Let's go see," Sasha said, and the four of them trooped from the chambers to Gloria's desk outside the door in a tight knot.

Gloria opened her top drawer and took out a thin stack of tapes, rubber banded together. A yellow sticky note was wrapped around the stack and secured with the rubber band. Someone—Gloria, presumably—had written "completed tapes; opinions signed" on the paper in slanted cursive writing.

She thumbed the stack. "They're all here," she said. "Five through eight."

"Yesterday was Tuesday," Russell spoke up. "Did that mean he was on tape two?"

Gloria smiled at the memory of the judge's methodical nature. "Oh, yes. Even though it didn't matter at all, the judge always used the tapes in consecutive order. He left number one on my desk Monday evening."

"Where's that one?" Sasha asked.

She swiveled her desk chair to the side return adjacent to her desk and pulled open a short filing cabinet that sat beneath the desk. She took out a mini-tape recorder and her smile disappeared. Tangled around the tape recorder were the wires from a pair of earbuds.

She worked through the mess of thin wires, unwinding them from around the recorder. Once the wires were out of the way, she looked down at the cassette deck.

A hand flew up to her chest. "It's gone!"

She popped open the cassette deck to show them it was empty.

~ ~ ~ ~ ~ ~ ~ ~ ~ ~ ~

Gloria offered to drive out to Sal's Trattoria on the outskirts of town and bring back a pizza for lunch. Bob's would be abuzz with the news of Judge Paulson's death, and, she added, Marie had confided that Bob was no longer ordering fresh produce or meat, as the clock was ticking down to his closure and the launch of the Café on the Square the coming weekend. It appeared Bob didn't plan to go out with a bang, unless it happened to involve listeria.

Sasha, Russell, and Connelly agreed eating in was the better choice. Plus, the errand would get rid of Gloria for a while.

Once she'd left, they reconvened in the judge's chambers.

Russell spoke first. "So, Gloria's lying." His tone was glum and his disappointment was plain in his face.

"She sure is," Connelly agreed.

Sasha just nodded.

Connelly continued, "About some of it, not all of it."

"Right," Russell said, "she lied about whether or not she noticed if there was a tape in the recorder. Her eyes shifted to the left."

Connelly agreed again. "True, but she told the truth about it still being in his hand. She looked to the right then."

Russell nodded and said, "I guess you took a course in truth detection through a suspect's verbal and nonverbal cues, too, huh?"

"No," Connelly said. "I teach one."

"Okay," Sasha said, hurrying to interrupt the chest-thumping. "So, we're all in agreement that when she said she couldn't remember whether there was a tape in the recorder, she looked to the left."

The theory was a person trying to recall a visual image looked to the right; a person trying to create a visual image looked to the left. Assuming the person was right-handed. The process was reversed for southpaws, but Sasha had already noted that Gloria was a righty.

"She also lied about whether she touched the recorder," Connelly continued. "She evaded the question by answering with another question—'why would I?' An attempt to answer without having to lie outright."

Sasha jumped in. "And, then, when I pressed her, she said 'actually, no.' Just about every time I've deposed someone and they preface a yes or no question with 'actually,' they've been lying."

It amazed her, how much people could disclose without meaning to.

"But all of the rest of it—the process they used with the tapes, being surprised by the empty tape recorder—that all seemed genuine." Connelly said.

He made a point of soliciting Russell's input. "Do you agree?"

"I do." Russell sat a little straighter in his chair, glad to be consulted.

Sasha was pleased to see Connelly and Russell were male bonding, because she really didn't have the patience or the time to deal with any alpha male nonsense. She had a killer to catch.

The issues swirling around the judge's death were, unfortunately, multiplying. Why had the sheriff tried to break into the judge's apartment? Where were the missing tapes? Who had been threatening the judge? Did Danny Trees and PORE have anything to do with any of it?

And, most troubling, what was Gloria hiding and why?

22.

AFTER CRAMMING THE GOOD, BUT greasy, pizza from Sal's down her throat, Sasha needed to take a constitutional of her own.

Connelly and Russell had their heads together over the crime scene photos, not exactly her thing on a full stomach. So, Sasha told Gloria she'd be back in thirty minutes and headed out the door into the hallway.

As she pulled the door shut behind her and turned left toward the stairwell, she narrowly avoided colliding into a pinstriped chest. She stopped short and looked up. A breathless Drew Showalter was applying the brakes, as well, one hand up to soften any impact.

"Sorry," Sasha said.

"No, no, I apologize," he said, "I was distracted. I'm glad to run into you, as it were."

"Oh?"

"Yes. I read about your appointment, of course. Front page of the *Clear Brook Crier*, you know. Congratulations; that's quite an opportunity."

He said it matter-of-factly, but she wondered if the local lawyers had been put out by it. She guessed it really wasn't her problem.

"Thanks, I guess. I'm sure we'd all rather the judge be alive."

Showalter reddened and stammered, "Absolutely. And I'm sure you're quite busy, but, as I mentioned in my voice-mail message last week, I do need to speak with you about our little discovery matter."

He inclined his head toward the judge's chambers. "Can you spare a few moments?"

She stifled a sigh. "I was just heading out for a quick walk. Why don't you join me? We can walk and talk."

She strode toward the stairwell without waiting for an answer, leaving him no choice but to join her if he wanted her ear.

He scissored his long legs to match her brisk pace.

"What can I do for you?" she asked over her shoulder, pushing open the fire door. "As I understood your message, you just wanted to make sure I don't have any questions about the materials. I don't."

He cleared his throat twice before answering. "I'm sure the VitaMight matter is on your back burner now, what with the investigation, but there's a small matter regarding my client's document production."

She turned toward him. "Which is?"

He coughed out another throat-clearing grunt.

Then, in a rush, the words tumbled out. "We've made an inadvertent disclosure. I'd like you to return the e-mail and attachment Bates labeled KP 00476 through 00477."

Inadvertent disclosure. She allowed herself a small smile. That was a lawyer's way of saying "I screwed up. Badly."

Then she frowned. Inadvertent disclosure meant Showalter had accidentally turned over privileged documents—usually, it was a communication between the client and the attorney or a memo the attorney had created in preparation for trial. But, she had a near-photographic recall and was certain she hadn't reviewed any privileged materials on the disk he'd sent.

"You're claiming privilege?"

She stopped on the landing and looked him square in the face.

"Not exactly."

He cranked his neck to the side and grimaced.

"Well, what exactly are you claiming?"

It was easy enough to think the polite thing to do would be to give back whatever Showalter had given her in error, but the reality was, she was obligated to do whatever was in her client's best interest. The Disciplinary Board didn't award points for proper etiquette. And, as she understood it, Pennsylvania law required her to return privileged material produced in error and nothing more.

She couldn't even imagine what other ground he'd have. This wasn't a case that involved trade secret or proprietary information, unlike a lot of her business litigation matters. In those cases, the parties would sign a confidentiality agreement, promising not to use each other's client lists or pricing matrices or whatever. But, she and Showalter hadn't entered into such an agreement because they had a straightforward breach of lease case.

Showalter took his time forming an answer.

"The documents in question are not relevant to the issues in the case and, as such, aren't responsive to your document requests. They were produced in error. Let's not make a federal case of it, eh?" He shot her a too-wide grin.

Relevance? Responsiveness? Was he kidding? Nobody, literally nobody, would try to get back documents because they were irrelevant. In fact, most of the attorneys she knew deliberately padded their document productions with irrelevant, useless documents to bulk them up and waste opposing counsel's time.

She pushed open the door to the lobby and shook her head.

"I'll take a look at the documents and talk to my client, but my inclination is no, Drew. What's the big deal, anyway?"

He trailed behind her as she pushed through the ornately carved doors leading to the courthouse steps.

"Sasha, please. I need them back."

He squinted at her in the sunlight.

"I said I'll talk to my client."

She was more confused than irritated. After reviewing his electronic files, she hadn't understood why he'd fought the document request in the first place, now he was making an extraordinary request that only piqued her interest in the documents.

He leaned over her, blinking rapidly.

"A refusal is not the act of a friend," he said in a soft voice. Then he popped an antacid out of a foil roll and stuck it in his mouth.

Sasha looked at him for several seconds, but she couldn't think of anything to say in response. So she turned and walked down the wide white steps to the sidewalk.

Had she turned around, she would have been surprised to see a satisfied smile spread across his face.

23.

"A REFUSAL IS NOT THE act of a friend." Connelly and Russell were still poring over some papers spread out on the late judge's desk; they jerked their heads up when she yanked open the door to chambers and spat out the sentence. She'd turned the phrase over in her mind while she'd walked through town and still didn't know what to make of it.

"*The Godfather*," they said in unison.

Another reference to *The Godfather*. Men and their movies, she thought with no small amount of exasperation.

"Figures." She craned her neck to get a look at the papers, "Is that the coroner's report?"

"Nope. Better." Russell's eyes gleamed with excitement. Over his shoulder, Connelly shot her a skeptical look.

"Really? What?"

"On a hunch, Stinky paid Danny Trees a visit. He wanted to know if Jay had been back. Everyone in the house said they hadn't seen him, but the sheriff asked Danny for permission to search the room Jay had used. The duffel bag was still in there and these were right on top." He picked up the papers and waved them at her.

Sasha took the crumpled papers. The top was a printed sheet on generic white printer paper. It read "Lunch at Bob's every day. Then he stands at the window and dictates." Underneath was a printed list of sporting goods stores in a fifty-mile radius. It had come from a website called The Huntsman and was dated two days earlier.

Connelly spoke up, "We've called several of the stores on the list. They all sell ammunition; no one admitted to selling the 120-grain Nosler Partition to anyone fitting Jay's description."

She turned to Russell, "So, he's been back? The printout's only two days old."

"Looks like. The thing is—and this is credible—Danny doesn't keep tabs on the weirdos living in his house. People come and go. He never locks the side door. So, this Jay character could have easily slipped back in and then out."

"The sheriff thinks Jay's the shooter?" she asked.

"Well, yeah."

"Did you ask him about the judge's keys?"

Russell frowned. "No. He flew in here very excited and left in a hurry. He's arranging a press conference."

"Press conference? Don't you think he's jumping the gun?"

Russell shook his head. "This wasn't all that was in Jay's bag. He had the missing tapes."

That changed things.

"All of them?"

Another shake of the head. "All but number 2, the one from the dictaphone. We figure he must have it on him. Listen, Stinky's all hopped up now. He wants to talk to you before the press conference. He said to come see him as soon as you get back, okay?"

Russell looked miserable. His adrenaline was pumping, flooding him with excitement about having a suspect. But, the suspicion that Stickley was up to something picked at him under the surface. Sasha could read it on his face.

Seeing no reason to compound his discomfort, she just nodded and turned to go find Stickley.

Connelly followed her out. In the hallway, he pulled her into the stairwell.

Even now, after all these months, her heartbeat ticked up when he touched her. He kept his hand on her arm and leaned close, searching her face.

"Jay's not your guy. You know that right?"

His warm brown eyes, flecked with gold, clouded with concern.

"I don't know anything, Connelly. And neither does Stickley. I'm going to tell him his media blitz is premature, but the only evidence we have certainly does suggest Jay is the killer."

Connelly gave her a sharp look. "What about the attempted break in? You think some random hippie waltzed in to the sheriff's office and took the keys from the evidence locker?"

She shrugged. He had a point.

"No, I still think that was Stickley, trying to cover up his slipshod job of securing the scene. But, it could have been Russell. Or the receptionist. You're right, there's something else at play here, but we do need to find Jay. And fast. Even if it's to clear him so we can move on."

"You're not going to find Jay. And making a lot of noise about looking for him is going to have consequences."

She narrowed her eyes. "Connelly, if you have something to say, say it. I don't have time for the intrigue and innuendo."

His jaw tightened. Then he let out a long, slow breath and said, "I've said all I can say, Sasha. You need to get Stickley to back off Jay."

He took her by both shoulders. "Trust me, okay?"

She removed his hands. "I do. You, however, obviously don't trust me. If you did, you'd just come out and say whatever it is you're driving at."

She dropped his hands and stalked off in search of the malodorous sheriff.

24.

CARL SAT WITH HIS FEET propped up on his scratched wooden desk, the phone receiver jammed between his shoulder and ear, and glared at the phone's base as if Griggs could see him.

"It's done. We have a press conference in a half hour. Your pretty little prosecutor and I will announce there's a suspect in the murder of Judge Paulson and ask for the public's help in finding him and bringing him to justice."

He paused to pick at his front teeth. There was nothing between them. But, the habit had developed when he switched from cigarettes to hard candy. He was always finding slivers of peppermint or butterscotch stuck on his teeth. Still, he was glad he'd finally kicked the habit.

Of course, everyone said his food would taste better after he quit. Turned out that wasn't the case, since he'd lost his sense of smell entirely thanks to the damned cigarettes. With no sense of smell, everything just tasted bland. He took a second to think about the injustice of it all before continuing.

"You just better hope nobody finds the damned hippie, Bob."

The attorney general brushed off his warning and said, "You'll jump off that bridge when we come to it, Sheriff.

He gave a loud guffaw at his own stupid joke.

Carl made a jerking off motion with his hand and really wished the asshole could see him.

"Did you find a judge who will play ball?"

Griggs said, "Jesus, Stickley, not over the phone. We'll talk about it when I come to get the tapes tonight. You better find that last tape in the meantime."

The sheriff bristled. He considered giving the man a piece of his mind but swallowed it. They had to work together long enough to make the commissioner happy and get paid. Maybe, after his bank account was swollen with cash, he'd let Griggs know just how much he hated his puke guts.

A rap at his door jarred him out of the fantasy of telling off the attorney general.

"I have to go," Stickley said. "I'll see you to-night."

25.

ASHA WAS RAISING HER HAND to knock again on the sheriff's door, when he called out, "Come in."

She took a long breath of the hallway air before pushing through the door and into an enclosed space with the sheriff. He swung his legs off his desk and made a halfhearted movement, as if he were going to stand to greet her, but instead just slumped back into his chair.

"Do you have a few minutes to talk about our investigation, Sheriff?" she asked, hanging back near the door.

He flashed a toothy grin. "Did you come to congratulate me? I had a feeling about that hippie bastard who attacked you."

He waved her toward a guest chair.

She walked over and took a seat while she tried to formulate a way to back him off Jay as his only suspect without insulting his police work.

She settled in the rickety chair before she said, "Well, I understand from Deputy Russell that the Sheriff's Office is convinced this Jay guy shot the judge?"

"Damned straight," Stickley agreed, punctuating with a vigorous head bob.

She gave him a cool look. "Why don't you go ahead and run your theory and the evidence that supports it by me?"

He raised his eyebrows but didn't speak.

"I'm the special prosecutor, remember? Seems like I have a say in this."

"Well, now, I don't know about that," he said. "Seems to me, you were appointed to make sure one of our fine barristers wasn't mixed up in this, in light of the threats Judge Paulson had been getting. But, some lefty wacko environut, who's shown a propensity for violence? Nah, wouldn't say that's in your purview."

Anger flared in her chest. She focused on keeping her pulse low and steady and her breathing slow and even. As a rule, showing anger put a person at a disadvantage in a negotiation. She tried hard to only let her temper show when doing so would throw her adversary off his footing or otherwise benefit her cause.

When she was sure she could speak calmly, she said, "Why don't you just run it by me anyway? Call it a dress rehearsal for your upcoming press conference?"

He stared at her trying to decide and then shrugged.

"Sure, okay. Jay Last Name Unknown has been on the sheriff office's radar ever since he viciously attacked an unarmed female attorney in the municipal parking lot. He appeared to believe she was involved in the hydrofracking industry, based on comments made before the attack. That led us to tie him to the local environmental protesters known as PORE. Led by one Daniel McAllister. Although the suspect is currently a fugitive, he left a bag of clothing and other possessions at the residence of Mr. McAllister, who gave this office permission to search it."

He paused here and scratched his neck, digging under his yellowing collar with dirty fingernails.

"The bag contained, among other items, a document that set forth Judge Paulson's afternoon routine, and a list of sporting goods stores, which may have been where the suspect acquired the hunting rifle used in the attack, the ammunition, or both. We are following up on that now. Also in the bag were four mini-cassette tapes that appear to have been stolen from the judge's chambers."

Sasha cut him off.

"What's your theory on how Jay gained access to chambers? It was an active crime scene. Russell was posted at the door during business hours and you took the keys into evidence."

She didn't plan to mention tape number two. She'd see what, if anything, Stickley said about it.

Stickley appraised her with a measured look. Then he leaned forward and spoke in a soft voice.

"I'll tell you my theory but it is not for public consumption. Are we clear?"

"Yes."

He yanked open his top desk drawer and took out a manila tag with a number printed on it.

"I haven't shared this piece of evidence with anyone yet, but the duffel bag also contained the evidence tag from the judge's set of keys, which were removed from the evidence locker by person or persons unknown at some point yesterday evening. The keys themselves remain missing."

He held up the tag toward her for a minute and then returned it to his drawer.

"I believe Jay is working with someone in this office—quite possibly Deputy Russell, as much as it pains me to say it. Russell cannot know the evidence tag was in the duffel bag. Understand?"

Not Russell. Stickley was just trying to misdirect her. Stickley took the keys; so, of course, he'd have the tag. It didn't implicate Russell.

She stopped herself. She didn't know Russell from Adam. Or Stickley or Gloria, for that matter. She didn't know any of these people. She was making snap judgments based on the fact that Russell made good coffee, Stickley stunk to high heaven, and Gloria seemed nice.

That was foolish. And dangerous. Daniel, her Krav Maga instructor, had a mantra: Niceness isn't a character trait. It's a tool.

People are nice in an effort to gain something. A person could be pure evil to the core and make the decision to be nice to get his way. Her job was not to be taken in by a display of niceness.

She considered the sheriff.

"Do you really believe it's Russell?"

He shook his head, "I don't know what to believe. But the sooner I flush out this Jay bast—, er, character, the sooner I'll know. Now, if you'll excuse me, I need to prepare for our press conference."

He pushed his chair back and moved toward the door.

She stood up to follow him. "Wait. Our press conference?"

He jerked the door open and gave her another big smile.

"Why, yes, ma'am. You're going to thank this office for its diligent work and announce that your investigation is closed. Go on, now, I'm sure you'll want to check your makeup or what have you."

~ ~ ~ ~ ~ ~ ~ ~ ~ ~

Sasha stormed back to her temporary workspace and sped by Gloria without saying anything. She shut herself up in the office and tried to decide what to do next.

Connelly really didn't want Jay to be named as the suspect, and she didn't know why. Stickley was hell-bent on tying up the investigation with a big red bow and sending her on her way. She had serious reservations about his investigation. And about Gloria's truthfulness. And maybe about Russell, too.

A band of sharp pain radiated from above her left eye out around her ear and toward the back of her head. Tension headache.

She walked over to the window with its cardboard square marking the bullet hole and stood, looking out over the square. Trying to cut through the noise in her brain and formulate a plan.

Her ringing phone interrupted her efforts. She picked it up from Judge Paulson's desk and checked the display. *Unknown Caller.*

"Sasha McCandless."

"Sasha, it's Bob Griggs."

"Sir."

"Just calling to congratulate you on your fine, fine result. I understand we have a lead suspect." The attorney general's voice was upbeat, almost jolly.

"I can't really take credit for that," she said.

She paused, considered what she was about to do, and then forged ahead. "In fact, I have some concerns that the sheriff's office is rushing to judgment, sir."

His tone got serious fast. "What makes you say that?"

"Well, a number of things. For one—"

He cut her off. "Actually, it really doesn't matter, does it? You were appointed because the chief judge had concerns that a member of the bar was involved. Have you found any evidence of that?"

"No, but my investigation isn't even twenty-four hours old. I think—"

He jumped in again. "And, of course, you don't have any law enforcement experience, so your judgment of the sheriff's investigation can best be called uninformed, don't you agree?"

That stung her into silence for a second, but then the words came out before she could stop them. "With all respect, I have the same qualifications I had yesterday when you appointed me the special prosecutor."

He softened. "Of course, of course. I don't mean to offend you. The Attorney General's Office—indeed, the Commonwealth—is grateful to your service on short notice and under the circumstances. I'll have the press office draw up a very complimentary release. Now, with my personal thanks, your service is no longer required."

The band of pain spread from the back of her head and circled all the way around to her right temple, creating a halo of pressure. She considered how best to argue against this course of action, and the image of Judge Paulson and Chief Justice Bermann smiling into the camera at some chicken dinner flashed into her head.

"Has Chief Justice Bermann agreed to shut down the investigation?"

He answered with an undercurrent of warning in his voice.

"The chief justice would never presume to meddle in a criminal investigation. He's well aware of the division of power. Now, it's time for you to go back to Pittsburgh and savor your victory. Add it to your resume and move on."

26.

SASHA'S CHEEKS STILL BURNED WITH impotent anger. Having to stand next to the rank-smelling sheriff and smile and nod while he puffed out his chest and trumpeted his great detective work to two local newspaper reporters and a field reporter for the nearest television station had not improved her headache.

She'd made a beeline from the courthouse steps to Gloria's house. She wanted to get out of town as quickly as possible.

She was throwing files into her briefcase, haphazardly, and perhaps with more force than was strictly necessary. She had already shoved her clothes into the overnight bag and tossed it by the door.

Judge Paulson's cats had sensed the gathering storm as soon as she'd come into the apartment and had slunk under the judge's bed to wait it out.

Gloria tapped on the door and eased it open slightly.

"Sasha, may I come in?"

"Sure," she said without looking up from her packing.

Gloria approached her, holding a cardboard recipe box that bore a drawing of a rooster on one side and the words "Kitchen Favorites" in a flowery font on the other.

"Here, I know you wanted my stew recipe and my sourdough bread recipe."

She thrust the box toward Sasha like it was burning her hands.

Sasha took it and stared at the woman.

"Uh . . . thanks?"

She had complimented Gloria's cooking at dinner, both to be polite and because the food had tasted good. But, Sasha most certainly hadn't asked for any recipes. She'd sooner change the brakes in her car than attempt to make bread from scratch. Maybe Connelly had asked for them.

Gloria went on, "I know you're in a hurry, so I didn't take the time to copy them. Those are the originals, but I don't need them. Goodness, I have them memorized."

Sasha shrugged and tossed the box on top of the papers in her bag. She fastened the briefcase's buckle and scanned the room, looking for any items she'd forgotten to pack.

"Well, I guess that's it. Is Leo downstairs?"

"Yes, he and Jonas are on the porch. Are you sure you aren't going to stay for the memorial service? Luke and Linnea are coming in tomorrow; I'd like for you to meet them." Gloria's eyes got soft at the mention of the service.

The woman was a cipher. She seemed so kind, but she was clearly keeping secrets.

Whatever. It wasn't Sasha's problem anymore. She'd been dismissed.

"I really need to get back to Pittsburgh, Gloria. I'm sorry. I'd like to meet your children some time. They sound like great people. And I wish I could stay for the memorial service, but I'm a one-woman show and my work is really piling up."

It was true, she had plenty of work waiting for her at home. But the reality was, she wasn't sticking around for the memorial because she wanted to lick her wounds in private.

Gloria nodded. "I understand."

The cats, sensing a drop in the tension in the room, emerged from the bedroom, stretching and preening.

"Did you say goodbye to Deputy Russell?" she asked, petting Atticus Finch.

"I left him a message. I'm not sure where he is, actually. He didn't show up at the press conference."

Sasha's doubts about Russell were growing. Again, whatever. Not her concern.

She sighed and hefted the bag onto her shoulder.

"Gavin's a good man, Sasha. I know it. He may have gone out to visit with his folks. They're kind of isolated out there in Firetown and now that the last well on their land is active, they're keeping to themselves even more."

"Why's that?"

"Oh, it's so hard to explain what's happened here. At first everybody thought fracking was going to save the town. So much money was coming in. Everybody was for it, even people like us, who don't own property on the Shale."

"And now?"

"Well, now, the town's fractured, I guess, you'd say. Brothers and sisters not speaking. The school board voting to lease the rights under the playground and the parents up in arms. People lighting their well water on fire and posting it on YouTube. But, then you have people like Bob, selling the diner, and cashing out, retiring to Florida. Or even us; I mean, look at Luke. He just graduated and has a good, secure job thanks to the Shale. It's a mess is what it is."

Sasha didn't know what to say.

"And poor Judge Paulson, so worried about every decision and its impact on future generations. He never said anything, mind you, but I could tell. It was taking him longer and longer to get out his decisions that involved the Shale. I wonder what will happen with a new judge?"

It was a question without an answer.

Gloria made an awkward move toward her, and Sasha realized the woman was going to hug her.

She hugged her back, surprised at the intensity of Gloria's embrace, and said, "Thank you for everything. Take care of yourself."

She bent to pet the cats, who were now rolling around, exposing their furry bellies in a bid for attention.

Then she walked through the door and down the stairs.

27.

LEO WAS GLAD HE AND Sasha were cara-
vanning back to Pittsburgh in their separate
cars. Sasha was still smarting from having
been fired, and he hoped the hypnotic rhythm of
highway driving would soothe her enough that
she'd be ready to talk about it when they got home.
Plus, he wanted to make a phone call without her
in earshot.

As he followed her car over a hill and down into
a small valley, he noticed the scenery that he'd
missed on the drive up in the dark. Drilling equipment rose up among the trees, sitting in muddy
patches of earth, surrounded by large green tanks,
pumps, batteries, and vehicles. Sand trucks, trailers,
pickups, and other trucks formed rings around the

derricks. Interspersed between drilling sites, capped wells dotted the fields.

A lot of activity. And a lot of activity meant a lot of money.

He picked up his phone and dialed from memory a number at the Environmental Protection Agency's Criminal Investigation Division.

"CID. Special Agent Ortiz."

"Manny, it's Leo Connelly."

The clipped businesslike tone that Manuel Ortiz had used to answer his phone dropped away, replaced by genuine joy. "Leo! How you doing, man?"

Leo smiled. Manny Ortiz had been a student in the very first class he had ever taught at the federal law enforcement training center. Leo had stood in the front of the sweltering room, cooled by a fan and an underpowered air conditioner that was no match for the Georgia heat, looked out at all the serious, eager faces, and wondered what the hell he'd gotten himself into.

His stomach had dropped when he realized they were waiting for him to dazzle them with his brilliance. But before his nerves had gotten the best of him, he'd been beaned in the forehead by a sheet of ruled paper fashioned into the shape of an airplane.

The room had erupted into laughter, and a slight, dark-skinned man sitting in the approximate middle of the room had shot a fist into the air and shouted, "Yes! A direct hit on the air marshal."

Leo had managed to keep a straight face, but he'd been grateful for the room's lightened mood. So much so, that when he asked Manny Ortiz to stay after class, it was to thank him, not reprimand him.

That exchange had led to a beer, which had led to more beer and some karaoke at a dirt-floored country bar. And, like that, the man had become a fixture in Leo's life. He always thought of Manny as a Hispanic elf. Mischievous and jolly.

"Good, good. It's been too long," Leo said now. "How's Josie? And the kids?"

Manny's voice swelled with pride and love as he detailed the achievements of his three children and his wife's work as an interior designer. He interrupted his own story about his middle daughter's exploding science fair project and said, "Eh, that's not why you called. Leo Connelly doesn't make personal calls on company time. What's up, brother?"

Leo chuckled. Manny couldn't resist pointing out his more uptight character traits. "As it happens, I need some information on an outfit called Big Sky. Know them?"

It was Manny's turn to chuckle. "Yeah, I know them. Huge player. Oil and gas giant out of Texas. What do you need to know?"

"Are they dirty?"

Manny fell silent, thinking about the question. For all his joking, Manny took his work seriously. Leo knew whatever Manny told him would be accurate and well-researched.

Finally, he said, "Nah. We've investigated them nearly a dozen times—including two cases I worked personally. If they were dirty, we'd have found something by now, but nada. Every time, the tip that started the thing just peters out. They play hardball, which pisses people off, man, but nothing illegal. They go right up to the line but don't cross it. They don't have to. Do you have any idea how many lobbyists they have? Politicians are throwing themselves at the oil and gas industry. Especially these guys."

"Any chance they're just that good at it? They're playing dirty but getting away with it?"

Most law enforcement personnel would have bristled at the suggestion. Not Manny. He gave it a moment's consideration.

"Anything's possible, but I don't think so. We've crawled all over them, more than once. They have too many employees; if they were breaking the law, someone would have slipped up somewhere. They're clean."

"Okay," Leo conceded.

"Can you tell me why you're asking?"

"No real reason. This isn't an air marshal investigation. You hear about the state judge who got killed up in Pennsylvania?"

"Sure, out in the middle of nowhere."

"Sasha's mixed up in it. Or she was. Anyhow, the whole town's divided over fracking and Big Sky seems like the biggest player in town."

"Almost certain to be," Manny said. "They're the big dogs in the industry. Their Marcellus Shale strategy is very straightforward: they just sue everybody who interferes. They tried the whole PR blitz and got mixed results, so now, anybody who complains about the drilling, they just sue 'em. Sick kids, contaminated water, noise pollution, whatever. People start griping and Big Sky runs to court to get an order declaring whatever they're doing is legal. Gotta keep the lawyers fat, eh?" Too late, he remembered Sasha was a lawyer and added, "Not to insult your lady, man."

"No worries."

"What'd you mean, anyway—she's mixed up in the murder?"

"She has a case up there and the judge appointed her to represent some local guy on an unrelated matter. Then the judge happens to get killed on a day she's in town. Next thing you know, she's appointed special prosecutor because there's a theory the shooter was a member of the local bar."

Spelling it out like that, Leo realized Sasha's appointment made zero sense. At least for the stated reason.

"And she thinks, what, Big Sky hired somebody to kill this judge?"

"She doesn't even have a working theory. The sheriff announced this environmental protester as his chief suspect and the state AG shut down Sasha's investigation about twenty-four hours after he appointed her."

Manny's confusion beamed up to a satellite and into Leo's ear. "The sheriff's running the homicide investigation? Are they in the Old West?"

"It's a mess up there, Manny. But, I was thinking maybe this protester was a plant, like Big Sky sent him in to cause trouble and maybe got a little too enthusiastic. He has no ties to the area, he's vanished, and . . ." Leo paused.

He didn't want to share with Manny that he'd run an unauthorized search of the Guardian database.

He went on, "My contacts can't or won't tell me anything about this group. Something's up."

"Nah, nah," Manny said.

Leo could picture him shaking his head, his dark hair flipping from side to side.

He got thoughtful, dragging out his words. "Not their style."

Maybe not, Leo thought, but he knew whose style it was.

28.

T HE ROAD HAD ROLLED OUT ahead of
Sasha in a ribbon leading her away from
Springport and back to Pittsburgh, and her
headache had eased with each passing mile. By the
time she swung the car into a parking spot at her
condo at dusk, she felt almost human. She turned
off the ignition and watched Connelly's headlights
rise over the speed bump and fall, before turning
in to the spot next to hers.

She stepped out of the car, ready to apologize
for her earlier crankiness. He stayed in his car but
buzzed the window down and waved her over.

"Listen, Connelly, I shouldn't have—"

He put his hand up like a crossing guard. "Forget about it, okay? You're under a lot of pressure.

But, I need to run out to the field office to take care of something. I won't be long."

He reached across to the passenger side floor and lifted a soft-sided cooler he'd borrowed from Gloria. It held his long-delayed Thai chicken. He handed it to her out the window and spoke slowly, "Are you listening?"

She nodded.

"Okay, in the cabinet under your sink there's a stainless steel slow cooker. Do you know what I'm talking about?"

She huffed. One time, one time, she mistook his rice cooker for the slow cooker and she was never going to hear the end of it. It wasn't her fault all his appliances were sleek, modern, and had the same shape.

"Of course I do."

His raised an eyebrow but just pressed ahead. "Put the chicken and the peanut sauce in the slow cooker. Plug it in. Set it to the lowest level. Put the noodles in the refrigerator and then walk away. Don't touch anything else. I'll finish dinner when I get home. I'll be two hours, tops. Probably less."

Home? Had Connelly just called her loft home?

"Sasha? Do you understand?"

"Yes, I'm not a moron."

"No, you're not. You are, however, an unmitigated disaster in the kitchen." He said it like he meant it but softened it with a crooked smile.

"Whatever. See you later."

She gave a little wave and turned to gather her bags as he put the car into reverse and backed over the speed bump.

She pushed through the front door of her condo, her arms full of bags, and left her keys dangling in the door while she dumped the bags on the kitchen counter and turned on a light.

Before she could forget, she crouched and retrieved the slow cooker from its home under the sink. She slid the chicken out of its container and into the vessel, dumped the sauce on top of the chicken, plugged in the appliance, and turned it on. She stepped back and waited for the beep to tell her she'd done everything properly.

She figured while the food heated she might as well run over to her own office and catch up on all the administrative details that she'd ignored while in Springport. She started up the stairs to her loft bedroom and remembered the keys in the door. She reversed course and fetched her keys then jogged up the stairs to change into her running clothes.

Back in the kitchen, she eased her laptop out of the briefcase and into her padded backpack. Wriggled into the pack and clicked the straps closed across her chest. As she pulled her hair back into a low ponytail, her eyes fell on Gloria's recipe box, still in the briefcase. She placed it on the counter, next to the slow cooker, so she wouldn't forget to give Connelly the recipes. She looked around for a piece of paper to leave a note for Connelly, then decided there was no need; she'd probably be back before he was.

She inhaled the aroma of the peanuts and ginger, and switched off the lights.

~ ~ ~ ~ ~ ~ ~ ~ ~ ~ ~

Sasha had poured her anger at Griggs and Stickley into a speed workout. Now she caught her breath and waited on the sidewalk, one hand on the wall while she stretched her hamstrings, until there was a pause in the flow of pedestrians past her office building. Then she cupped one hand around the keypad and punched in her access code with the other.

Most random crimes were random only in that the victim didn't know her attacker. But they were targeted in that criminals don't generally waste a lot of energy gaining access to their victims in a stranger crime. Two homes, side by side—one locked up tight, with good security lighting, the other with open windows, overgrown hedges, and an unlocked door—no contest.

With the first floor of the building vacant, Sasha could have been a sitting duck. But, she took steps to remedy that. Changed her key code regularly; used a different code for the pad outside her office; locked herself in when she was working after hours. She couldn't do anything about the landlord's lighting choices, she thought, as she mounted the steps to her office in near darkness. She'd have to remember to clip a flashlight to her backpack next time.

She moved cautiously through the darkened second-floor hallway and felt for the keypad by the door. She tapped the numbers and the soft electronic click told her the door had unlocked. She reached into the mailbox mounted beside the keypad and retrieved a fistful of mail.

She hurried in, hit the lights, and locked the door behind her. She removed a Nalgene bottle from one of the backpack's side pockets and filled it from the water cooler that sat next to her coffee maker. Then she took out her laptop and booted it up, flipping through the mail while it cycled through its startup processes.

A legal magazine, a pamphlet advertising a CLE program, a Westlaw invoice, and an envelope containing a check from VitaMight.

The payment from VitaMight reminded her of Showalter's bizarre inadvertent disclosure request. She put the stack of mail to the side and rolled out her desk chair. She typed her password into the start screen, and sat staring at the screen and tapping her nails against the desktop while the electronic database that held a copy of the files on Showalter's CD launched.

"00476 through 00477," she muttered to herself as she scanned the database for the document bearing those numbers. She hadn't written them down when Showalter ambushed her earlier in the day, but her memory was sound.

Her former coworkers had insisted she had a photographic memory, but that wasn't the case. She just had a great memory—almost total recall. It was both a blessing and a hindrance. A blessing because she could, at will, remember a line from a deposition transcript, the amount of an outstanding balance, or her sister-in-law's dress size and favorite color. A hindrance because her mind refused to prioritize or weed the information it retained. So, the pinpoint page cite to the leading case on an important issue had to share space with her best friend from third grade's telephone number, which had been disconnected when her family moved to Iowa in 1985.

Curiously, the one piece of data she couldn't seem to retain reliably was the names of men she'd dated. When she ran into them, she'd panic—was it Jon or Joe? Mark or Martin? Someday, she figured to make a therapist rich delving into the issue.

She found the document in the spreadsheet and double-clicked the numbers to open the image. An e-mail with a PDF attachment filled the screen. It was an internal e-mail Keystone Properties had sent to its employees inviting them to a pizza lunch for a candidate for county commissioner. The attached PDF was a color flyer with a cartoon picture of a stereotypical mustachioed Italian chef, holding a steaming pizza aloft. It set out the time, date, and location for the lunch, which had occurred nearly a year earlier.

Could she possibly have misremembered the numbers?

No question, it was irrelevant to her document request, but surely Showalter couldn't seriously want this document back.

She leaned back in her chair and stretched her arms over her head to think. What was even remotely interesting about this document? Not the pizza. It had to be the politics. She read it again.

The candidate Keystone Properties was backing was Heather Price.

She knew that name. She played back the previous several days' interactions in her mind, spooling through her conversations with Russell, Gloria and her husband, the sheriff, Attorney General Griggs and Chief Justice Bermann, until finally she landed on Jed. Jed had told her Heather Price was the commissioner who had held Big Sky's permits hostage until it contracted with her trucking company.

Could it just be a coincidence that Showalter was desperate to get back an otherwise-innocuous e-mail that showed his client had supported Heather Price's bid for county commissioner? Maybe Keystone Properties was also playing ball with Ms. Price.

Sasha rocked back in her chair and thought it through, chewing on the end of her pen as she did so. It hung together. Showalter still wasn't getting his document back, but at least it made some sense.

She reached for the phone to call and break it to him, then she froze. She thought she heard the jangle of the bells over the exterior door downstairs.

The only other people who had the code were Connelly and the landlord. Connelly, having learned the hard way, knew better than to startle her. The landlord was best described as absentee. It was unlikely to be either of them.

With her hand suspended midway to the phone, she listened hard. Heard nothing. She was just spooked from the incident in the judge's chambers.

She picked up the phone and began to punch in the numbers. She thought she heard the faint squeak of floorboards.

She placed the receiver back in its cradle, careful not to make any noise, and crept to the door. She strained to hear over the thump of her heart.

There was no reason the landlord would be there after hours and no reason he'd be sneaking up on her.

The door's locked, she told herself. Just wait it out.

She pressed her ear against the door. The door to the street creaked on its hinge and the bells rang again. Someone was there, and he was going back outside.

Her gut told her it was a trap.

She fought the urge to fling open the door and run down the stairs, outside to perceived safety. The impulse to flee was almost irresistible. But, of course, she was safer staying put.

She rushed over to the window and looked down on the sidewalk below. There was no one walking away from the building in either direction. She looked across the street, searching for a lone figure. She watched for several minutes. Couples, holding hands, on their way to dinner. A group of college students, loud and laughing. No ninjas.

She told herself it could have been the wind. On a gusty night like this, it could shake the door hard enough to dislodge the bells.

She picked up the phone to call Showalter, but her hands were still shaking from the jolt of adrenaline. She put the phone down and paced around the office like a trapped animal.

She considered calling Connelly and asking him to come pick her up. He'd do it, of course. Then she tossed her head, snapping her ponytail behind her. Don't be pathetic, she told herself, you are not going to call your boyfriend to rescue you like some hysterical female.

She dragged the yoga mat out from under her desk and unrolled it. A moon salutation would slow her heart and calm her down.

She starting from standing and raised her arms overhead. She did a deep backbend and imagined the anxiety and fear rolling off her arms onto the floor. Then she folded herself forward, hands interlocked and arms outstretched in front of her as she brought her forehead as close to the mat as she could.

Her heart slowed to a normal rhythm. She released her hands and came up into a high lunge. The fear had vanished.

She worked through the rest of the poses, finishing in the same standing mountain pose she'd started from.

She rolled up the mat and returned it to its place under the desk, then she took a long drink of water. She was glad she hadn't called Connelly and blabbered about being scared.

She shut down the laptop and stuffed it into the backpack. After she wriggled the pack onto her shoulders, she turned out the lights and stepped out into the short hallway. She tested the knob to make sure the door locked behind her then started down the hallway.

29.

ASHA HURRIED DOWN THE DARKENED hallway to the stairs and took them lightly, one hand sliding along the railing. She could see the door, illuminated by the emergency exit light hanging above it.

Almost there.

Her feet hit the landing at the bottom of the stairs and she moved forward, toward the door.

A tall figure stepped out from the entrance to the empty deli space to her left and stood between her and the exit, blocking her way. The exit sign shined down on him, casting a red glow on his sharp, bony face, feral eyes, and long, stringy pony-tail.

Jay. And this time he didn't have a stick in his hand. He had a gun.

She stood, motionless, and waited for him to tell her to put her hands up. Then it would be a fluid series of moves and she would have his gun while he had a broken trigger finger and, unless he was luckier than Connelly had been, a broken nose.

"Turn around," he said, gesturing with the gun.

She was going to need a new plan.

She did as he said.

He moved close behind her and pulled her wrists together behind her back. In a fast, fluid motion he snapped a set of handcuffs around her wrists.

"We need to talk," he said.

He grabbed her by the shoulders and pushed her into the retail space. He guided her into a chair that sat at a dusty laminated table.

The deli owners had sold off most of their fixtures before they'd vacated the space, but a few tables and chairs were left behind, scattered across the room. Standing guard over them was an empty, unplugged drink cooler, its SoBe juice sign darkened and its door hanging ajar.

She ran through the scenario in her mind. She was in an abandoned building with a suspected killer who had previously attacked her. Connelly would eventually start looking for her; but he would likely call her office line, get no answer, cross it off the list of places to look, and search elsewhere. Less than ideal facts.

Fighting her way out had just become a remote possibility. She'd have to put her oral advocacy skills to work and talk her way out.

"Jay," she began, "I don't think you've thought this through."

He smiled. "No?"

He took a seat across the table from her and splayed his long, thin hands out across the table.

"Is this the part where you show me the error of my ways and convince me to confess to killing Judge Paulson and turn myself into that idiot pig sheriff?"

She smiled back, ignoring the cold stainless steel digging into the undersides of her wrists.

Well, yes, it was. But, when he put it that way, it sounded like a fairly lame plan. It was, however, the only one she had at the moment.

He didn't wait for a response.

"Here are the flaws with your plan, if that is what you're thinking. First—and this is a pretty big one—I didn't kill Judge Paulson. And, as if that weren't enough, second, your ill-advised press conference may have compromised my investigation. The Bureau's not going to be happy about that."

He leaned back and smirked as comprehension flooded her face.

"The Bureau? You're with the FBI?"

Relief coursed through her body in a wave. She figured she was in some amount of trouble, but she wasn't going to be raped or killed or both.

"Correct. I apologize for the ambush, but this is an unofficial visit. Given your propensity for violence and apparent belief that I'm a killer, well, the cuffs seemed advisable."

She decided not to point out that he also had a propensity for violence.

"Am I under arrest?"

"Not at this point."

"Then, how about you take off the handcuffs? I promise not to beat you up again." She smiled.

He shook his head. "Hilarious. No, sorry. I didn't track you down just to have you take off on me. This thing is big, nationwide. I can't risk you doing any more damage than you've already done."

She considered forcing the issue. He had no legitimate reason to keep her in restraints. But, she was too curious to hear about his investigation to push it.

"So, you're undercover?"

"Correct. And you and that moronic sheriff have jeopardized a massive domestic terrorism investigation."

"You're investigating PORE? As suspected terrorists?"

"PORE and others. McAllister has been on our radar since '08, when the natural gas boom hit Clear Brook County in a big way. McAllister seized on hydrofracking as the issue that would catapult him from drum circles in the woods to the national spotlight. We watched and waited, looking for an opportunity to infiltrate his organization. Once he started the website, boom, I had my in."

"I thought PORE was nonviolent."

Russell had told her that, until the attack on her, the most destructive act PORE had undertaken was when Danny chained himself to a collection tank, which resulted in a work stoppage for most of a morning while the crew and the state troopers looked for a pair of wire cutters to cut him free and drag him off the property.

No one had been harmed but Big Sky had been furious. The company pressed trespassing charges and threatened to file a civil suit as well, claiming it had sustained lost profits of nearly a quarter of a million dollars because of his stunt. According to Russell, Danny had hired Marty Braeburn to negotiate a quick confidential settlement and the criminal charges had gone away, as well.

The FBI agent had a different view of Danny Trees's shenanigans.

"PORE's original focus was on economic terrorism, aimed at harming the oil and gas companies' bottom line, but, as you experienced firsthand, they've recently moved on to destruction of personal property and physical attacks. In addition, they're loosely affiliated with a network of similar cells, spread throughout the country. Some of their compatriots in the Pacific Northwest have ramped up the violence recently."

She looked at him closely. He didn't seem to be joking.

"Okay, I'm pretty sure Danny slashed my tires, and I think you and Danny both pelted me with rocks, but everything else was you, remember? You tried to smash my windshield. Everyone else split, but Danny tried to stop you, Agent . . ."

"Stock. Agent Jared Stock. The details aren't important. McAllister participated in a violent attack on an unarmed woman in furtherance of his radical environmental agenda."

The laugh escaped before she could stop it.

"Agent Stock, let's be serious. He couldn't convince you to stop, so he left. Then you attacked me with your stick. Or tried to, at any rate."

Stock's nostrils flared. "What was that move you used? Jujitsu?"

"Krav Maga."

He gave her a rueful look. "You caught me off guard."

"And, it's a good thing I did. Otherwise, you'd have viciously beaten me, and the hapless Danny Trees would have faced terrorism charges for an attack incited by and ultimately carried out by a federal agent. Is that right?"

"I'm not going to sit here and try to convince you of how very dangerous PORE and organizations like it are, Ms. McCandless. Your government has deemed domestic ecoterrorism to be a profound threat to national security. If you disagree, write your congressman. I'm here because I need you to convince the sheriff to find himself a new suspect and get that sketch of me off the news. I didn't murder Judge Paulson, but someone did. Quite possibly, that someone's a member of the PORE cell. That fits with the evidence allegedly found in my bag. Someone in PORE could have killed him then conveniently framed the guy who had disappeared."

"Which of the dangerous ecoterrorists do you suspect? Melanie? Or maybe Flower?"

"As I said, I'm not going to debate national security with you. Will you help me or not?"

It wasn't as though she had much free choice in the matter, given the handcuffs and the gun. But the reality was, she didn't have any power to help him.

"If you saw the press conference, then you know the attorney general shut down my investigation. It's over, Agent Stock."

He banged his open palm against the table. "Get him to reopen it. There's a killer out there."

Sasha thought. "Did you search Judge Paulson's office on Tuesday evening? Or try to get into his apartment later that night?"

He met her eyes with a level gaze.

"No. And, no. Up until the press conference I had no professional interest in the judge's murder. I didn't have any reason to believe anyone at PORE was involved. In fact, McAllister seemed to regard Judge Paulson as a fair judge—as close to a friend as the movement was likely to have among the local decision-makers. He was optimistic the judge would rule against Big Sky on the county commissioners' decision to consider the drilling moratorium petition he'd presented."

"Then nobody affiliated with PORE would want to see the judge killed," Sasha said. "Why do you think a PORE member framed you?"

"Who else had the means and opportunity?"

Lots of people, including Stickley and Russell, for starters, she thought, but kept it to herself.

Instead, she said, "But no motive. You just said they considered the judge to be a friend. So, it stands to reason that PORE wouldn't have any reason to see Judge Paulson dead. But, if Big Sky shared Danny's assessment of the judge's leanings, then the company might."

Stock shifted his weight in the chair and launched into doublespeak. "I can neither agree nor disagree with that working theory. PORE considered the judge to be friendly on the drilling moratorium issue. I have no information as to whether other issues before the judge might have caused a PORE member, acting alone or in concert with others, to murder him."

She stared at him. She got the distinct feeling that morass of qualifiers and cautions contained a message, but, she'd be damned if she could untangle it. She knew who could, though.

"There's someone you should meet."

~ ~ ~ ~ ~ ~ ~ ~ ~ ~ ~

Sasha walked into her condo with Agent Stock by her side. He'd finally agreed that the handcuffs were overkill, but he'd kept a firm grip on her right hand during the trip from her office to the condo. Which just showed how observant he was: she was a lefty.

Connelly stood at the kitchen island, plating the chicken and peanut noodles. He'd set the walnut dining room table he'd convinced her to pick up at an estate sale so they didn't have to eat his lovingly prepared meals at the kitchen island. Two balloon glasses of red wine shone, reflecting the light from the candles that sat in the center of the table.

"Better set another place," she said by way of greeting. "We've got company."

"So I see," he answered, wiping his hands on the dish towel he'd tucked into his waistband. He came around to the small foyer and extended a hand, "Special Agent Leo Connelly, Department of Homeland Security."

Hardly a social greeting, but, in his defense, he was addressing a disheveled wildman who was manhandling his girlfriend.

Agent Stock eyed him coolly. Then he nodded and dropped Sasha's hand and shook Connelly's.

"Agent Jared Stock. I'm with the Bureau. Domestic Counterterrorism."

Connelly shot Sasha a look.

"Also known as Jay," she explained.

Connelly half-nodded with a knowing expression. "Let me guess. You're on the frontline of the nation's fight against ecoterrorists, specifically PORE."

"Correct. My assignment is—or was—to monitor their actions, particularly any planned violent protests or criminal activities they may engage in to raise money for their cause. As I explained to Ms. McCandless, the Springport sheriff's idiotic theory that I killed that judge poses some serious problems for my continued ability to perform undercover work and for a nationwide investigation into radical environmental groups."

Connelly bobbed his head in understanding.

Sasha narrowed her eyes and looked hard at Connelly. "Why don't you seem surprised by this development?"

"The reason I went to my office was to run down a hunch," he told her. "I thought 'Jay' might be a plant, but I was thinking Big Sky had placed him in PORE to stir up trouble. A source at the EPA CID told me that wasn't Big Sky's style. It occurred to me, though, that it is *our* style. So, I did a little checking. All the information I tried to access about PORE was locked down—DNTK—demonstrate need to know. Even when I called in a personal favor, I hit a brick wall. That smelled like someone had an undercover agent in place or, more likely, several undercover agents spread out throughout a network."

Stock frowned. "And what precisely is your need to know, Special Agent Connelly?"

Connelly reddened.

Before he could open his mouth and get himself in trouble, Sasha jumped in.

"I reached out to Special Agent Connelly as part of my now-defunct investigation," she lied.

Stock raised a brow. "You thought the Federal Air Marshal Service would be the appropriate agency to help you track down an ecoterrorist?"

He looked meaningfully at the table set for two to let her know he wasn't buying what she was selling.

She continued to spin her tale. "I thought perhaps he—you—had fled the jurisdiction and might be traveling by plane. As you may have surmised, Special Agent Connelly and I have a personal relationship. So, I asked him to put Jay Last Name Unknown on the TSA's watch list."

Stock just stared at her.

"But, I'm sure we broke some regulation. Why don't you report it? Make sure you mention that you ambushed and handcuffed an officer of the court at gunpoint in that report."

He moved on.

"So where are we now?" he asked.

"Where we are now," Connelly said, having made a full recovery from his earlier tongue-tied state, "is eating dinner. Pull up a chair."

Over mouthfuls of chicken and peanut noodles, washed down by a robust merlot for Sasha and Connelly and tap water for Stock, the three dissected Stickley's story about the keys and his convenient discovery of the tapes and notes in Stock's bag.

Sasha was forthcoming about the fact that she thought Russell was clean but couldn't be sure. She left out her conviction that Gloria was hiding something, and Connelly didn't mention it.

Stock wiped his mouth with his napkin and pushed back his chair. "Good eats. Thanks."

He looked from Sasha to Connelly and his prickishness fell away, replaced by anxiety. "Look, I'm up for a promotion. I can't get tagged with a blown cover. Not now. I really need your help. I'll do what I can to get you information on the QT. Okay?"

"Of course," Connelly said immediately, as Sasha knew he would.

His ready agreement annoyed her, as she also knew it would.

"Let's start with this information," she said. "I know Connelly's contact said Big Sky was clean, but I've heard the oil and gas companies have to play ball with the county commissioners if they want to get the gas out of Clear Brook County. Can you pull background information on the commissioners? Start with Heather Price."

Stock furrowed his brow, "I have, of course. The Wilson family has had a hard time recovering from the scandal back in the 70s, but, by all accounts, Ms. Price has made good."

She furrowed her brow right back at him. "What's that have to do with anything?"

For all his pokes at Stickley's intellect, Stock wasn't exactly coming off as a genius.

"Price is the daughter of Clyde Wilson, local businessman turned pauper."

"Wait. Heather Price is Wilson's daughter?"

"Affirmative."

"Shelly Spangler, the town doctor, is her sister?"

"Again, affirmative."

30.

SHELLY CHECKED HER WATCH. Eight p.m. on the dot. She stood by her car at the trailhead and waited for Heather. Her sister was always late. As if Shelly's tight schedule meant nothing.

Shelly rubbed her hands together. It was too dark and too cold for a walk on the trail, but Heather refused to move their weekly power walks to a mall or the Y. She had always been an out-doorsy person, her younger sister's comfort be damned.

Stop it, Shelly told herself.

Heather was the only family she had left. Their relationship, for all its faults, was her tie to her childhood. She sometimes wondered whether it wouldn't be better to loosen that tie completely and let her youth, with all its sorrow and suffering, float off into the sky, far away.

But, in the end, she couldn't. She did love Heather. And she valued where she came from. She couldn't dismiss how she'd grown up, despite the pain.

High beams swept the parking lot as Heather sped in, bumping over the uneven ground, and came to a stop across two spots.

"Sorry I'm late," she said in a not-at-all sorry voice, as she hopped out of her truck.

She fell into step beside Shelly, and they walked onto the dark and empty trail.

Shelly was glad for the tall lights that Heather and her fellow commissioners had voted to install every one hundred feet on the trail. She just wished they had been spaced a little closer.

"How's everything?" she asked, as they quickened their pace.

Their goal was to cover three miles in under thirty minutes. The Wilson girls always achieved their goals.

"Good," Heather huffed, her arms pumping like pistons. "Business is good. I'm going to need to expand the fleet if the drilling keeps up like it's been."

"That's great," Shelly said and meant it.

She had no ownership stake in the trucking company, but under their arrangement, they each got a cut of all the money that flowed, directly or indirectly, from the fracking leases. That meant Shelly got a percentage of the take from the trucking contracts with the oil and gas companies, just as Heather got a percentage of the mineral leases Shelly signed. They carried their own expenses, so it didn't matter to Shelly if Heather had to invest in more trucks, just like Heather didn't care about all the hours Shelly spent filling out those blasted annual reports to the Orphans' Court on all the properties. The only expense they shared, and it galled Shelly to do it, was the cost of keeping Stickley cooperative. At least Heather footed the bill for Bob Griggs.

"It is, and it isn't," Heather said now. "These oil companies need to slow down and start listening to public opinion somewhat. It wouldn't take much. Sponsor the wellness fair. Or donate some books to the library. But, if they keep coming across as money-hungry outsiders, the tide is really going to turn."

That would be bad, especially now, because their newest venture was heavily dependent on fracking being around for the long term.

Shelly felt her chest squeeze and reassured herself. Heather wouldn't let that happen. Not out of any sisterly love, but out of her own self-interest.

They reached the 1.5 mile marker and turned around. Shelly checked her watch. It was just a quarter after eight. They were ahead of pace. And she figured she had at least twenty minutes before the call came summoning her to the hospital. The timing was perfect.

"You're still planning to come to the grand opening, right?" Heather interrupted her calculations.

"Wouldn't miss it," she said. Although Café on the Square was Heather's project, she'd already promised Shelly a cut of all the catering contracts she could manage to force down the oil companies' throats.

"Good. Wear something festive. The way some people are carrying on, you'd think we killed Bob instead of buying him out."

No, Shelly thought, you'd only kill him if you couldn't buy him out.

31.

Pittsburgh, Pennsylvania
Tuesday, 9:10 p.m.

AFTER STOCK LEFT, with a promise to dig further into the personal lives and business dealings of Heather Price and Shelly Spangler, Sasha and Connelly cleared the table. She rinsed the dishes and loaded the dishwasher while he used the other side of the double sink to wash the cooking gadgets and array of pots and pans he seemed to need to create any meal, even one that came from the slow cooker. Not that she was complaining. The end result was fabulous.

She ran a dish under the water, her mind on the water in Clear Brook County and the Wilson sisters.

"You okay?" Connelly asked.

"Yeah, just thinking." She turned the faucet, stopping the flow of water, and slid the plate into the dishwasher. "All done. You want me to dry?"

"No, I'm about finished, too. Grab your wine and relax. You can keep me company."

No need to ask her twice. She dried her hands and reached for her glass on the gleaming countertop. Gloria's recipe box caught her eye.

"Oh, I almost forgot. Gloria sent some recipes home with me. I assume you wanted them?"

He looked at her, puzzled. "I didn't ask her for any. Her food was good, though. I'll check them out."

He placed the last pot on the drying rack and wiped his hands on a towel. Then, he reached across her for the recipe box and looked inside.

"Oh."

"What?"

"Look." He held the box out to her.

She put down her glass and took the little cardboard box. Contrary to its name, it held no recipes. Just one mini-cassette tape marked "2."

She ran to her desk and fumbled in the top drawer, pushing paper clips and highlighters aside until she found her old handheld recorder. She hadn't used it since college. No chance the batteries would still be good.

Where was the charger? She shoved a box of envelopes to the side and rifled through the next drawer down.

"Slow down," Connelly told her. "It's not going anywhere."

He was right, but she ignored him. Her heart was racing and her hands were shaking. This could be it. The key.

"I can't find the charger." She could hear panic in her own voice and forced herself to speak more calmly. "We're going to need to get batteries."

"Okay, the 7-11's open. It's a nice night. We can walk."

His deliberate calm was rubbing off on her. She felt her anxiety level falling.

"Sure."

They were putting on their jackets when Sasha's phone rang. It was Marty Braeburn, apologizing all over himself for calling so late.

"It's not a problem," Sasha assured him, the phone jammed between her ear and her shoulder as she zippered her fleece jacket to her chin. Spring might come in March, but April in Pittsburgh still carried a chill.

"I thought you'd want to know, Jed Craybill has been admitted to Clear Brook General. He's incoherent and dehydrated. There's no next of kin and his health care power of attorney names his late wife. The county's going to step in. Dr. Spangler's here. I assume you have no objection to her making his medical decisions?"

The air went out of Sasha's diaphragm, like she'd been gut punched.

Jed had been fine—better than fine—just one day earlier. How could he have gotten into such bad shape so fast?

"Thanks for calling, Marty. Mr. Craybill has a new physician. Dr. Alvin Kayser, a geriatric specialist here in Pittsburgh. Dr. Kayser and I are on our way. The county is not authorized to act on Mr. Craybill's behalf, absent a verifiable medical emergency, in which case, I expect an ER doc to call my cell phone first. Are we clear?"

She grabbed a piece of paper and scrawled Dr. Kayser's telephone number on it from memory then shoved it into Connelly's hands. He could get through to the doctor's answering service and have him on the line by the time she was off the phone with Braeburn.

Connelly nodded; he understood what she wanted him to do. He pulled out his phone and walked over to the window to make the call.

On the other end of Sasha's phone, Braeburn huffed. "A specialist from Pittsburgh? This is beyond the pale. I called you as a courtesy—"

She cut him off. "A courtesy that I greatly appreciate. Now, I'm returning the favor, and letting you know I will raise holy hell if anyone up there takes steps beyond keeping my client alive until his doctor arrives."

"This specialist doesn't even have privileges up here, I imagine. This is absurd!" He was sputtering.

"Are you telling me the county hospital isn't going to grant my patient's personal physician the right to evaluate him and have him moved to another facility?"

"Of course not. I just . . . Okay. Please get here quickly, though. I don't know how much time he has." Braeburn's voice softened and took on a sad note.

"We'll be there as fast as we can. Thanks again for the call."

"You're welcome. You should know I plan to make some calls and see if Judge Paulson's replacement has been named yet. I'll be requesting an emergency hearing."

"That's fine, Marty."

She ended the call and joined Connelly by the window.

"We'll pick you up, sir." He jotted an address on the sheet of paper Sasha had given him and hung up.

"He's getting dressed. Grab your stuff and let's go."

He slid the phone into his pocket and hurried to the bedroom, where he kept a change of clothes and some toiletries.

"Are you sure you can come back up there? I can handle it myself. I know you have a job of your own." A job he seemed intent on jeopardizing for her.

He took her by the shoulders. "I don't know what the hell's going on up there, but I know you aren't walking into it alone."

She smiled up at him. "Let's go, then."

They flew around the loft, throwing clothes and papers into bags. Sasha strapped on her backpack. Connelly carried their overnight bags. On his way out the door, he reached over the counter and grabbed the tape recorder and Judge Paulson's tape.

32.

THIRTY MINUTES PAST MIDNIGHT, SASHA, Connelly, and Dr. Kayser pulled in to the dark parking lot of Clear Brook County General Hospital. They'd made the four-hour drive in a little better than three and a half hours, thanks to Connelly. Sasha had spent much of the tense drive with her eyes squeezed shut, as Connelly weaved around drivers who dared to follow the posted speed limits.

The three stretched their legs and backs in the cold night air of the lot and then stepped into the blindingly bright lobby. The wide glass doors closed behind them with a soft pneumatic whine.

Sasha blinked and took in the reception area. It was quiet, clean, and, as apparently was mandated by some regulation, just as relentlessly beige as every other hospital lobby she'd ever seen. Behind a high, faux-wood counter, a woman wearing green scrubs with an alternating teddy bear and heart pattern spoke in urgent, hushed tones into a hands-free telephone headset clipped to her ear.

Sasha pitched her empty coffee cup into the recycling receptacle just inside the door and made a beeline for the desk, with Connelly and Dr. Kayser trailing behind her.

It's all in the presentation, she told herself. She worked up some moisture in her dry mouth and wet her lips before she spoke.

"Excuse me." She was glad to hear her words come out with some authority rather than as a squeak.

The nurse or whatever she was sighed and looked up. She gave Sasha the "wait a minute" signal with her index finger and threw in a side of stink eye for good measure.

"Don't get the frozen shrimp," she said into her tiny mouthpiece, "get the peeled and deveined stuff behind the counter—it's on special. Make sure you use my bonus shopper card."

She imparted these instructions with an urgency that would have been impressive if it had related to a patient but that seemed disproportionate to a shellfish sale. She flipped through her Shopping Kart ad, making no move to wrap up her personal business.

Great.

Sasha squared her shoulders, stretched up on her tiptoes, and reached over the counter to depress the button and end the woman's call.

The woman's head snapped back, and her dangly earrings swung wildly.

"Excuse you?! Who do you think you are?"

Sasha exhaled. "Attorney Sasha McCandless, ma'am." She gestured over her shoulder. "This is Special Agent Leo Connelly with the Department of Homeland Security and Dr. Alvin Kayser, our forensic medical expert. As you may imagine, we're not here about the special on shrimp down at the grocery store."

The woman blushed, red blotches blooming on her neck first, then spreading to her cheeks. Despite her apparent embarrassment, she just continued to glare at Sasha, arms folded across her chest.

Sasha plowed forward. "We need to speak to the physician treating Jed Craybill immediately. If he or she isn't out here in three minutes or fewer, I'll be speaking to your supervisor." She squinted at the woman's name tag. "Are we clear, Doris?"

"Yes," Doris answered in a sour voice before hustling through a door marked "Staff Only."

She disappeared down a narrow hallway.

As soon as the door swung completely shut behind her, Connelly burst out laughing.

"Way to trip your bitch switch right out of the gate, Sasha."

She swung around and gave him a warning look. He swallowed the rest of his laughter.

"You're really worried about your client," he said, reading the concern behind her anger.

She didn't trust herself to answer, so she just nodded.

The doctor looked away, giving them some minimal amount of privacy, and Connelly pulled her close for a brief hug.

He released her as Doris came bustling back through the door with more than a minute to spare. A harassed-looking young doctor was on her heels. His brown eyes were tired and his hair mussed, as though she'd roused him from a nap, but his demeanor was crisp and all business.

"This is Dr. Brown," Doris said, waving her hand toward him, before retreating to the relative safety of her desk. Out of the direct line of Sasha's ire, she immediately returned to her grocery circular.

He stepped forward and scanned the group, trying to decide which of them to address, even though Doris had almost certainly told him the little crazy woman seemed to be in charge.

Sasha made it easy for him. "I'm Sasha McCandless, Mr. Craybill's attorney. This is Dr. Alvin Kayser; he's a geriatric specialist who recently examined Mr. Craybill."

Sasha looked back at Dr. Kayser and motioned for him to come take over the discussion.

Dr. Kayser blinked rapidly behind his glasses but stepped forward with his hand extended.

"Sam Brown, sir," the younger man said, visibly relieved to be talking to a fellow doctor instead of the lawyer or the unnamed federal agent looming behind her.

"Please, Dr. Brown, call me Al." Kayser smiled encouragement at him. "Can you give me a quick run down on our patient's condition?"

Brown cleared his throat and gathered his thoughts. Then he slipped in the long-abandoned role of resident on rounds and launched into a clinical recitation, falling back into the pattern of precise, quick speech that marked an eager-to-impress medical student.

"The patient was admitted at 20:30 hours, dehydrated, delirious, and febrile."

Sasha jumped in. "Who brought him in?"

He frowned at the interruption but answered the question. "Deputy Gavin Russell."

A look passed between Sasha and Connelly.

"What was your diagnosis at intake, doctor?" Dr. Kayser asked.

"With the caveat that I'm not board-certified in geriatrics, I think this situation arose out of a simple case of inadequate self-care, likely as a result of age-related dementia. Mr. Craybill was severely dehydrated. He clearly had not been consuming sufficient fluids, and his primary—uh, former primary—physician, Dr. Spangler, suspects he also hadn't been taking his medication as directed."

Dr. Kayser put up a hand like a crossing guard. "What medication would that be?"

Sasha called up Kayser's expert report in her memory. He hadn't referenced any meds.

Brown scrunched up his forehead and tried to remember, "Uh, I'd have to check the chart. It was one of the OTC antihistamines. Can't recall which one offhand."

"Moving on," Dr. Kayser said in a tone that betrayed nothing. "What were your initial orders?"

Brown glanced over at Sasha and Connelly before deciding to sell out Doris. He cleared his throat and then said, "There was. . .an error. Someone at intake believed, or assumed, Dr. Spangler was the patient's treating physician. After all, she is the doctor of record for most of our patients. So, she was called in to participate in the treatment plan."

He shot an apologetic look at Kayser. "She neglected to mention that you had taken over Mr. Craybill's care."

Technically, Dr. Kayser had examined Jed for the sole purpose of writing his expert report. But Jed had been livid at the thought that Dr. Spangler had gotten the ball rolling on the incapacitation petition and, according to Kayser, had said he would never seek treatment from her again, under any circumstances. Jed had asked Dr. Kayser to take him on as a patient, and the two had been trying to work out the logistics.

Jed may not have communicated his new plans to Dr. Spangler, but Sasha was confident he would rather be treated by Dr. Kayser. She was less confident that wish would stand up under the law. No need to share that tidbit with Dr. Brown.

Brown continued, "When she arrived, Dr. Spangler ordered intravenous fluids and canceled orders for tests I had already written. She said we were to take comfort measures only until she sorted out the 'mess' with the patient's attorney."

Kayser's woolly white eyebrows crawled up his forehead but he let the younger man continue.

"She said there was some sort of active court case as to the patient's capacity to make his own decisions. Until she got the go-ahead from the judge, we were to keep him stable, but beyond that, it was hands off."

"In your opinion, did that seem like a prudent course of action?" Sasha asked.

The doctor took his time formulating an answer.

Finally, he said, "Look, I took this position because this is an underserved rural community. Three years here, and the government forgives my student loans. I don't know all the nuances of the local scene. Me, personally, I would have run the battery of diagnostic tests. The patient presented in a pretty severe state, but the underlying cause could be something serious or it could be something exceedingly simple and easy to reverse. The only way to know is to run the tests. But, it wasn't my call. Dr. Spangler said he was her patient. And I heard her attorney tell her not to do anything because he'd spoken to you."

"Her attorney? Marty Braeburn?"

"Yes. He came flying into the exam room and pulled her aside. He told her you had refused to consent to the county acting on Mr. Craybill's behalf and that you were on your way here with some hotshot geriatrics specialist. She lit into him about it, and they argued. I went out to find a nurse to start a line so we could get fluids into him. When I came back, the lawyer was gone, and Dr. Spangler was all smiles. Like nothing had happened." He ended with a little shrug.

"Can we see Jed now?"

"Sure. I have to tell you, he's floating in and out of consciousness, and when he has been conscious, he hasn't been lucid. Don't expect much in the way of conversation, and don't stay too long. If nothing else, he needs to rest."

~ ~ ~ ~ ~ ~ ~ ~ ~ ~

Jed looked bad. Worse than bad, if Sasha was being honest. His skin was gray and papery. He opened his eyes and stared at the ceiling with clouded, dull eyes. He was a shadow of the ranting man she'd sat across from on Tuesday afternoon.

"Jed," she said and heard the break in her own voice.

He turned toward her voice and struggled to lift his head from the pillow.

"Yes, honey?" He smiled at her, kind and vague.

He didn't recognize her. Her stomach lurched.

"Excuse us for a minute." She forced the words out around a lump that had taken up residence in her throat and motioned for Kayser and Connelly to follow her.

They huddled in the corner furthest from his bed. Jed folded his hands over his stomach like he was praying and waited—a picture of patience and understanding,

Sasha kept her voice low. "What's going on with him? He's being so docile. He clearly doesn't know who we are. Did he strike you as a man who would just smile and nod at a bunch of strangers in his hospital room?"

Doctor Kayser placed a gentle hand on her arm. "No, I can't say that he did. Sometimes dementia causes people to act out of character. Usually, we see some kindly little old lady who never curses fly into a sudden rage. When such an outburst occurs, we chalk it up to a misfire in the brain. Here, in Mr. Craybill's case, this more pleasant demeanor is equally unusual and likely the result of disease."

"Could dementia really set in so fast? It's only been a day and a half since I saw him. He was eating pie. He was fine!"

Kayser made a motion with his hands, palms skyward. "Who can say? Dr. Brown is right. We need to run those tests to rule out the simple stuff."

"So, do it." Connelly said. "You're his doctor."

Sasha and Kayser shared a look.

"What?" Connelly demanded. "Isn't that what the guy said he wanted?"

"Yes. Absolutely . . ." Dr. Kayser trailed off.

"But?"

"But," Sasha said. "Dr. Kayser has never taken him on as a patient. He evaluated him for my case, that's all. Officially, Jed hadn't transferred his records or taken any other action that manifested his intentions to fire Dr. Spangler. Under ordinary circumstances, that wouldn't matter so much. But, here, it gives Braeburn an opening to claim Jed wasn't competent to hire a new doctor, or he made the decision under duress, or—who knows what he'll say, but it's not so cut and dried."

"And," Dr. Kayser added, "because he doesn't seem to know who we are, if he is asked to reaffirm that decision now, who knows what Mr. Craybill will say."

The three stood silent for a minute and waited for a brilliant idea to strike one of them. Nothing.

Kayser reared his head back and sneezed, a violent burst. Another. One more. Then he reached into one of the pockets of his trousers and pulled out a package of travel-sized tissues.

"Gesundheit," Connelly said.

The doctor wiped his nose, found the pedal-operated trash can near the foot of Jed's bed, and disposed of his tissue before responding.

"Thanks. Allergy season. The trees in Pittsburgh don't bother me, but if I go any further north than Tarentum this time of year, look out."

"That's miserable," Jed piped up from the hospital bed. "You should see a doctor. Pretty gal I go to told me what to take. Dried everything right up."

Kayser turned toward Jed. "Your doctor? Is that Dr. Spangler?

"Yep."

"Do you know the name of the medication?"

"Afraid not."

"How long have you been taking something for your allergies? I mean, this year?"

"Welp, the pollen and ragweed just started getting bad up this way. So, just a day or two."

"Did you have a recent appointment with Dr. Spangler?" Sasha asked. If he had, he hadn't mentioned it to her, but she found his sudden lucidity encouraging.

"Who?"

"Dr. Spangler."

"Spangler? Who's he?" Jed looked at her blankly, then turned to Connelly. "Aren't you my doctor?"

Without waiting for an answer, he returned his head to his pillow and his eyelids fluttered twice, then shut.

~ ~ ~ ~ ~ ~ ~ ~ ~ ~ ~

Sasha escaped to the hallway. She ducked into a little alcove next to the stairs, pressed her back against the cool tile wall, closed her eyes, and tried to erase the image of Jed, pale and quiet, his blue veins stark against his rice paper skin, looking up at her with a face full of confusion and hope then drifting to sleep without warning.

Her vibrating cell phone buzzed against her thigh. She removed it from her pocket and checked the display. 717 area code. Harrisburg. She didn't recognize the number but answered the call anyway.

"Sasha McCandless."

"This is Justice Bermann." Despite the late hour, the chief justice sounded fully awake. And not particularly happy.

"Hello, your honor."

He ignored the greeting and got to the point. "Ms. McCandless, I just received a phone call from the court administrator from the Supreme Court, who was interrupted by her babysitter while out for an anniversary dinner. It seems she had received a panicked call at home from Judge Canaby, whom I just this afternoon appointed to hear Judge Paulson's docket. Judge Canaby, I am told, received an urgent call from a Martin Braeburn earlier this evening, asking the judge to preside over a telephonic emergency hearing because you're trying to prevent Mr. Craybill's physician from treating him."

His tone—sharp to begin with—grew increasingly irritated until, by the end of the summation, he was unmistakably scolding her.

She fought her urge to apologize and waited. If he wanted her to say something, he'd ask her a question. If he just wanted to rant, then so be it.

"Well, what do you have to say to all that?" he snapped.

"I'm Mr. Craybill's court-appointed attorney. I can't really discuss my representation of him with you, your honor."

"Don't be cute. What are you even doing up there? You should be in Pittsburgh. The attorney general informed my clerk this afternoon that your investigation had been closed because you and Sheriff Stickley had almost immediately determined no members of the local bar were involved in Judge Paulson's murder. Go home, Ms. McCandless."

"Your honor, I did go home, but my client needs his attorney, so I'm back. I have a duty."

His voice got crisp and official. "Okay, Ms. McCandless. I'll give you some rope. Try not to hang yourself. But, I've no intention of saddling Judge Canaby with this morass. Tell Mr. Braeburn

I'll hear his emergency motion. Have him call this number in ten minutes and we'll get this done."

"You?   Respectfully, can you do that, your honor?"

Justice Bermann laughed. "I'm the chief justice of the commonwealth's supreme court, Ms. McCandless. I most assuredly can."

He was still laughing when he ended the call.

She slipped the phone back into her pocket and went in search of Braeburn.

She found him in the twenty-four-hour coffee shop, hunched over a sudoku puzzle. He looked up as her shadow fell across his number grid.

"Ms. McCandless." He half-rose and gestured to the empty seat across from him.

"No, thanks. I just got off the phone with Chief Justice Bermann," she said.

Braeburn's sleepy eyes were instantly alert.

"Is that a fact?" he said.

"Yes. And it looks like you're getting your emergency hearing. Right now."

Braeburn folded his paper and slid it into his briefcase in one smooth motion, all business.

He stood quickly and said, "Before whom? Judge Canaby?"

Sasha shook her head. "Nope. The chief justice himself is going to hear it."

Braeburn's head snapped back. "Can he do that?"

"Apparently."

33.

RAEBURN SCURRIED OFF IN SEARCH of Dr. Spangler, and Sasha raced back to Jed's hospital room to try to prepare both him and Dr. Kayser for what was about to happen. Connelly, lost in the flurry of hurried pre-hearing preparations, wandered away.

As Sasha explained the purpose and procedure of the emergency hearing, Jed's eyes fluttered open and closed. He asked no questions, but he smiled weakly and said he understood. Dr. Kayser stood at the head of his bed and shook his head at Sasha.

"You know you can't let him testify," the doctor said in as low voice.

She knew.

"It's all going to rest on you, Dr. Kayser," she told him.

She was overwhelmed with gratitude that he'd agreed to come. She took a quick minute to appreciate the charm her Nana Alexandrov had exuded until her dying day. But for Nana, Jed wouldn't even have a fighting chance.

He blinked behind his glasses. He cleared his throat with two short coughs and began, "There's something you need to know before the . . ."

He stopped abruptly when the door swung open and Braeburn rushed in, followed by a stunning redhead. She wore a tight-fitting lab coat over a silk blouse and an equally snug black skirt. Sasha was suddenly and acutely aware that she was wearing running clothes and had her hair pulled back in a ponytail.

The woman sashayed—there was no other word for it—across the room, her hand extended. "Shelly Spangler," she said to Dr. Kayser, her eyes never leaving his face.

He nodded and took her hand. "Nice to see you again, Dr. Spangler. I'm Alvin Kayser. We met at the Pennsylvania Medical Society's retreat a few years back."

Her lips turned down into a small pout, "Oh, I feel so foolish. Of course, Dr. Kayser, how could I forget?"

Sasha thought it incredibly likely that Dr. Spangler had forgotten meeting the kindly older man almost instantaneously.

With a toss of her hair, the taller woman pivoted to greet Sasha. "And you must be Jed's attorney," she said with a wide smile.

Sasha shook her hand.

"Sasha McCandless," she said, trying to get a bead on Dr. Spangler. Was the sex kitten persona some kind of act?

Dr. Spangler dropped Sasha's hand without ceremony and walked over to Jed's bedside. She pursed the pouty lips and placed two fingers on the underside of his wrist, as if she were checking his pulse. The touch stirred him and he opened his eyes.

"Dr. Spangler," he said in a dry, creaky voice. He smiled at her.

She shed the vixen act and smiled back at him, her eyes warm and shining. "How are you feeling, Mr. Craybill?"

"Tired," he croaked.

She patted his hand. "Let me get you some nice cold water."

She held the large plastic pitcher with one hand and guided the flexible straw into his mouth with the other.

"Now, you go ahead and rest. We have to talk to a judge about you, but you can go back to sleep."

"Harry? Is Harry coming?" Jed looked around, searching for Judge Paulson.

Dr. Spangler gave him a sad smile, "I'm sorry, Mr. Craybill, but Judge Paulson passed away. Don't you remember?"

"Harry's dead?" Jed said, his voice rising in confusion.

Sasha closed her eyes so she wouldn't have to see the glow of victory in Braeburn's. She inhaled, filling her lungs, and let the air out as slowly as she could. Then she snapped her eyes open.

"Okay, let's do this."

They arranged themselves around Jed's bed. Braeburn and Dr. Spangler on his left; Sasha and Dr. Kayser on his right. They pulled the tray table out from the side of the hospital bed and rested the phone on it. Jed was already sleeping again.

Braeburn hit the speaker button and dialed Chief Justice Bermann's home number.

He answered on the second ring.

"This is the chief justice."

"Sir, it's Martin Braeburn and Sasha McCandless calling. Can you hear me okay?" Braeburn held his tie down with one hand and leaned over the bed to speak into the phone.

"I hear you fine, counselor. You are on speaker phone, as well. I wasn't able to scare up a stenographer at one a.m., so I am going to record this call and have it transcribed tomorrow. Do either of you object to that course of action?"

"No, your honor," they said in unison.

"Good. Now, one more housekeeping matter. Mr. Braeburn, I spoke earlier to Ms. McCandless ex parte, as I am sure she told you. When we had our conversation, this matter obviously was not before me. I must tell you that I called Ms. McCandless to reprimand her for her shenanigans, and it was my suggestion, not hers, that I preside over the emergency hearing. I assume you have no objection?"

Braeburn flashed Sasha a cold smile. "No objection, your honor."

Her heart sank. She hated to lose. She really hated to lose against a stacked deck.

"Wonderful. Why don't you tell me who's in the room and we can get started."

Braeburn spoke first. "I'm Martin Braeburn, representing the Clear Brook County Department of Aging Services. With me, I have Dr. Shelly Spangler, who is Mr. Craybill's physician and the county's proposed guardian for Mr. Craybill."

"Sasha McCandless, your honor. I'm Jed Craybill's court-appointed attorney with regard to the issue of whether a guardian is required. With me, is Dr. Alvin Kayser, a board-certified gerontologist, who is my expert witness for the upcoming incapacitation hearing. He also happens to be Mr. Craybill's new doctor. And, of course, Mr. Craybill is here, as well."

She looked at her client whose eyes were still closed. He was breathing evenly.

"But, he appears to be sleeping at the moment. We're gathered in Mr. Craybill's hospital room."

"Mr. Braeburn, you requested this hearing on an emergency basis, correct?"

"Yes, your honor."

"What relief are you seeking?"

"Well, your honor, in light of Mr. Craybill's current condition, we cannot simply follow the briefing schedule that Judge Paulson set and then wait for Judge Paulson's replacement to schedule the incapacitation hearing. Mr. Craybill was admitted to Clear Brook County General Hospital this evening. He is not doing well. I'll leave the medical part to Dr. Spangler, but he's going in and out of consciousness and he seems quite confused when he is awake. Important medical decisions need to be made, and he's in no condition to make them. Because of the pending hearing and the county's request that Dr. Spangler be appointed Mr. Craybill's guardian, I called Ms. McCandless as a courtesy to let her know that Dr. Spangler would be making

Mr. Craybill's medical decisions in her current capacity as his treating physician. She objected to that course of action and asserted that Mr. Craybill had selected a new doctor. So, we're asking the court to appoint Dr. Spangler as guardian immediately."

"Ms. McCandless, do want to say anything before Mr. Braeburn puts up his witness?"

Sasha took a step closer to the phone.

"Yes, your honor. Mr. Braeburn neglected to mention that the reason Judge Paulson postponed the incapacitation hearing and ordered briefing is that, just last week, the county sought to have Jed Craybill declared totally incapacitated, which would result in a guardian being given carte blanche to make all of his decisions—medical, financial, quality of life, everything. But, despite the extraordinary power and control the county requested, it failed utterly to set forth any factual basis for its request. The county submitted no expert report and failed to propose less restrictive means that would enable Mr. Craybill to maintain his independence, perhaps with support—such as a limited guardianship. It was a naked power grab, your honor. And Mr. Craybill was quite vocal about the fact that he would not consent to it; he wanted to continue to live independently, as he has done for years."

Sasha could hear her voice rising.

Jed opened his eyes for a minute and looked around with mild curiosity, then drifted off again.

She continued in a quieter voice. "Last week, I retained Dr. Kayser to perform an assessment of Mr. Craybill to determine if he could continue to manage his own affairs. Dr. Kayser will testify as to his opinion of Mr. Craybill's capacity."

She paused. She wanted to mention the conversation between Jed and Dr. Kayser, where Jed had told the doctor he no longer wanted to be under Dr. Spangler's care. It was a delicate thing, though. Jed was the logical person to testify about it, but, at the moment, he wasn't competent to testify—a bad fact for their position. If she introduced the conversation through Dr. Kayser, Braeburn would almost certainly object to it as hearsay.

She stifled a sigh and looked at her client. Trying to pretend he wasn't presently incapacitated was a lost cause. Better to own it. Her motto as a trial attorney was if she could frame the issue, she would win the argument. So she needed to frame it. Spin it to her advantage.

She plunged in, talking a little faster than she would have liked with the hope that it would discourage Braeburn from interrupting. "In addition, Mr. Craybill advised Dr. Kayser that he intended to end his relationship with Dr. Spangler and inquired as to whether Dr. Kayser was taking new patients. Although Mr. Craybill had not yet transferred his records to Dr. Kayser when he fell ill, his then-present intention is of paramount importance—especially now, when I think all parties would agree that Mr. Craybill is in no shape currently to tell us his wishes."

Her eyes darted to Braeburn. He opened his mouth, thought the better of it, and closed it again. Fast, like a fish gulping. Dr. Spangler glared at him, her eyes cracking.

On the other end of the phone, Justice Bermann exhaled heavily. "Okay, people. Let's hear from the county. In an effort to get this thing finished before sunrise, please limit yourselves to five minutes on direct and five minutes on cross for both sides' witnesses."

It didn't sound like a lot of time. But, Sasha knew it would feel like an eternity to the doctors. She'd once had an expert witness describe testifying as what he imagined it would have been like to have defended his dissertation while naked and being pelted with vegetables by a panel of ex-girlfriends.

Braeburn arranged his papers on Jed's tray table and turned to Sasha. "I guess we should swear in our own witnesses?"

She shrugged, but the chief justice rattled off the oath over the phone, and Dr. Spangler raised her right hand and was sworn in.

Braeburn ran her through her vitals and background information in a hurry, then got right down to business.

"How long have you been Jed Craybill's treating physician?"

"Oh my, forever. For as long as I've been practicing medicine, I mean."

"And how long has that been?"

"Let's see . . .it's going on twelve years, now."

Sasha did some rough calculations in her head. That meant Dr. Spangler was probably in her mid-forties, if not older. She looked like she was twenty-five. Tops.

"And, had he ever indicated that he was displeased with the quality of care he received from you?"

"Never." Dr. Spangler leaned forward here and smiled at the phone, as if Justice Bermann could somehow see her through it. "I treated his wife Marla, too, until she lost her battle with cancer. They both seemed perfectly happy with my care; although, I suppose, Jed stopped coming in after Marla died. That was concerning. You see that sometimes with elderly couples."

She turned and gazed sadly at Jed before continuing. "The first one goes and the survivor sort of stops taking care of himself or herself. So, when I ran into Jed at the gas station over the winter and he mentioned that he'd fallen, I got to thinking about him being all alone out there at his place and not coming in for routine checkups. I was worried."

She'd rambled far beyond the bounds of Braeburn's question, but Sasha didn't intend to object. Let her run on and eat up Braeburn's time; given the late hour, she doubted the chief justice was going to be generous in response to requests for additional time.

"What did your worry lead you to do?"

"He'd injured his arm—not seriously, thank goodness—and I kept thinking how much worse it could have been. I prayed over it, and I decided I had a duty to report my concern to the Department of Aging Services."

She turned again and looked at Jed's sleeping form with liquid eyes.

Sasha jotted a few notes on her notepad and waited.

"What happened next?"

"I met with the director of Aging Services, and she determined it would be appropriate to file a petition to have Mr. Craybill declared incapacitated. She asked me if I would serve as the guardian. I agreed, of course. As the town's population has aged, I have had to take on that role more and more for patients and others who can no longer manage on their own. It's a sad fact of my practice these days."

Braeburn nodded with understanding, and Sasha refrained from rolling her eyes. They were laying it on pretty thick, considering the judge couldn't see them and Jed was off in la-la land.

"Now, in your medical opinion, Dr. Spangler, as we sit here today, is Mr. Craybill incapacitated?"

"Objection," Sasha said in the direction of the phone.

"Would you care to share the basis, counselor?" Justice Bermann cracked in a bored voice.

"Relevance, your honor."

Braeburn telegraphed his outrage. "Relevance? Mr. Craybill's incapacitated state isn't relevant to a petition to have him declared incapacitated? Your honor, I don't even know how to respond to that."

"Ms. McCandless, please explain."

"The county is conflating Mr. Craybill's current state and his state when it filed the petition. Assuming, for the sake of argument, that Mr. Craybill is currently incapacitated, it doesn't lend any credence to the petition. The county couldn't have known Mr. Craybill would be in this state today back when it filed. Unless Dr. Spangler has psychic powers that Mr. Braeburn forgot to tell us about?"

"Mr. Braeburn, what do you say? Isn't this a case of bootstrapping?"

"Absolutely not, your honor," he sputtered. "The county obviously believed he was incapacitated when it filed the petition; hence, the filing of the petition. His current incapacitation serves to confirm the correctness of that belief and to highlight the urgent need for this court to appoint a guardian immediately—before Mr. Craybill declines further and so that Dr. Spangler can treat his condition appropriately."

Braeburn waved his hands around in wide, fast circles as he warmed to his argument.

"Indeed, this crisis situation is a direct result of Ms. McCandless's refusal to consent to the appointment of a guardian at the initial hearing. An appointment that almost certainly would have prevented Mr. Craybill from engaging in the self-neglect that has brought us all here. To now say that his condition shouldn't be considered, well, isn't that a bit like the old chestnut of the boy who killed his parents then pleaded for mercy from the court because he was an orphan?"

He finished and gave a satisfied nod.

This time, Sasha couldn't stop her eye roll.

"Oh, come on," she said. "Your honor, I take exception to counsel's suggestion that I am responsible for Mr. Craybill's condition. I carried out his wishes, as I was required to do as his attorney. I understand Mr. Braeburn wanted me to ignore that duty and play ball, as it were—"

"I've heard enough. The objection is overruled. Dr. Spangler, you may answer."

The doctor let out a throaty laugh. "If I can remember it."

Braeburn smiled and said, "Let me repeat it for you, doctor. In your medical opinion, based on your examination of Mr. Craybill earlier this evening, is he incapacitated?"

"Yes."

"Is he capable of making his own decisions about his medical care?"

"No, he is not."

"Thank you. I have no further questions." Braeburn picked up his notepad and returned to his chair.

Dr. Spangler's warm, open manner dropped away. She straightened her back and held her hands stiffly in her lap. Here was a woman who had testified enough times to know what was coming.

Sasha stood and claimed the spot on Jed's tray table for her notes.

She started with a neutral tone. "You testified that you became concerned about Jed this past winter when you learned he'd fallen, correct?"

"Correct."

"When was this encounter with Jed at the gas pumps, if you recall?"

Dr. Spangler frowned, thinking. "Right after the holidays. So, early January?"

"So, in early January, Jed told you he fell, and you were sufficiently worried about his ability to take care of himself that, after prayerful reflection, you felt you had to report the situation to the Department of Aging Services, is that right?"

"Yes."

"When was that?"

"Excuse me?"

"When did you tell the director of the Department of Aging Services that you thought Jed Craybill could no longer function independently and needed to have a guardian appointed?"

"Hmmm . . . I'm not sure." She flashed Sasha a fake apologetic smile.

Sasha gave her a fake helpful smile right back. "Was it in January?"

"I don't remember. Sorry."

"February?"

"I don't know." Irritation crept into her voice.

"March?"

Braeburn shot out of his chair. "Objection! She's badgering the witness. She said she doesn't remember."

"Ms. McCandless, move along."

Well, at least she knew the judge hadn't fallen asleep on the other end of the phone.

"Yes, sir," she said, then turned back to the witness. "Let me make this easy for you, doctor. The incapacitation petition was filed on March thirtieth. That's roughly ten weeks after you would have run into Jed at the gas pumps. So, did you wait two and a half months to report your concern to the Department of Aging?"

"I'm sure I didn't wait that long."

"The Department of Aging sat on your report for weeks, if not months, then? Is that what happened?"

"I didn't say that!"

"But, it stands to reason: either you didn't report it right away or you did, but the Department of Aging Services didn't do anything about it right away. You agree it has to be one or the other, right?"

Dr. Spangler narrowed her eyes but didn't answer. Instead, she glared at Braeburn, who shrugged. The question wasn't objectionable, and he knew it.

"Do I need to repeat the question, doctor?"

She shifted in her seat. "I don't know what to say. At some point after I saw Jed, I raised my concerns with Aging Services. At some point thereafter, someone there instructed Attorney Braeburn to file the papers, and then, apparently, they were filed on the last day of March."

Sasha liked the way the doctor laid it at Braeburn's feet. It showed Shelly Spangler looked out for one person and one person only: herself.

If there'd been a jury, Sasha would have gone after her once or twice more, just to beat her up and get her back up, but Justice Bermann understood the point and, more important, was running a clock on her.

"Approximately how many times did you check on Mr. Craybill between the January encounter and the filing of the petition at the end of March?"

"None."

"None? Didn't you testify that you were worried about your patient living alone in a remote area?"

"Yes."

"So worried that you couldn't be bothered to follow up with him to make sure he was okay?"

Braeburn was back on his feet. "Your honor!"

"Yes, counselor?"

"This is uncalled for. Ms. McCandless is—"

Justice Bermann cut him off. "Cross-examining the witness, I believe it's called."

"It's not that I couldn't be bothered," Dr. Spangler said, drawing out her words in an effort to buy herself some time. "It's that Mr. Craybill is . . .was . . .someone who valued his independence. He wouldn't take kindly to me checking on him."

"Knowing that quirk of character, you didn't try to talk to him before you sought to have him declared incompetent? Perhaps you could have suggested that he hire a part-time home aide or ask a neighbor to stop by periodically. Did you do that?"

"No."

"Did you do anything to help him access resources that would have supported him?"

"No." Her voice took on a petulant tone.

"Now, you mentioned you have a number of patients for whom you serve as court-appointed guardian?"

"That's correct."

"How many?"

"I don't know offhand."

"But you can estimate, can't you?"

"I don't know—maybe, three to five percent of my patients?"

Sasha was getting tired of the doctor's coyness. "How many patients do you have, Dr. Spangler?"

"I treat most of the residents of the town proper and a good portion of the surrounding county. The last time I checked my database, I had nearly three thousand patients." She finished with a self-satisfied smile.

"Three thousand?   You're a practice of one, right?"

"That's right."

"Forgive me, doctor. Can you explain how you can possibly adequately treat three thousand people?"

The smile turned modest. "Well, first off, the fact that a patient is registered in my database simply means I have treated him or her. Many of my patients are like Mr. Craybill, in that they don't come in for annual checkups or well visits. I see them when they have the flu or sprain an ankle, but it might be years between visits. And, second, as you've surely noticed, Springport is fairly rural. There's not much drawing people to the area; well, there wasn't until the fracking started, at least. Although some businesses are moving into the area, there aren't currently a lot of other options for medical care. So, some of my patients may see me for routine issues just because it's handy, but they seek treatment in Johnstown or elsewhere for other conditions. I understand that. I'm just a simple country doctor, after all."

She fluttered her eyelashes and looked down at her lap, like she was waiting for Sasha to come put a halo on her head.

"Okay, let's do some math. We'll be conservative. Three percent of three thousand is ninety. I got that right, didn't I?"

"Yes."

"So, there have been at least ninety of your patients, possibly more, who—in your view—needed to be declared incapacitated. Did you manage to get yourself appointed as the guardian for all ninety?"

"You say it like there's some kind of conflict." Her dark eyes flashed a warning at Sasha.

A warning she chose to ignore. "Isn't there?"

"Not hardly. It's a great deal of work and responsibility. If there's a family member or friend willing to take it on, I always ask them to do so before I go to the Department of Aging Services. But, sometimes, there's no one."

"No one except you."

"That's right."

"You're paid by the county for doing this, right?"

She laughed, a wide open laugh. "A pittance."

"So, that's a yes?"

"Yes."

"And serving as guardian gives you complete control over the person, his finances, everything, right?"

"Yes. Well, subject to the court's oversight, of course."

"Of course. I don't imagine you have time in be-tween caring for your three thousand patients to provide the level of support required to help ninety or more incapacitated individuals stay in their homes?"

"No, unfortunately, that's just not possible. And, unlike more metropolitan areas, we don't have any social work agencies qualified to serve as the guardian. It's just me."

"A simple country doctor, right?"

"You got it."

Sasha switched gears fast, while the doctor was still basking in her self-sacrifice. "When did you last see Mr. Craybill before today?"

"I can't recall. It's been awhile."

"You didn't speak to him recently and recom-mend an allergy medication?"

Dr. Spangler's face clouded. "Who told you that?"

Sasha looked at her impassively and waited for her to answer.

"I . . .don't believe so." She wrinkled her brow and stared at the ceiling. Her eyes shifted to the left corner of the room. "Not that I recall."

"Hmm. Are you sure?"

This time her eyes met Sasha's straight on, but the doctor raised one hand to her mouth before saying, "Actually, I am."

Liar, Sasha thought and tallied the tells: she'd answered the question with a question; looked up and to the left; touched her face; and, finally, prefaced her answer with "actually."

"Just one last question. What was Mr. Craybill's score on the MMSE you administered?" Sasha threw the question over her shoulder, casual and relaxed, as she headed back to her seat.

"Um, I didn't give him a test." She said it in a resigned voice.

"Pardon?" Sasha said, wheeling around to face her again, letting her face register disbelief.

Dr. Kayser, who had been so silent and still that she'd forgotten he was there, choked back a laugh at the theatrics.

"I said," the doctor repeated, louder this time, "I didn't give him a test."

"I have no further questions for this witness," Sasha said.

Justice Bermann spoke before Braeburn had a chance to ask for redirect. "Excellent. We are adhering nicely to our schedule. Call your expert, Ms. McCandless, and let's keep this ball rolling, shall we?"

Braeburn was too busy whispering furiously with his red-faced client to ask the judge for any leeway, so Sasha motioned with her head for Dr.

Kayser to hurry up and take the seat Dr. Spangler had just vacated.

"The defendant calls Dr. Alvin Kayser."

The simple country doctor grabbed her four-hundred-dollar couture handbag and stormed out of the room while the chief justice administered the oath to Dr. Kayser.

A weary Braeburn stipulated to the gerontologist's qualifications as an expert in geriatric medicine. It was a concession that Sasha wouldn't normally want nor ask for, even at a bench hearing. Judges were, after all, people, and people were impressed by a long string of medical credentials. Dr. Kayser's were more impressive than most, and, ordinarily, Sasha would have loved to have trotted out every award, certification, and publication to his name. But, she didn't have that kind of time.

She got to the point as soon as he'd settled in his chair.

"Dr. Kayser, can you tell us what method you employ to determine if someone is incapacitated?"

"Certainly. First, I perform a complete physical examination, including extensive blood work. Typically, I'd be looking for changes in the patient's health that either could cause incapacitation or could result from it. That sounds convoluted; would you like an example?"

He was a pro, Sasha thought. He got out in front of the confusing matter right away, with no prompting.

"Please."

He fell into his rhythm. "An obvious example of a condition that could render a person incapacitated is Alzheimer's Disease, mid-stage or later. An example of a condition that might be caused by a patient's incapacitation would be diabetic ketoacidosis in a patient whose diabetes had been controlled by insulin but who, as result of dementia-related forgetfulness, has stopped taking insulin or eating a proper diet."

"What would your next step be?"

"Next, I would administer a mini mental state examination or MMSE to screen for cognitive impairment. If the patient's score on the MMSE indicated mild to moderate impairment, I would gather additional psychosocial information and perform a safety assessment of the patient's home. Based on all that information, I would determine whether there were services that could be provided to support the patient, despite the impairment."

He paused and took one of the clear plastic cups stacked by Jed's bedside. He picked up the water pitcher, poured himself a drink, and took a sip.

Then he said, "Obviously, a severely impaired person, such as someone in advanced late-stage

Alzheimer's Disease would not be able to care for himself or herself, regardless of the level of support available. But, in most cases involving even moderate impairment, in my experience, complete guardianship is not warranted."

"Did you evaluate Mr. Craybill?"

"Yes. Last Thursday, I visited Mr. Craybill in his home and performed a physical and MMSE. The results of the physical indicated that he was in relatively good health, and he scored 29 out of a possible 30 points on the MMSE, which indicated no cognitive impairment. His home was clean and well-maintained. He was cogent and engaged. In my opinion, as a board-certified geriatric specialist, he was not, at that time, incapacitated in the least."

Sasha steeled herself and asked the question. "What's your opinion of his current condition?"

"Sadly, he is currently not capable of making medical or other decisions. He appears to be disoriented, confused, and incoherent, at times."

"How could such a precipitous decline occur in a week?"

"I'm afraid I can't say. I would need to examine him and run some tests, which I am told Dr. Spangler has forbidden—"

"Objection!" Braeburn was on his feet in a flash. "Hearsay, your honor."

"Sustained," came the ruling from the phone.

"I'll rephrase. To your knowledge did Dr. Brown order any tests at intake?"

"Yes."

"Were those tests ultimately performed?"

"No, they were not."

"In your opinion, should they have been?"

Dr. Kayser leaned forward and said, "Without a doubt."

Good enough.

"Now, previously, did Mr. Craybill tell you he was looking for a new doctor?"

"Objection. Hearsay."

"It's not being offered for the truth of the matter asserted, your honor, but to show Mr. Craybill's state of mind."

Hearsay was the biggest evidentiary hurdle in most trials. Neither side could introduce an out-court-statement to prove the truth of the statement. There were, however, several exceptions to the hearsay rule. Some of them deemed an out-of-court statement to not be hearsay under certain circumstances; some of them permitted the admission of hearsay statements for limited purposes if the speaker was unavailable to testify in court; and some of them permitted the admission of such statements regardless of whether the speaker was unavailable.

Sasha had learned early in her career that most attorneys were terrified of looking like idiots with regard to hearsay, so she had simply memorized all of the exceptions and key cases that set them forth. Knock a guy down on hearsay a few times early in a trial and he'd think twice about objecting again. It was the same principle she applied to self-defense: make the first punches count.

"Mr. Braeburn?" Justice Bermann prompted her opponent.

"Your honor, um . . .," Braeburn was thinking hard.

Sasha could guess what was coming and tried to keep her smile at bay.

Braeburn walked right into the trap she'd sprung. "Even if Mr. Craybill said that, the statement is inadmissible because it is irrelevant. There's nothing to suggest he did ultimately switch doctors."

"Ms. McCandless."

"Under the Hillmon Doctrine, your honor, a statement of intent is a present mental state and relevant to show the intent was carried out."

The chief justice's amusement was evident in his tone. "Hillmon, eh?"

"Yes, your honor, the United States Supreme Court ruled in Mutual Life Insurance Company of New York v. Hillmon that a declaration of intention is credible evidence of that intention and, as such, is admissible as an exception to hearsay."

"Refresh my recollection; what year was that case decided?"

"1892, your honor."

"This court isn't about to ignore a hundred-plus years of precedent. The objection is overruled."

Sasha nodded at Dr. Kayser to answer the question.

"Yes. He was furious at Dr. Spangler for initiating the incapacitation proceeding. He asked me if I would take him on as a patient. I was willing, but I expressed concerns because my practice is in Pittsburgh, which is a good distance from here. I told him I would see if I could associate with a hospital up this way. He said that regardless of whether I began treating him, he was not going to see Dr. Spangler again."

"Did you officially accept him as a patient?"

Dr. Kayser spread his hands wide, "I can't answer that. It's not like being a lawyer, where there's a formal process for a client to leave and find new representation. Some patients immediately transfer their medical records, others may make the decision to leave a doctor's practice but take no overt action until they need to make an appointment with a new doctor. If Mr. Craybill had called my office seeking an appointment, my staff would have given him one."

"As a gerontologist, you've had patients who have been deemed incapacitated, haven't you?"

"Oh, yes."

"Have you ever done what Dr. Spangler did— report your concerns about a patient to a county agency?"

"Have I ever determined a patient to be incapacitated and without support, then reported it to the appropriate service agency? Yes, I have. Have I ever made that determination solely on the basis of a chance meeting in a parking lot? Certainly not."

"Have you ever served as guardian for one of your patients?"

"No, I have not. Nor would I."

He was a dream witness. Having had no opportunity to prep him beforehand, she had to rely on his instincts and experience as an expert to understand where she was headed and follow her there. But, he was a step ahead of her.

"Why is that?"

"In my view, it would be unethical for me to deprive someone of his decision-making power and then take control of that power myself. It could too easily lead to abuse."

"Thank you, Dr. Kayser." Sasha turned to Braeburn. "Your witness."

"Dr. Kayser, I have only one question for you."

The doctor, having been cross-examined more than a few times before, raised an eyebrow in open disbelief.

Braeburn chuckled. "Well, depending on your answer, there might be one or two more. But, let's start here: you do not have privileges to practices at this hospital, do you, doctor?"

"Well, no. I suspect I could easily—"

"You've answered my question. Dr. Spangler does have privileges, correct?"

"I don't know firsthand, but I would imagine she does."

"Mr. Craybill needs care right now, doesn't he?"

"He does, indeed. But Dr. Spangler has apparently instructed—"

"Again, doctor. You've answered my question. Now, you testified about the steps you took to arrive at your opinion that, as of last week, Mr. Craybill was not incapacitated, did you not?"

"I did."

"You also testified that, in your view, Mr. Craybill is now, in his current state, incapacitated, correct?"

"Yes."

Dr. Kayser shot Sasha a look. She gave him a half-shrug, glad the judge couldn't see her. She knew where Braeburn was going with this line of questioning, but she didn't see a way to stop it.

"Now, did you examine Mr. Craybill this evening, give him an MMSE, or inquire into his social support systems this evening?"

"No, of course not. He's not lucid."

"But, even without having taking any of those steps, you were willing to testify under oath that Mr. Craybill is incapacitated now?"

Dr. Kayser sighed heavily and stared at Braeburn. "Correct."

"Thank you, doctor. That's all I have."

"And I'm ready to rule," Justice Bermann informed them.

Sasha and Braeburn took a step closer to the telephone and stared down at it. Jed's chest rose and fell in an even pattern as he slept. Dr. Kayser sat attentively, like a school child, and waited. As if on cue, Dr. Spangler slipped back into the room and stood against the wall.

"I find that Mr. Craybill is incapacitated and needs to have a court-appointed guardian. I have grave reservations about the potential conflict of appointing Dr. Spangler. Similarly, I find credible Dr. Kayser's testimony that Mr. Craybill intended for Dr. Kayser to be his physician going forward, but as Dr. Kayser himself noted, it would be unethical for him to serve as the guardian for one of his patients. Accordingly, I appoint the emergency room physician who admitted Mr. Craybill as his temporary guardian. What was the doctor's name?"

"Brown," Sasha said. "Sam Brown."

"Thank you. Dr. Brown has decision-making authority for Mr. Craybill until his condition changes and someone petitions the court, by which I mean Judge Canaby, to modify this order in the ordinary course. Good night, counselors. And good night, Dr. Spangler and Dr. Kayser. The court thanks you for your time." He ended the call without further niceties.

34.

SASHA TOLD HERSELF THAT A loaf was better than none. At least Dr. Spangler hadn't been named Jed's guardian. But, this didn't feel like half a loaf. If felt more like the bread heel—the nasty, crusty heel that her brothers would leave in the wrapper growing up and their mother would dutifully toast and eat with her morning tea. A crummy heel.

She paced along the long hallway, trying to shake off her disbelief that Justice Bermann hadn't ruled in her favor. Dr. Kayser overtook her a third of the way down the hallway.

"Sasha, I'm sorry. I walked into that, but it's true. I don't think a treating physician should be the guardian. At least he didn't name Dr. Spangler." His kind eyes wrinkled with concern that he'd let her down.

"Don't be sorry, Dr. Kayser. You told the truth. But, don't you see?"

"See what?" He stared at her in confusion.

"If Dr. Brown is the guardian, he can't be the treating physician, per the judge's order. You don't have privileges here. That leaves guess who as the treating physician."

Understanding spread across his face. "Dr. Spangler."

She just nodded. Any victory they'd achieved was Pyrrhic. Not only was Dr. Kayser out in the cold, but with the incapacitation issue decided, she presumably was no longer authorized to represent Jed. She felt tired. Tired and defeated.

His expression reflected the same emotions briefly, then he perked up. "But, what I was starting to tell you before the hearing. I took the liberty—"

He stopped mid-sentence as Connelly came toward them, running full out, and skidded to a stop beside them.

"Gloria's had a heart attack," he said, catching his breath.

Sasha felt tears pricking at her eyes. What next?

Ashamed to let Kayser and Connelly see her cry, Sasha bowed her head and hung back as Connelly led them to the cardiac care unit.

Connelly and Kayser had just entered the stairway, headed down a flight of stairs, when her cell phone rang.

She backed out of the doorway and leaned against the wall to check her display. Justice Bermann was calling. Sasha never thought she'd see the day she received a call from the Chief Justice of the Pennsylvania Supreme Court, let alone the day she contemplated letting that call roll in to voicemail.

She thought about it for three rings before deciding she didn't have the nerve.

"Your honor."

"Counselor."

She waited and listened to his even intake and exhale as he thought something over.

Finally, he said, "I realize this call is highly unusual. It has nothing to do with your incapacitation matter. I—I need to know if you're truly satisfied with the investigation into Harry's . . . Judge Paulson's death. Please."

His slip of the tongue—using Judge Paulson's nickname so familiarly—and the break in his voice forced her to tell him the truth.

"No, your honor, I'm not. I have good reason to believe the suspect the sheriff identified publicly is a dead end. Something else is going on. It's like a web up here, sir. Everyone and everything seems to be entangled and interconnected. I haven't yet gotten my arms around the hows or whys."

"A web."

There was a long pause, then he said, "The last time I spoke to Judge Paulson, on Sunday, he told me he felt like a fly being eyed by a fat spider. Two days later he was dead."

He spoke softly, talking more to himself than to her.

Then, his voice regained its timbre. "I'm authorizing you to unofficially reopen your investigation into Judge Paulson's death."

"Unofficially?"

"Yes. If you believe there's a cover up or conspiracy or what have you going on, then look into it. But, do it quietly. And carefully. Don't involve the sheriff's office. You'll report to me, privately, and not to the attorney general. Do you understand?"

Oh, she understood. She understood this was a spectacularly bad idea.

He was asking her to poke around with no true authority, no support from the attorney general's office, and no backup from local law enforcement if anything went wrong.

She also understood that she lacked the ability to look at a bad—potentially dangerous—situation that involved her only tangentially, if at all, and decide it wasn't her place to get involved. She hadn't been able to walk away from the plane crash the previous year, and here she was again, about to walk headlong into some mess.

What she should do, she thought, was just swear the man to secrecy, tell him about Agent Stock, and make the whole thing his problem.

Instead, she said, "I do."

"I thank you. Harrison Paulson was a good jurist and a good man." He hung up without waiting for a response.

She slipped the phone back into her pocket and took the stairs down one flight and emerged into a hallway identical to the one she'd just left. She wandered around until she found an orderly who pointed her to the coronary care unit and Gloria's room.

Gloria lay in a bed, its head elevated so that she appeared to be sitting. A breathing tube was taped to her nose and a monitor beeped out her heart rate. With her glasses off and her eyes closed, she looked younger and vulnerable.

Jonas sat at her side, straddling a metal chair backward, both of his hands wrapped around those of his wife. His eyes were distant and disbelieving. Behind him, Deputy Russell rocked on his heels, looking everywhere in the room except at his

coworker. Connelly and Dr. Kayser stood a respect-
ful distance away, leaning against the room's one
long window.

Sasha walked straight to Jonas and crouched beside his chair. "What happened?" she asked, resting
a hand on his knee.

She surprised herself with the gesture but he
seemed to welcome it.

He shook his head slowly. "She was getting the
kids' rooms ready for them. You know, they were
coming in for the memorial service. I walked by and
she was leaning against the door frame. Clutching
her chest. Said she couldn't catch her breath. I
called Dr. Spangler and she told us to come straight
to the hospital. I can't believe it. A heart attack."

He stroked Gloria's hand absently while he
spoke.

Sasha squeezed his knee, then turned her head
to give him some privacy. She stood and gestured
for the others to follow her into the hallway. They
huddled against the wall and talked in low hushed
tones.

"How bad is it?" Sasha asked, directing the question to Dr. Kayser.

"You just missed Dr. Spangler," he answered.
"She seems to think it was a minor myocardial in-
farction. Probably stress induced. Prognosis for a
full recovery is good."

The door opened, and Jonas peered out at them.

"She's awake," he said. "She'd like to speak to Sasha."

He slid through the opening and held the door for her. "The kids are on their way. Linnea went to pick up Luke at the airport. Try not to wear her out, okay?"

"Of course," Sasha said, ducking under his arm to enter the room.

Gloria had managed to prop herself up with the flat hospital-issue pillows and was patting her hair down when Sasha walked in.

"I must look a sight," she said. "Can you hand me my glasses?"

Sasha took the glasses from the bedside table and unfolded the arms. She placed them on Gloria's nose and adjusted the earpieces behind her ears.

"Ah, that's better. Thanks." Gloria blinked a few times behind the lenses.

"How are you feeling?"

"I don't know. Scared."

"You gave everyone a scare."

Gloria nodded. "Listen, the kids will be here soon. Did you have a chance to try out my recipes?"

She peered at Sasha over the glasses, searching for a reaction.

"Not yet. We were about to, when I got the call about Jed."

Gloria wrinkled her brow. "What about Jed?"

"He's here, too. One floor up. Gavin Russell stopped by his house and found him in bad shape. Confused, dehydrated—they don't know exactly what's wrong yet."

The older woman nodded. "Goodness. It's a lucky thing Gavin happened by."

"It is," Sasha agreed. "I wonder what he was doing out that way?"

"Probably he went out to see his folks," Gloria said, half to herself.

"His folks?"

"Oh yes, the Russells are Jed's closest neighbors."

"Oh?"

"Yep. Now, Jed doesn't have much use for Mikey and Rita Russell, what with all the disagreements they've had about them leasing their land to the frackers, but Gavin will usually check on Jed when he's out that way. Good people, the Russells."

Sasha filed the nugget of information away for later. She needed to get the story behind the tape before Luke and Linnea arrived to see their mother.

"About your recipe. Did you . . . try it?"

Gloria picked at the sheet tucked over her chest with a nervous bird-like motion. "No. I wasn't sure what to do with it. I thought you should have it, though."

Sasha dropped the coded speech. "It's crime scene evidence. How'd you get it?"

Gloria closed her eyes and leaned back against the pillows.

She was so still Sasha thought she had drifted off to sleep, but after a minute she opened her eyes and said, "It's like I told you. When I knocked on the door and the judge didn't answer, I went in. At first, I didn't realize what happened. I saw the papers fluttering on his desk and realized the window was broken. Then I saw . . . him. On the floor. His face was, well, part of it was missing and there was so much blood. I knelt beside him. To see if he was alive."

Her chest heaved and the monitor beside her began to bleat with increased urgency.

Sasha took her hand. "Gloria, please, stay calm. Breathe. Please."

She worked to keep the urgency out of her voice, but her own chest tightened.

Gloria swallowed and nodded. "I'm okay," she said, although the monitor continued to beep louder and faster.

"The tape recorder was still in his hand, like I said. But, I lied about not touching it. I can't explain what made me do it—I honestly can't—but I just reached in and popped out the cassette and put it in my pocket. Then, I called Sheriff Stickley." She widened her eyes. "Am I in trouble?"

Probably, Sasha thought.

"Let's not get ahead of ourselves, okay? I'll listen to the tape and we'll take it from there."

"Okay. Thank you."

Gloria relaxed into the pillows. Her face was gray and drawn, but the monitor had returned to a steady, reassuring pace.

35.

Friday Morning

ASHA WOKE UP AFTER ONLY three hours of sleep because someone was tickling her nose. She opened one eye. Sir Thomas More was perched on her upper chest, almost on her neck, his long fur fanned out over her face. He was staring at her. She stretched, raising her arms above her head and pointing her toes. In response, Atticus Finch pounced on her moving feet and swatted at them through the covers. She pulled back her feet and clambered out of bed.

"Guess you guys are looking for some breakfast," she said to the cats as she followed the aroma of freshly brewed coffee out into Judge Paulson's kitchen.

When she'd emerged from Gloria's hospital room, it had been two thirty in the morning. Dr. Kayser had vanished. Dr. Brown had assigned a medical student to chauffeur the gerontologist back to Pittsburgh. Apparently, being a medical student was not much different from being a junior associate at a law firm. Aside from the occasional saving of a life, it seemed to be an existence devoted to low-level scut work and the performance of demeaning errands for one's superiors.

In the days before e-mailed PDFs were the preferred method of exchanging counter-signed legal documents, she had once been tasked with babysitting a fax machine in her old firm's office for an entire weekend, with instructions to hand deliver a settlement agreement to the partner's home the minute the papers stopped curling off the fax. At least this hapless medical student/chauffeur had good company for half the trip: Dr. Kayser had probably asked a dozen questions to make the kid feel involved and important.

In any case, Dr. Kayser had left and Jonas had insisted that she and Connelly stay the night in the judge's apartment. They'd been too tired to do anything but gratefully accept the offer. Sasha had tried to talk Connelly into finding an all-night market where they could get batteries for her tape recorder, but he'd promised to run out first thing in the morning.

Given that she was alone in the apartment, save for two hungry felines, it looked like he'd kept his promise. He'd even had the foresight to beg some coffee off Jonas before he'd gone, judging by the large work thermos sitting on the counter.

She was working on her second cup of coffee, while the cats licked the vile-smelling fishy juice leftover from breakfast off their dishes, when Connelly returned. He held a plastic convenience store bag aloft, like a trophy.

"Morning," he said. He leaned in for a kiss. "Do you know I had to drive all the way to Copper Bend to find a store that (a) was open and (b) sold batteries?"

"Where the hell is Copper Bend?"

"My point exactly." He poured himself a mug of coffee from the thermos and tore at the hard plastic packaging around the batteries.

"Oh," he added, looking up, "I forgot to tell you this—last night, Dr. Kayser said he needed to talk to you and would give you a call this morning."

"He tried twice to tell me something last night but there was so much chaos, he never got to say what was on his mind."

"I like him," Connelly said.

Sasha nodded, glad his impression of the doctor lined up with hers.

"You met Dr. Spangler in Gloria's room last night?"

"Mmm-hmm," he said from behind his coffee mug, his tone careful.

"What did you think of her?"

Connelly looked stricken.

"Relax, Connelly, I'm not going to ask who you think is prettier. Did she seem, I don't know, kind of off to you?"

His relief at not being put on the boyfriend hot seat palpable, Connelly considered the question. "Off how?"

"Inappropriately sexual? Or, I don't know, just not the way you'd expect a doctor to behave."

"I guess she was sort of flirtatious—with everyone, I mean, Russell, Jonas, and Dr. Kayser, too—but she seemed genuinely concerned about Gloria. I need scissors or a knife."

He tossed the batteries on the counter in frustration. His struggle to free them from their plastic prison had yielded nothing but a bashed-in package.

"Here."

Sasha took the kitchen shears from the judge's knife block and snipped off a corner.

She found the tape recorder and popped the cover off the battery compartment. Before she figured out which direction the batteries went, her cell phone rang.

She thought it might be Dr. Kayser, so she abandoned the batteries and answered the call.

It wasn't the good doctor. It was the annoying opposing counsel.

"Sasha, good morning. It's Drew Showalter. With my apologies for calling so early, have you made a decision about returning our inadvertently produced document?"

Seriously? It wasn't even seven o'clock. This guy was too much.

"I have. I looked at the document. It's a flyer about a pizza luncheon. There's no way a court would rule in your favor on this. There's no privilege, nothing confidential—there's no basis for you to claw it back. To be honest, Drew, I don't know why you called attention to it. All you've done is highlight it."

She expected him to bluster and pound the table, but instead he conceded defeat immediately and almost happily.

"I understand. My client asked me to try, so I tried."

She ended the call with the distinct feeling that he had just wanted to make sure she'd looked at the document. She shrugged off Showalter's increasingly bizarre behavior and inserted the batteries into the back of the tape recorder.

She hit play and sat the recorder on the breakfast bar. Connelly came over to hear better and they leaned over the bar together, listening.

Judge Paulson's baritone voice rumbled out of the tiny speaker. "This is the Court's order and opinion in Big Sky Energy Solutions Incorporated versus the Clear Brook County Commissioners. Counsel for the plaintiff is Martin K. Braeburn, Esquire, of the Law Offices of Martin Braeburn. Counsel for the defendant is Drew J. Showalter, Esquire, of the Law Offices of Drew J. Showalter."

Sasha was moderately surprised that the two attorneys she knew in Springport were both involved in the case, but then she figured they probably both had a hand in almost every case in town.

She reached across the counter and pulled a pen and notepad from her bag. She scribbled a quick note. Drilling ban? Had the judge's last act been to rule on Big Sky's motion that it was unconstitutional for the county council to consider a moratorium on drilling?"

The judge went on, his voice rhythmic and slow. "This matter is before the Court on Plaintiff Big Sky Energy Solutions Incorporated's motion for a declaratory judgment. Plaintiff seeks a declaration that Defendant's approval of Springport Hospitality Partners LLP's plans to build a ninety-eight room hotel on a parcel of land located at Lot 14, Block 60 in Firetown was improper and failed to consider a memorandum of understanding entered into between Keystone Properties and Plaintiff regarding the mineral rights located on the property."

Judge Paulson paused on the tape, maybe to gather his thoughts, and Sasha hit the pause button on the recorder to gather hers.

She rubbed her temples.

"What?" Connelly asked.

"My case for VitaMight is against Keystone Properties. And the distribution center is located at Lot 14, Block 60 in Firetown."

"Are you sure? The same address?."

"I'm sure."

She'd read the lot and block number on the lease. She wouldn't forget.

"I'm just not sure what it means."

"Coincidence?" Connelly suggested.

She raised an eyebrow. "Seriously? No way."

When Keystone Properties had booted VitaMight from the site, they'd refused to give a reason for the eviction. That decision had puzzled Sasha from the beginning of the case. It almost guaranteed a victory for Sasha in the breach of contract case; the only real question was the amount of damages, provided she could skirt the liquidated damages clause in the lease. It looked like the judge's opinion might provide the reason.

"I'm going to jump in the shower," Connelly said.

"Okay," she replied, ignoring the hint of invitation she thought she heard in his voice. Not that she wasn't interested, but she had work to do.

By the time Connelly emerged from the bedroom, dressed in khakis and a sweater, she'd listened to the entire opinion and had written four pages of shorthand notes.

"So," Connelly said, "did you hear anything worth killing the judge over on that tape?"

"Maybe. Listen to this—" Before Sasha could launch into her theory, her phone rang.

This time it was Dr. Kayser. "Shoot, it's the doc. Let me see what he wants."

Connelly nodded and pulled out his own phone. Probably to check his e-mails while he waited.

"Good morning, Dr. Kayser," Sasha said.

"Yes, it certainly is. I have something you're going to be very interested to hear." Excitement buzzed in his voice.

"In that case, do you mind if I put you on speaker? Agent Connelly's here with me."

"By all means," he replied.

Sasha hit the speakerphone button and Connelly returned his phone back to his pocket.

"Can you both hear me?" the doctor asked.

"Clear as day," Connelly assured him.

"Very good. Well then, this is a bit awkward, but I did try to tell you last night, Sasha. After you left Jed's room the first time—before the telephone hearing—I considered Agent Connelly's suggestion that we just do the blood tests notwithstanding the uncertainty about whether Jed had left Dr. Spangler's practice. I felt I really didn't have the right to do that, but I did track down Dr. Brown. And, I convinced him to run the tests."

"How did you do that?" Sasha interrupted. "I thought he was afraid of Dr. Spangler."

"He was, or is, I suppose. But, he's also not planning to spend the rest of his career in Clear Brook County. I suggested that I knew many chiefs of staff and hospital administrators throughout the Northeast and that, perhaps, it would behoove him to have me make some inquiries on his behalf after he'd served out his commitment at County General."

His tone was equal parts ashamed and proud of himself.

"I see," said Sasha.

It struck her as a fairly shady thing to do, and she was thankful he hadn't told her of his plan in advance. She was, however, thankful he'd done it.

"Dr. Brown called this morning with the results. Jed Craybill has extremely high levels of an over-the-counter antihistamine decongestant combination allergy medication in his bloodstream. A known side effect of these drugs in the elderly population is an anticholinergic effect that can result in dementia-like symptoms, including dehydration, confusion, inability to concentrate, and memory loss."

"Jed's condition is being caused by his allergy medication?"

"Quite possibly. The drugs block acetylcholine, a neurotransmitter that helps with memory and concentration. The effect is more pronounced in older adults because the natural levels of acetylcholine decrease as we age. Thus, a higher percentage of the neurotransmitter will be blocked in an older person. And, Mr. Craybill seemed to be taking a rather high dose of his medication."

"Once the drugs are out of his system, will the effect go away?"

Sasha could feel the excitement rising in her chest.

"It should. However, Dr. Spangler ordered another dose, which was administered late last night, so it could be another twenty-four hours before we know if that's the cause of his symptoms. It was a curious decision on her part to order another dose, because he's not exhibiting any seasonal allergy symptoms currently. Which is to be expected, given that he's in a HEPA-filtered, closed air environment at the hospital."

Connelly spoke up. "Are you suggesting Dr. Spangler is deliberately medicating him to cause him to be incapacitated?"

Dr. Kayser answered carefully. "I can't say that. I can say I see no reason for him to be taking an antihistamine at the moment, and I would never, under any circumstances, prescribe an anticholinergic drug to an elderly patient. It's simply not justifiable, given the ready availability of effective, allergy medications that do not have such side effects."

If he had tried to keep the judgment out of his voice, he'd failed.

"So, what do we do? Medically, I mean."

"Dr. Brown, in his capacity as Mr. Craybill's temporary guardian, has agreed to inform Dr. Spangler she is not to order any additional medications. He's also going to instruct the nurses not to administer any, even if Dr. Spangler does order them. The poor young man is quite nervous, though. It would be a help if Agent Connelly could go to the hospital to provide support when Dr. Brown talks to her. And perhaps he could stay in or at least near Mr. Craybill's room to ensure the instructions are followed?"

"Sure thing," Connelly said.

"Why Leo?" Sasha asked.

"It was Dr. Brown's suggestion. Apparently, Dr. Spangler became agitated to learn that a federal agent was present last night. She asked Dr. Brown several pointed and, as he described it, panicky questions about who Agent Connelly was, which government agency employed him, and how he was connected to the incapacitation matter. Dr. Brown may be afraid of Dr. Spangler, but he seems to think she's afraid of Agent Connelly."

~ ~ ~ ~ ~ ~ ~ ~ ~ ~

Sasha was drying her hair when she heard the apartment door creak open and then shut. She watched through the bathroom window as Connelly climbed into his car on the street below and sped away from the curb without having said goodbye.

Fine, let him pout. She still couldn't believe it.

In the middle of everything—a murdered judge, an undercover EPA agent, an incapacitated client, a new friend in the cardiac care unit—Connelly had decided it was the appropriate time to start a conversation about where their relationship was headed.

She'd hung up with Dr. Kayser ready to take action. She would shower and head to the courthouse while Connelly babysat Jed.

She'd downed what remained of her lukewarm coffee in a single large gulp and grabbed her toiletries from her overnight bag. As she'd hurried past Connelly with her hands full of shampoo, shower gel, and lotion, he'd reached out and put a hand around her waist.

"Mac, slow down a second," he'd said.

"Is something wrong?" she'd asked, her leg jittering and her voice impatient.

"We need to talk."

The serious way he'd said it had worried her. So, she'd allowed the bottles to tumble from her arms onto the table and had taken his hands in hers.

"What is it?" She'd searched his face for a clue but found none.

"I know this probably isn't the best time," he'd begun, not meeting her eyes, "but I need to know."

"Need to know what?"

"Sasha, what are we doing here?"

She'd wrinkled her brow at the question, and, unbidden, her mother's voice had filled her head, sounding a warning about frown lines.

"What are we doing here?" she'd repeated, baffled. "I'm going to go to the courthouse and pull some documents I think might shed some light on the case before the judge. I thought you were going to go give Dr. Brown moral support and then make sure Spangler stays away from Jed. What am I missing?"

"No. What are we doing here? I've told you, more than once, I love you. I'm in love with you, Sasha. But, your response to that is . . .nothing. A smile or a kiss. I feel like my life, my career, everything is in suspended animation waiting for you to tell me how you feel."

Was he serious? He wanted to do this *now*?

She'd waited until the blood pounding in her ears like a wave had subsided, then had said, "Connelly, I care about you. We have a good thing, a really good thing, I think. But, now is not the time. I'm sorry, it's just not."

To his credit, he'd nodded.

"You're right, I know. But when is the time, Sasha? When are you going to answer me? You owe me at least that."

She'd nodded right back and said, "That's true, I do. But, I can't even think about us right now with everything going on. You don't want to back me into a corner. Trust me."

"It's not an ultimatum; it's a question."

She'd stretched up onto the tips of her toes and kissed him. "And I'll answer it. I promise."

Then she'd gathered her bathroom supplies from the table and had gone into the bathroom and closed the door before she could say something she'd regret.

Now, as she brushed her unruly curls into obedience, she shook her head at herself in the mirror. She didn't have time for this nonsense.

Someone had murdered a judge, and Chief Justice Bermann was counting on Sasha to find out who and why. Jed Craybill may have been poisoned by his doctor and was counting on Sasha to get him out of her hands. Drew Showalter was desperately waving a flyer about Heather Price in her face.

She'd be damned if she'd let her very real responsibilities disappear into a cloud of hearts and flowers.

36.

ASHA COVERED THE SHORT DISTANCE from the Burkes' home to the courthouse at a good clip. Her heels tattooed a staccato rhythm against the pavement that almost kept pace with her racing thoughts.

She'd put the scene with Connelly out of her mind entirely. If there was one trait she considered a strength, it was her ability to compartmentalize. When she was focused, it was impossible to distract her. Growing up, her brothers had viewed it as a challenge to try to get her attention when she was engrossed in a task. It had never worked. It had occasionally backfired, like that time Patrick had accidentally set the shed on fire. She allowed herself a small smile at the memory.

She'd keep her promise to Connelly and give him an answer when she could, but right now she had other questions that needed answers.

She checked the time. It was just almost eight o'clock. Naya would be in the office by now. She hit Naya's number, programmed into her phone, and the legal assistant answered on the second ring.

"Mac, how's it hanging?"

Sasha could hear the printer in Naya's office churning out paper.

"Are you busy?"

"A little bit. Saving yet another junior associate's ass. Someone didn't realize his complaint needed to be verified. Just got a pdf of in-house counsel's signature and I'm working some last-minute arts and crafts magic before I walk this puppy over to the courthouse."

"Okay, I'll keep it short. Is anyone at P&T pulling mineral leases up in Clear Brook County?"

Sasha assumed her former employer would be up to its elbows in hydrofracking work, but she hadn't recognized any of the oil and gas suits warming the hall benches as Prescott attorneys. In itself, that didn't mean anything, though, because she hadn't really dealt with too many transactional attorneys while at the firm, and the ones she did know were mid-level associates or higher. If Prescott & Talbott was sending bodies to Springport, they'd be newly minted lawyers, paying their dues.

Naya laughed. "Hell, yeah. It's a rotating assignment. And this month, the lucky winner is Jessie Stewart."

The name didn't ring a bell.

"Do you know anything about her? Or him?"

"It's a her. Jessica Stewart graduated in the top five percent of her class at Pitt. Daddy was fraternity brothers with Cinco himself. She's got short blond hair and a developing nicotine addiction. Usually see her at my nine-fifteen smoke break. She's already down there, almost done with her morning cig."

"Naya, you need to quit."

"Yeah, yeah, yeah. Anyway, that's the book on Jessie."

"Is she, uh, a stickler for the rules?"

"Doesn't seem to be. I don't know her well. Why?"

"Oh, I need somebody to pull a lease for me."

"You doing mineral rights work now?"

"No, don't you read the paper, Naya? You're talking to the Special Prosecutor assigned to investigate Judge Paulson's murder."

"Yeah? I've been under the gun for about a week. Marcus is going to trial, the pro bono guys are filing a petition with the U.S. Supreme Court, and dumbshit junior associates have been forgetting to get their complaints verified. I *did* hear your name being tossed around, come to think of it, but I just assumed it was your usual notoriety, not any new celebrity. Well, rock on, sister."

Sasha laughed. She had left Prescott & Talbott under unusual conditions, to say the least. According to Naya, it had made her a bit of a legend.

"So, when are you going to take me up on my offer, Naya?"

Naya had an open invitation to join Sasha as her legal assistant.

Naya said, as she always did, "Mac, you know you can't afford me."

She was right. It wasn't the salary that was the problem, but there was no way she could match Naya's benefits, bonus, and the promise of paid overtime. Not yet, at least.

"Yeah, but I'm more fun."

"Yes, you are. That's why I'll meet you for happy hour tomorrow. You free?"

"I hope so."

Sasha had no idea at this point when she'd be back to Pittsburgh.

"Good. You can bring fly boy."

~ ~ ~ ~ ~ ~ ~ ~ ~ ~

"Morning," Sasha greeted the deputy at the entrance.

It wasn't Russell, but a younger guy, whose hair curled down almost to his shirt collar. She'd never seen him before.

"Ma'am," he said, touching the brim of his hat with two fingers.

She hoped Russell was at the hospital, checking on Gloria. She didn't care if she ran into Stickley, because he struck her as lazy enough that he wouldn't bother to inquire into what she was doing, but Russell would ask questions. Questions she wasn't prepared to answer.

She paused to look at the framed photograph of the open-eyed Lady Justice that hung near the directory and then pushed through the door leading to the stairs. She took them two at a time, running her hand along the smooth polished banister and planning her next move.

She loitered in the hallway until the Prothonotary's Office opened its doors to the public at eight-thirty. While she waited, she couldn't help think of Naya and her introduction to the Prothonotary's Office.

It might have been Sasha's third day of work when Naya had hauled her over to the Allegheny County Prothonotary's Office.

"Listen," Naya had explained, after she'd introduced Sasha to the clerks and walked her through how to use the office's on-line document retrieval system at the computer terminal near the door, "it's my job to traipse over here and pull whatever stuff you need to have pulled or to file whatever stuff you need to have filed. It's your job to understand how the office works, so you don't send me over here looking for stuff that doesn't exist. Got it?"

Sasha had nodded.

"And don't you ever send me over here with pleadings that don't conform to the rules. No excuses. Your crappy papers get kicked and these clerks will bust a gut laughing because a lawyer from the high-and-mighty Prescott & Talbott screwed up."

Sasha had nodded again.

Then, Naya had said, "Any questions?"

"Just one. What the hell's a prothonotary?"

And with Harry S. Truman's famous question, posed to the Allegheny County Prothonotary during a 1948 campaign stop, Sasha had won some small measure of Naya's respect. She might have been a wet-behind-the-ears attorney, but at least she had some understanding of history and a passable sense of humor.

Sasha smiled at the memory. Prothonotary was a pretty impressive-sounding title for a clerk of court, but that's how the Commonwealth of Pennsylvania rolled.

The doors opened, and she hurried inside. The public terminal was just inside the door, and one of the clerks had already started it up. The cursor blinked, waiting for her to start her search.

Sasha searched the Orphan's Court records and found all the cases in the past three years in which Dr. Spangler had been appointed guardian of an incapacitated person. It wasn't the ninety that she'd testified to, but it was a good number of them. Picking thirty at random, Sasha pulled up the docket sheets and printed off the defendants' addresses.

She walked through the quiet office to the counter to pay her bill and collect her printouts.

The clerk looked at her over her half-glasses. "You 104765?" she asked, reading Sasha's Pennsylvania bar number off the summary sheet.

"Yes, ma'am." Sasha was more than willing to be nothing but a number to this woman, what with the unofficial nature of her investigation.

"Let's see. That'll be twenty-two dollars even. Is there a firm account you'd like to charge it to?"

Tempted though she was to charge it to Brae-burn's firm, she shook her head. "Cash okay?"

"Always."

Sasha handed over a twenty and two ones, and the woman gave her the pile of printouts and a receipt.

"Thanks," Sasha said.

"You bet."

From the Prothonotary's Office, she headed straight for the makeshift waiting area, or holding pen, for the oil and gas suits outside the Recorder of Deeds' Office. It wasn't yet nine a.m., but the hallway was already standing room only.

She edged her way onto the fringe of the group but took care not to make eye contact with anyone. She summoned her shallow reserve of patience and let the snippets of conversation wash over her, not really listening, while she waited. She passed the time skimming the printouts. She'd give them a closer read through later.

At nine o'clock, she put the stack of papers away and started watching the suits.

At four minute past the hour, a serious-looking younger woman with short blonde hair leaning against the wall across from Sasha and down a bit began to fidget. She tapped her long, unpolished nails against the wall and stared at the deli counter display as if she were willing the numbers to change.

At seven minutes, she started to jiggle her leg.

Ninety seconds later, she grabbed her purse from the floor beside her and took off toward the ladies' room.

Sasha waited until she was almost to the restroom door then followed after her. By the time she pushed through the door, the young woman had already pushed open the screenless window and was perched on its wide sill, blowing her cigarette smoke out into the alley.

The girl's head spun toward the door, guilt splashed across her face.

Perfect.

"Don't mind me," Sasha said. "I won't rat you out."

The girl sighed. "Oh, thanks. I just need a quick drag."

She returned her attention to her cigarette, careful to keep the ash outside the window.

Sasha moved to the sink and took a lipstick from her purse.

"Who wouldn't? I mean what an assignment, cooling your heels outside the Recorder of Deeds Office."

After a deep drag, she answered. "Tell me about it. I thought I'd be negotiating deals and this is what I'm doing. Don't get me wrong, the pay's good, but the work's soul-crushing, you know?"

Sasha made a sympathetic clicking noise with her tongue. "Oh, I know, all right. I used to work at a big firm in Pittsburgh."

"Hey, I'm from Pittsburgh," the girl said.

Sasha opened the lipstick and considered her reflection. She waited until she caught the girl's eye in the mirror.

"Wait a minute, you're Jessie Stewart, aren't you?"

She worked the tube around her lips.

"That's right? Do I know you?"

Jessie crushed the cigarette against the window sash, then flicked it through the open window to the alley below. Then, she hopped down and came over, her hand extended to shake.

Sasha rubbed her lips together and returned the lipstick to her purse, then turned and took Jessie's hand.

"Well, we've never met, but we used to work at the same place. Sasha McCandless."

Her eyes widened. "You're Sasha McCandless? I thought you looked familiar."

The awe in her voice made Sasha want to laugh, but she needed to cash in on her fame, such as it was.

"In the flesh."

"What are you doing here?"

Didn't anyone read the newspaper anymore?

"I'm working on Judge Paulson's murder investigation."

Jessie looked dutifully impressed. "You do criminal law, too?"

"Sometimes. Hey, would you like to help out?" She said it casually.

Jessie's entire face brightened. "Really? Like, how?"

"Like, when your number gets called, while you're pulling whatever deeds Prescott wants, you could also pull a few for me."

A glint of interest shining in her eyes, Jessie nodded. "Okay, sure. Do you have the property descriptions?"

Sasha took out the stack of printed addresses. On the top sheet, she'd written the address of the VitaMight distribution center.

"Okay, I need thirty-one. Can you do that many?" Naya's boot camp had been limited to training her in the prothonotary's office and the federal clerk of court's office. She had no idea if the deeds were computerized, on microfiche, or bound up in dusty leather volumes tied with string.

Jessie frowned. "I dunno. That's a lot."

"Well, get what you can. What's your ticket number?"

She pulled the deli ticket from the pocket of her trousers and read it off. "218. Probably won't get in until just before lunchtime."

She said it with the knowing air of someone who'd wasted too many mornings riding the hard wooden benches in the hallway.

"Okay, I'll meet you outside the office right at noon."

"Sure. If you're looking for a place to hang out til then, you're stuck with Bob's. Too bad it's not next week—Café on the Square is opening over the weekend. From what I hear, it's going to be upscale, local cuisine. I can't wait. And the new owners plan to open a hotel, too. Like a real one, with wireless internet and Starbucks in the rooms. How awesome would that be?"

Sasha stared at her for a minute, then said, "Make that thirty-two deeds. Get me the deed to Bob's Diner, too."

37.

CARL STICKLEY TWISTED HIS CAP in his hands, working the brim back and forth. He wasn't sure where to look, so his eyes roamed around the room. And, damn, if that woman didn't seem amused by his discomfort. He wanted to tell her to put on some goddamn clothes but he didn't dare.

Heather Price licked her lips and broadened her smile, as if she could read his mind. She lounged against the high, curved back of her chair and draped a bare arm over the side. Her silk negligee displayed quite a bit of cleavage but at least it was long, covering her legs. Except when she shifted positions to re-cross her trim legs—then the deep slit fell open to reveal a flash of tanned thigh.

"So, Carl, why don't you tell me what's so urgent that you felt it necessary to drop by unannounced?"

Stickley cleared his throat and tried to remember the speech he'd rehearsed on the drive over. As unnerved as he was by her near-naked state, he was equally nervous because Heather Price was his biggest campaign contributor, easily the most powerful person in the county, and effectively his boss in this . . .side venture. Now, standing in her bedroom, his planned explanation sounded weak in his head, so he decided to just blame everything on Griggs.

"Well, Mrs. Price, here's the thing. That tape is nowhere to be found. It's just gone."

Behind her thick eyelashes, her eyes flashed. "It can't be just gone. It has to be somewhere. Find it." She waved her hand in the air.

"I've checked his chambers, top to bottom. It's not there. I checked his apartment, too."

Gloria's unfortunate heart attack had been well-timed for his purposes. After Sasha had put her tail between her legs and left town, he figured he'd give the apartment another late night visit since his first had been interrupted.

But, when Russell rushed into his office with the news that Gloria was over at County Hospital, he'd headed straight to her house, let himself in the front door, and searched the judge's apartment at a leisurely place. Nothing.

Heather kept a level gaze and waited.

"So, here's what I think happened. Griggs fu— messed up when he appointed that lawyer girl. I told him not to. But, she has to have the tape. It's the only thing that makes sense. I told Griggs he needs to take care of her, but . . ."

Heather raised a hand. "Stop. I don't need to hear about your petty problems with the attorney general. You're sure this woman has the tape?"

He was pretty sure. "Yes, ma'am."

"And the attorney general doesn't have any thoughts on getting it back?"

"No, ma'am."

He'd called Griggs before he'd decided to involve Heather, but Griggs had pulled that politician bullshit and evaded the issue of how they were going to get the tape.

So here he was. He knew what he would do if it he were in charge, but it wasn't his call to make. Heather had made it clear that this was her party.

Her dark almond-shaped eyes narrowed under their sleepy lids. "And this woman is back in Pittsburgh?"

"Uh, no. She's actually here in town, thanks to your sister."

As soon as the words were out of his mouth, Stickley wanted to pull his service revolver from the holster and shoot himself in the head.

She sat straight up. "My sister?"

Stickley sighed. He didn't understand women. But, he especially didn't understand the gorgeous, overtly sexual, competitive, quick-tempered Wilson sisters.

Heather was waiting for an answer.

"Uh, Judge Paulson appointed the lawyer to represent old Jed Craybill. I guess Doc Spangler reported him to the county, said he couldn't care for himself properly."

"Yes, I know all this, Carl," she said, tapping the arm of the chair. "Bob explained it when he told me she'd been appointed to investigate the judge's death."

She stopped the tapping and raised her arm, pointing at him now. "But you framed that hippie and Bob shut down her investigation. So, why is she back?" She flung herself back in the chair, exasperated.

"Well, I guess Jed took a turn for the worse. Deputy Russell found him, as it happens, and drove him to the hospital. Anyway, Marty Braeburn told your sister they had to call Ms. McCandless because of the active court case. She came flying up from Pittsburgh like a bat out of hell, with a federal agent and a geriatric doctor."

"A federal agent? Which agency?"

Stickley laughed. "Don't worry, he's just a sky cop, an air marshal. But, about McCandless and your tape, what should I do?"

She fluttered her fingers, displaying her dark red nails, then dropped the smile. "Just clean up your mess."

38.

BZZZT, BZZZT. Shelly Spangler's cell phone vibrated in the breast pocket of her lab coat. It was the fourth call in as many minutes. She excused herself from her conversation with the hospital's occupational therapist and ducked into an empty room.

"Spangler."

"Shelly, where have you been? I've been calling and calling," her sister demanded, her voice low and threatening,

Shelly summoned all of her patience before responding. "I'm at the hospital doing rounds. I can't talk now. Can I call you later?"

"No, honey, I have a packed schedule. I really need to talk to you. It's urgent." Heather's voice went breathy and dramatic at the end.

Of course she did. Shelly felt her irritation rise. Here was a woman who spent her days lounging around the house in her lingerie, perhaps, Shelly suspected, aimed at finally stopping her octogenarian husband's overtaxed heart.

To her older sister, a packed schedule meant she'd have to stop drinking her wine spritzers some time around three to go get her hair done before she poured herself into a cocktail dress to make an appearance at a fundraising dinner or, once a month, actually put on a suit to go sit through a county council meeting. Maybe once a week, she popped into the headquarters at the trucking company she'd sweet-talked her besotted, befuddled husband into signing over to her. Yes, clearly, Heather's schedule should take priority over her own day filled with rounds, examinations, minor surgeries, and the minutiae of running a medical practice. But, of course, that was the way it had always been.

"Of course, sis," Shelly said, careful to keep her annoyance out of her voice. "Is everything okay?"

"No, everything is not okay. What have you done?"

"What have I done?"   Shelly scoured her memory for something that would have pissed off Heather and came up empty. "I don't know, you tell me?"

"You did something to Craybill, didn't you?"

Shelly hissed into the phone, "I can't talk about that here, Heather."

"I know you did. That smelly old fool Stickley just left my house. Craybill just suddenly took a turn for the worse, and now the feds are in town. The feds, Shelly."

Shelly closed her eyes. She had hoped that somehow news of the federal agent's visit wouldn't make its way back to her sister. It had been a foolish wish, really. Heather had so many people who either owed her favors, were on her payroll, or both, that she probably knew what Shelly had for breakfast.

"He's not a problem, Heather. Trust me."

She hoped she sounded confident. Truth was, she was terrified. Dr. Brown had told her nothing useful at all about the federal agent or his reasons for being in town.

"Not good enough, Shelly. What were you thinking?"

"You told me Jed's property was the key. You came to my office and said that, remember, Heather? What did you want me to do?"

"I don't know, Shelly, but not *this*. You've done it too many times, given someone a little push into incapacitation and, now look, you're being investigated! What did dad always tell us? Pigs get fed and hogs—"

"Get slaughtered."

"That's right. If the feds start sniffing around the hotel deal because they're onto you, so help me God, I'll kill you myself."

Shelly's custom-fitted lab coat, tailored to show off her tiny waist and perfect breasts, suddenly felt constricting, as though she couldn't take a deep breath. Someone who knew Heather only in passing would have written off the tirade as venting. Shelly, who had suffered under Heather's sadistic thumb for sixteen years, until the bitch had finally graduated high school and moved out of their mother's house, knew it was no idle threat.

"Heather, I promise you, Agent Connelly isn't interested in our business holdings or my guardianship stuff. In fact, I think he's only hanging around because he's shtupping the lawyer. Russell said he spent the night with her at Judge Paulson's apartment."

"You'd better hope you're right, Shelly. Is Stickley right, this fed is an air marshal?"

Shelly had no idea. But, God, she hoped so.

"Yes, Heather. Like I said, he's not a problem." Shelly's voice betrayed her, quaking and breaking.

The anger left Heather's voice as quickly as it had appeared. Now, the charm was back. "Maybe you could do me a favor?"

"Sure, sis. Anything for you."

"If you get a chance—take care of that lawyer. I think Stickley's going to give it a try, but you know, he's so inept."

Surely Heather was kidding now. She couldn't have just copped to asking Stickley to kill the lawyer, could she? Over a cell phone?

"You know what else dad said, Heather? Don't write if you can speak; don't speak if you can nod; don't nod if you can wink."

Although their father had been nothing more than a failed furnace salesman, he'd fancied himself some kind of minor mobster because he had to bribe his suppliers out of Johnstown.

"I mean, just convince her to go back home, Shells. Tell her whatever she wants to hear about Craybill, so she'll go. Please? I know I said we need his land; we'll figure something else out, okay?"

Heather displayed no hint that she'd meant that she wanted the attorney to be killed, but the change in her tone and her use of Shelly's nickname confirmed for Shelly that her sister had said more than she'd meant. Now, she was backing away.

"Listen, I have to go. Don't worry about Craybill or this fed, okay? Everything's under control. I'll see you at the grand opening dinner, right?"

"Right," Heather said, her voice bright once again. "Love you, sis."

"I love you, too, sis."

Shelly ended the call and leaned against the wall by the door, gathering herself. What she had told Heather was true. The brooding federal agent did appear to be romantically involved with Sasha McCandless. She just hoped the tiny lawyer was the extent of his interest in Clear Brook County.

She had passed a sleepless night counting up the rules and regulations that her real estate venture had violated. She was reasonably sure most of them were state laws or medical ethical obligations. Really, nothing she'd done should have earned her any federal attention. If this guy really was an air marshal, he definitely wasn't interested in her dealings, but Stickley was wrong as often as he was right.

The genius of her plan was its simplicity. All she needed was one moderately lazy office drone at the Department of Aging Services, who was more than happy to have the county's most popular doctor take on the task of serving as guardian for the increasing number of older citizens who were finding it impossible to remain independent.

No one ever questioned her recommendations; they just forwarded them along to Marty Braeburn, who prepared the papers and then convinced opposing counsel, if there was one, to consent to an order granting the incapacitation petition. Apparently, the county's handful of attorneys were at least as lazy as the county government workers, because, until Judge Paulson had appointed that lawyer from Pittsburgh, no one had ever contested one of their petitions.

Once she had the papers giving her control over the incapacitated person's finances, she waited a decent interval, moved the old person to one of several nursing homes, and then let her contacts at the oil and gas companies know she was accepting bids for the mineral rights to the land. Everything was above board, with one small exception: when she filed the requisite financial reports with the court, she reported the lease income on behalf of the incapacitated individuals, but she understated the income from the hydrofracking leases by ten percent.

She liked to think of it as a finder's fee. Between that little slice of the pie and the fee the county paid her to serve as guardian, she had built up a nice little supplement to her income from practicing medicine. It was virtually risk-free. A cushion, just in case something ever happened to her practice. Even though, she did have to give Heather her cut.

It was pretty rich, though, Heather accusing *her* of being the greedy hog, when she was satisfied with a couple extra hundred thousand and her piece of the money Heather extorted for the trucking contracts. Heather was the one who wanted to branch out with the restaurant and the resort hotel.

Although, Shelly did have to admit that Heather's insistence that she get Jed Craybill's property was going to pay off, even if the hotel deal fell through. He owned one hundred and sixty acres of desirable land—that would get the oil and gas people salivating. She could probably get a bidding war started. That should make Heather happy.

First, though, she had to get Marty to appeal or do whatever he had to do to fix that stupid judge's decision appointing dopey Sam Brown, of all people, as guardian. In the meantime, she'd just have to keep a close eye on Dr. Brown to make sure he didn't undo all her work.

39.

ADRENALINE HUMMED THROUGH SASHA'S BODY as she sat tucked away in a corner of Bob's, soon-to-be the Café on the Square. Her fingers flew, the pen gliding over the notepad like it had wings. She stopped and took several long, slow breaths. She had to beat back her excitement, stay calm, and work her way methodically through the stack of documents Jessie had delivered.

The exchange had gone smoothly. Just before noon, she'd returned to the Recorder of Deeds Office and caught Jessie walking out of the office, her arms full of papers, engrossed in conversation with a man about her own age.

Judging by the smiles the couple exchanged, at least one romance had bloomed in the hallway.

That was no surprise. Every long trial or out-of-town document review Sasha had worked on had yielded at least one "summer camp" romance. Two bored attorneys, support staff members, or some combination of the two would get hot and heavy for the duration of the assignment. Usually, there'd be a halfhearted attempt to make a long-distance relationship work—a few weekend flights cross-country, the grownup equivalent of a flurry of letters before school started again and the summer romance faded with the leaves on the trees.

Every once in a while, a relationship took root and flourished, though; maybe Jessie and this dark-haired guy who didn't realize he was supposed to cut the fabric label off the outside of the arm of his suit jacket would beat the odds.

Sasha had caught Jessie's eye and nodded toward the restroom.

Jessie had tossed one last giggle over her shoulder and then trotted to catch up to Sasha. They'd walked to the ladies' room in silence.

Once inside, Jessie had checked under the stalls for feet, like she was in a made-for-tv movie, then handed over the papers.

"Jessie, I really appreciate this. Thanks so much." Sasha had dug into her wallet and fished out a fifty. "I know you said you didn't want money, but take this and buy dinner for you and Joseph A. Banks out there when the new restaurant opens.

"Joseph A. Who? Oh, you mean that tag on Brandt's sleeve. Good one." She'd rolled her eyes.

"Why don't you tell him to just snip it off?"

"I dunno. I don't want to embarrass him." She'd blushed, then laughed.

Now, reading over her notes, Sasha wished she'd given Jessie a hundred.

The pieces of two puzzles were falling into place. She had to hitch a ride to the hospital and talk to Connelly. She'd tried calling his cell phone, but it had rolled straight to voice-mail.

A familiar voice cut through the noise in her head.

"Thanks, Marie," Gavin Russell said, as he headed out the door with a pastry bag.

She threw the papers in her bag and tossed a ten on the table on top of her bill. She heaved the bag over her shoulder and called out, "Deputy Russell!"

He turned and looked over his shoulder while she ran over to him.

"Sasha, I didn't see you there."

"Listen, can you take me to the hospital?"

He hesitated.

"It's important. And, besides, I need to talk to you about Jed."

She watched him calculating, weighing Stickley's annoyance against whatever information she might have.

His curiosity won out and he nodded. "All right."

He held the diner door open for her and followed her out to the street.

~ ~ ~ ~ ~ ~ ~ ~ ~ ~

They drove in silence through the center of town, which was quiet on a Thursday afternoon.

"So?" Russell said, palming the steering wheel and turning onto the state road that led out to the hospital.

Sasha had been outlining her plan of attack in her head. She had to find out if she could trust him before they got to their destination.

"So, did you hear Jed's going to be okay?"

Russell took his eyes off the road long enough to give her a worried look. "I wouldn't get your hopes up, Sasha. He was in pretty bad shape yesterday."

"He was," she agreed. "Was he like that when you found him?"

"Yeah."

Time for the money question. "What made you just decide to stop in and check on him like that?"

Russell answered immediately. "Doc Spangler asked me to."

"She did?"

"Sure. I ran into her at Bob's, as a matter of fact. I was picking up one of Lydia's pies to take out to my parents. I have dinner with them every Wednesday, and I always bring dessert."

"Would Doctor Spangler have known about that routine?"

Russell wrinkled his forehead at the question. "Well, I imagine so. Her office is right next door."

"So, she approached you at the diner and asked you to visit with Jed after your dinner?"

"Right. So?"

"So, she had prescribed an over-the-counter allergy medicine for him that's known to cause dementia-like symptoms in older people."

The deputy's head snapped back like he'd been slapped. "What? Are you sure about that?"

"Yes. Doctor Brown ran blood tests. Once the medication's cleared Jed's bloodstream, his confusion and incoherence will disappear."

He jerked the car to the right and pulled off onto the shoulder. He parked on a wide gravel patch that led to a drilling pad about ten yards away. They watched as a hydraulic lift guided a huge section of pipe to the well head. Two mud-covered men in hardhats nudged the pipe into position and signaled to the drill operator.

Russell turned his body sideways so he was facing Sasha full on.

"You don't think she did that intentionally, do you?"

"Oh, I know she did. And she used you. She sent you out there knowing what you'd find."

Disbelief and anger clouded over his face.

She went on, more gently. "Gavin, she testified that she's had at least ninety patients declared incapacitated and serves as their guardian. I pulled thirty cases where her patients were deemed incapacitated and compared the addresses with recorded oil and gas leases. In all thirty cases, after Spangler took control of the patients' finances, she had them transferred to one of two assisted living facilities and then entered into hydrofracking leases on their property on their behalf."

He started to speak, but she kept going. "I compared the recorded leases with her certified annual reports to the Orphans' Court. She's been understating the royalty payments by ten percent. Assume the evidence carries through all ninety files. Ten percent of ninety mineral rights leases is a lot of money. Add in the fee the county's paying her to serve as guardian and, well, it certainly gives her a motive to create incapacitated patients, doesn't it?"

"But she . . . I . . ."

Russell pounded the steering wheel with his fist.

There was more, but she needed him to calm down and get her to the hospital. She touched his shoulder. "It's going to be okay. We're going to stop her."

"I have to radio Stickley," he said.

"Please wait until we get to the hospital and make sure she's even there."

She'd wait until they were at the hospital to fill him in on Stickley and Heather Price.

He nodded. "That's good thinking. Let's go."

He pulled out, as a convoy of equipment trucks came roaring up the road.

40.

EATHER SLAMMED THE CLOSET DOOR and smiled at her reflection in the mirror. She leaned in close to check her makeup, then hung her pocketbook over her wrist and turned out the light.

As she backed the pickup out of the driveway, she cursed Stickley and her sister. She didn't trust either one of them not to mess up. She'd just drive over to the hospital, find this federal agent, and see for herself whether he was a problem.

She punched Bob's number into her cell phone.

"Heather," Bob purred, "to what do I owe the pleasure?"

Although he was on the short list of husband candidates for when the old man expired, she ignored the flirtation.

"Things are spinning out of control, Bob."

She palmed the steering wheel and accelerated down the ramp to the interstate, cutting off one of her own commercial trucks, probably headed out to a drilling site.

"How so?"

"Well, let's see. We have a dead judge, but still no tape. That lawyer you appointed is hanging around town, stirring up trouble. And Stickley and my sister tell me there's a federal agent sniffing around."

"Sasha's back?"

"Yes. Although apparently, that's Shelly's fault. Listen, I think I can still salvage the hotel deal, if we can get that freaking tape. Stickley thinks the lawyer has it. Is he right?"

Bob took a minute to answer. "I doubt it, Heather. If she had the tape, she would have pushed back when I shut down the investigation. Stickley's just trying to cover his ass because he can't find it."

Heather breathed out. "Okay, that's what I think, too. I have an idea to keep your lawyer out of our hair, but it means sacrificing Stickley. I assume that's okay with you?"

Bob's only answer was to roar with laughter.

"Good then, we're in agreement."

She smiled and ended the call, then checked her rearview mirror. The left lane was clear, so she slid over and gunned the engine.

41.

LEO SAT IN A SMALL metal chair that he'd dragged over and positioned in front of Jed's hospital door. So far, the only person to come by had been Dr. Brown, who reported the drugs were clearing Jed's system and he was starting to come out of his haze.

With Dr. Spangler nowhere to be found, Leo, unfortunately, had plenty of time to mull over his earlier conversation with Sasha. He felt like a jerk. A needy, insecure jerk.

It wasn't like him to push an issue, but Sasha's blanket refusal to acknowledge his feelings had been eating at him. He wished he'd kept it to himself at least until they'd gotten a handle on the situation in this town. His regret and worry about their discussion was making his stomach flip. Or else he was hungry. He hoped Sasha'd show up soon, maybe with some lunch.

His cell phone vibrated in his pocket and he pulled it out. Not Sasha. A 202 telephone number. Looked like the Bureau, but not an extension he knew.

"Connelly."

"Connelly, it's Stock. I only have a minute. I have information for you. Can you talk?"

Connelly wasn't sure calling from the office was the smartest idea, if Stock was trying to operate under the radar, but it wasn't his neck.

"Sure," he said.

"Okay. My section chief called me in until this blows over, so I'm using my neighbor's office. If she comes back from lunch, I'm going to disconnect the call."

Maybe Stock wasn't entirely stupid.

"Understood. So what do you have?"

"Heather is the older sister by two years. Apparently, she was always the pretty, popular sister. Heather moved out at eighteen and tried her hand at modeling and acting. She spent time in New York and got a few commercial spots. Apparently, there was a pregnancy in the mid-80's, father unknown, pregnancy terminated either naturally or by abortion; it wasn't clear. She moved back to Springport and married a local businessman, Lewis

Price, who was thirty-some years her senior. By the mid-90's, she had taken over all his business interests. She ran for county commissioner for the first time in 1998 and has been reelected each term since then."

"What about Shelly?"

"Shelly was a late bloomer, studious and quiet. She went to Ohio State and was a pre-med major. Completed medical school at Temple and stayed in Philadelphia for her residency. She was briefly married to an accountant in Philadelphia. They divorced after a year and she moved home to care for her mother until the mother's death two years later. She remarried. Clint Spangler runs the hardware store. She opened her medical practice right after they married. She maintains a low profile, in contrast to her sister."

"Shelly and Heather are said to have a typical sister relationship, with periods of closeness and bouts of disagreements. Does that sound typical?"

"I don't know, I'm an only child."

"Yeah, me, too," Stock said. He continued, "Shelly supported Heather's various runs for office. Heather and her husband have the Spanglers over for dinner every Sunday."

"What about the thing Sasha heard. Anything about Heather using her position as commissioner?"

"Sure. Nothing solid, but none of my sources doubted that she does it."

Connelly stretched his leg out straight trying to get more comfortable on the chair and asked, "How are their finances?"

"Both sisters are cash-positive. Shelly's sitting on seven hundred and fifty thousand liquid or easily obtained. Heather's got more like a million cash, spread out across several accounts. Neither husband is a signatory on any bank account."

Connelly gave a low whistle.

"Yeah," Stock agreed. "I guess watching your father lose a fortune then eat a gun will make a girl want to have a nice-sized nest egg. Shelly keeps it simple, real estate concerns and the profits from her practice. Heather's got investments all over the place, probably as a result of all the *quid pro quo* arrangements she's got. She's got the trucking business, of course, and has an interest in a construction company. She's also a backer for the restaurant that's about to open in town and is pushing for some kind of hotel deal. The only real interesting thing is that the sisters both make fairly regular deposits to and withdrawals from their mother's old checking account. They're both signatories, so I guess it's okay that they still use it. But, they seem to be using it to transfer money back and forth. Heather deposits forty grand; Shelly takes it out. Shelly deposits twenty-five grand; Heather withdraws it. If you want to get the white collar fraud guys or the money-laundering pros involved, that's on you."

"No, not yet. Listen," Connelly began, but the sudden silence of a call being disconnected filled his ear.

It appeared Stock's office neighbor had returned from lunch.

Connelly tipped the chair back on two legs and considered Stock's information.

42.

JED PUSHED HIMSELF UP ON his elbows and tried to make sense of what the fresh-faced Dr. Brown had told him. Apparently, his allergy drugs were making him sick? His head was still thick and he had to struggle to remember, but the last thing he recalled was Gavin Russell pounding on his front door.

He'd just come back from feeding the ducks and was feeling woozy. He thought he might have fallen trying to answer the door, but he really couldn't be sure.

Whatever the case, he'd told young Dr. Brown he wanted to get out of this hospital room pronto. Jed knew how hospitals worked. When Marla had been sick, the bills from the hospital stays made him want to vomit right alongside her. Ten dollars

for an aspirin. Five more for a bandage. He'd refused to drink the water Dr. Brown had offered until he'd been assured it was free.

He reached for it now and took a long, cold
swallow. It tasted like heaven. Like the water in the
creek used to taste, before it took on the taste of
the salt and sand and God knew what else that was
being dumped in it.

Brown hadn't said it, but Jed could tell it was no
accident he was here. Doc Spangler was behind
this. He knew it.

What Brown *had* said was that Sasha was back
in town and would be coming to see him. Jed was
surprised by how glad that news made him. Despite her size, that girl packed a wallop. She'd get
him the hell out of here.

Harry Paulson had known what he was doing
when he put her on Jed's case. Poor old Harry.

Jed reached for the water again and, as he did,
he could have sworn his bed shook. He waited a
minute but nothing else happened. He figured he
must still be loopy from the drugs.

43.

A S ASHA AND RUSSELL HURRIED down the corridor toward Jed's hospital room, the rapid beat of their shoes against the tile caught Connelly's attention and he sat up straighter.

Sasha stopped in front of his chair. She hoped the way they'd left things at the apartment wasn't going to cause any awkwardness. She inclined her head toward Jed's door. "How is he?"

Connelly grinned. "Pissed off. Doc Brown thinks he can go home today."

A smile broke across Russell's grim face in response.

Connelly continued, "But only if Spangler signs off on it. She's still the treating."

Russell's smile vanished.

"How'd she take the news about the new orders?" Sasha asked.

Connelly shook his head. "She hasn't made her way over here yet. I talked to Jonas. Gloria is stable and in good spirits, by the way. Anyhow, Spangler started her rounds this morning and checked on Gloria. Brown said she disappeared late morning. But, she sets her own schedule. So, she can come by any time."

"Have you been sitting here all day?" Russell asked.

"Yeah."

"I'll spell you," he said. "Go get a cup of coffee or take a leak or whatever."

Connelly didn't protest. He stood up and motioned that the chair was all Russell's.

"Thanks, man." He turned to Sasha. "Walk with me?"

As they walked away, her shoulder brushed against his side and he gave her that lopsided smile that made her heart skip.

She was about to launch into her discovery, but he pulled her into a quiet hallway near a set of vending machines and said, "Agent Stock called me. I was talking to him when you called earlier."

He fed two quarters into the coffee machine and filled a Styrofoam cup. He fed two more quarters into the snack machine and scored a bag of hard pretzels.

Sasha grimaced, "I should have brought you something from Bob's. I didn't think."

"It's okay."

He tore into the package of pretzels and broke off a large chunk.

She waited until he finished chewing and asked, "So Stock?"

Connelly ran down the background information that Stock had provided. Then he said, "So, to summarize, they have a lot of money, but nothing illegal jumped out at Stock. Those transfers back and forth seem hinky to me, though. Might be something there."

Sasha raised an eyebrow. "There's something there, all right. Shelly specializes in boring state crimes that definitely wouldn't attract the attention of the FBI. But, I am sure Heather's getting a cut. Heather's more of an arm-twisting extortionist, but since she's paying off the local sheriff and the Pennsylvania Attorney General, I doubt anyone's brought it to the notice of the federal government."

Connelly leaned forward, instantly interested.

Sasha went on. "As far as I can tell, until recently, Heather's activities might have been considered self-dealing or greedy, but not illegal."

Connelly said, "And recently?"

"What do you call murdering a judge?"

Then the lights went out.

~ ~ ~ ~ ~ ~ ~ ~ ~ ~

Gavin Russell used the time sitting outside Jed's door to radio the sheriff.

"Sir, what's your location?"

"County General," Stickley replied. "Visiting with Mrs. Burke."

"Have you seen Doc Spangler?"

"Matter a fact, she just walked by."

Russell thought fast. "Can you grab her and bring her to Jed Craybill's room, sir. Craybill is in distress and I don't know where Dr. Brown is."

"Roger that."

Russell clicked off the radio. Sasha would be pleased that he'd lured Spangler to them, he thought. Just then the floor vibrated and his chair rattled against the wall behind him.

He heard Jed Craybill yell out from his hospital room. "What the Sam hell?!"

Then the lights went out.

~ ~ ~ ~ ~ ~ ~ ~ ~ ~

Heather was in the hospital lobby when the ground shuddered and the space was plunged into darkness. As the security guard came around from his station to try to calm the small crowd of visitors and patients milling around, she slipped into the stairwell and headed up the stairs.

She'd just have to walk around the hospital until she found Shelly. She didn't have time to wait until the power outage or whatever it was had ended. She'd start with the doctors' lounge. Maybe she'd get lucky and catch her there.

As she trudged up the stairs, Heather worked through the plan.

Shelly's office was right next to Bob's Diner. If Shelly happened to have been in the front of her building last Tuesday afternoon, Heather knew she'd have had a good visual on the shooter who picked off the judge.

The shooter, Heather knew, had taken up position in the narrow alley that ran alongside the squat Methodist church anchoring the west end of the square. The church provided cover from the side of the street where the courthouse sat, and, because of the massive stone wall that ran between the church and the alley, it also partially blocked the view from the east. But, from Shelly's front office window, one could clearly see if someone had set up a sniper's nest in the alley.

Shelly was going to remember seeing Sheriff Stickley in that alley. At the time, it wouldn't have seemed odd to her, but now, she was going to realize she needed to tell someone.

Heather hadn't quite decided if she was going to use a carrot or a stick to help Shelly with her memory, but figured she'd make that call on the fly.

As she passed the third landing, with just one floor left to go, the door from the third floor opened, and she looked over her shoulder to see Shelly and Stickley enter the stairway.

The door swung closed behind them and she turned to face them.

"I was looking for you," she said to her sister.

Shelly pasted on a smile and chirped, "You found me!"

Ignoring Stickley, Heather said, "Did you get rid of the lawyer like I told you to?"

"Um, not yet. I'm on my way to Jed's room now. Apparently, he's taken a turn for the worse, which is good. I'm sure Sasha will realize it's over and leave."

Stickley guffawed. "Right."

Heather turned to him, "I'm glad you're here, too. This will save me some time. Let's go."

Shelly and Stickley fell silent, and the three walked together up the dim stairs.

44.

WHEN THE EMERGENCY GENERATOR WHIRRED to life, a series of alarms sounded. Translucent boxes mounted at the end of each hall emitted a wail and a pulsing strobe light for a solid minute.

Then the loudspeaker system clicked on in a burst of static. A preternaturally calm male voice came through the speakers: "Do not panic. The hospital-wide earthquake plan is in effect. Shelter in place. Do not, repeat, do not attempt to leave the building. Take cover in a doorway, hallway, or against an inside wall. Stay with your patients. Turn off all nonessential equipment. Do not panic."

Sasha and Connelly ran along the hallway and skidded to a stop in front of Russell.

"Did he say earthquake?" Sasha asked.

"Yep," Russell said.

"There's a fault line here?" Connelly pressed him.

"Yep," Russell responded again. "A minor fault that had been inactive until Big Sky and friends started injecting wastewater into disposal wells situated along it."

"Fracking causes earthquakes?"

Russell remained unruffled. "More like tremors. The theory is the sustained pressure of the injection wells may cause minor seismic activity."

He shrugged and then said, "Oh, I have a location on Doctor Spangler. I asked the sheriff to tell her Craybill is in distress and we can't find Brown. They were leaving Gloria's room before the tremor hit."

"Stickley's with her?"

"Correct."

Sasha looked at Connelly, then back to Russell.

"We have a problem," she began.

Beside her Connelly made a sharp hissing sound.

She turned to see Spangler and Stickley hustling down the hall along with a bombshell in a tight, purple, boucle dress. The woman made Spangler look plain by comparison.

"How is he?" Spangler said, breathless.

"You know," Russell said, "I think it was a false alarm. He seems okay now." He smiled at her, sheepish and apologetic.

Annoyance flashed in her eyes. "I should check on him in any event."

Sasha cleared her throat. "I believe you need his guardian's approval, Dr. Spangler. And we can't seem to locate Dr. Brown."

The doctor turned to her and snapped, "Of all the petty, short-sighted nonsense."

The other woman spoke up. "Shelly, aren't you going to introduce me?"

Spangler bit her lip. "Sure, sorry. Sasha McCandless, this is my sister, Commissioner Heather Price. Heather, this is Attorney McCandless."

Price flashed a wide smile. "It's a pleasure to meet you, Ms. McCandless. Bob Griggs speaks so highly of you."

Sasha smiled back at her. Her mind was in overdrive. All the local players were here. What was going on?

Connelly cleared his throat. "Special Agent Leo Connelly, Department of Homeland Security," he said to the sisters.

"So," Sasha said, trying to ignore the questions swirling in her head, "Deputy Russell was just telling us about the fracking earthquakes, Commissioner."

Price nodded, "It's troubling, isn't it? That's one reason the commission thought it appropriate to vote to consider the drilling moratorium."

Spangler's eyes shifted between her sister and the sheriff.

She started to ease her way to the edge of the cluster, as if she might take off down the hallway. Connelly caught it and moved to stand between her and the door to the stairs.

Russell and Stickley each rested a hand on the butt of his weapon.

Only Price seemed completely relaxed.

Prevent. Avoid. De-escalate. Krav Maga's pre-fight mantra ran through Sasha's head.

Sasha moved so she was blocking the door to Jed's room. As she did, the floor shifted under her feet and she braced herself against the wall.

The movement triggered the strobe lights and the announcement.

As soon as it was quiet, Russell said, "Dr. Spangler, you might be interested to know that Dr. Brown ran some tests this morning."

Spangler's eyes darted from Russell to Price. "Heather," she bleated.

"What kind of tests, deputy?" Price asked.

Here we go, Sasha thought, not at all sure prevention was still viable.

"Turns out, old Jed's not suffering from dementia. He's suffering from an incompetent doctor. Or worse."

Spangler smiled. "I'm sure there's been some mistake."

Russell shook his head. "I don't think so, Shelly. How dare you use me."

He moved toward her, his handcuffs in his right hand.

"Sheriff," he said, "this woman has been having her patients declared incompetent so she can take over their land and lease the mineral rights. She's misusing civil process."

Stickley chewed his lip for a minute, and then snuck a peek at Price. Her face was a mask, providing no guidance, so finally he said, "Detain her. We'll take her to Dogwood Station. Make her their problem."

As Russell snapped the bracelets around her wrists, Spangler begged her sister to intercede.

"Heather, please!"

"Deputy," Price said in a soft, calm voice, "you might want to reconsider."

Russell looked at her in disbelief.

"Why's that, Commissioner?"

"Well, I think—and, Shelly, correct me if I'm wrong—but I think my sister has information about the judge's murder."

Stickley and Spangler both snapped their heads toward Price.

Russell turned and looked at the doctor.

Handcuffed now, she tried to raise her hands in a confused gesture.

"Heather, what are you talking about?"

"Tell them, Shelly. Tell them what you told me, how you saw Sheriff Stickley in the alley beside the church on Tuesday afternoon right before the judge was killed."

Spangler looked at her sister, confusion painted across her face.

"Wait? Wha—"

Stickley erupted at Price. "You dirty little tramp!"

He pulled his weapon.

Price mocked him. "Are you going to shoot me the way you shot the judge?"

Russell's eyes ping-ponged from Stickley to Spangler to Price.

Connelly moved around behind Stickley.

Price went on. "He killed Judge Paulson, deputy. Shelly has information placing him at the scene.

And I think, if you check the alley, you'll find the angle lines up."

Russell released Spangler and drew his own gun. He trained it on his boss.

"Sir?"

"She's lying, Russell. *She* shot Paulson because she wants that tape. All I did was go into the office to get it after she blasted him to kingdom come, but it was already gone."

Price laughed. "You don't seriously expect anyone to believe you, do you, Carl? Especially not when Shelly's willing to trade what she knows for some consideration on this misunderstanding about Mr. Craybill."

She looked meaningfully at her sister.

Stickley's face was red and his hand was shaking.

Sasha spoke to Stickley in a calm, quiet voice. "It doesn't seem fair, does it, sheriff? You've done everything she's asked. You stole the tapes, framed PORE, and even put up with the attorney general's interference. And now she's going to sell you out to save her sister? This is the woman you're in business with?"

The violet eyes flashed at Sasha.

"Shut up," Price warned in a low throaty voice.

Sasha turned to her.

"Or what? Don't you see it's over? For all of you. Springport Hospitality Partners has a paper trail, Commissioner. Everyone's going to connect the dots. It doesn't matter who pulled the trigger. The three of you are done. Griggs might weasel his way out of it, but you three are toast."

Connelly crept up behind the sheriff, ready to tackle him.

Spangler blurted out, "No, it's true. Like Heather said. I saw him."

Stickley turned from Price to Spangler and, as he did, Connelly knocked the gun from his hand. It skittered across the floor and landed at Price's feet. Sasha lunged for it, but Price got there first.

As Connelly restrained the sheriff with his own set of handcuffs, Price trained the gun on Sasha.

Spangler flattened herself against the wall, and Russell turned his weapon on Price.

Despite being on the business end of a gun, Sasha felt a perverse relief that they were now down to four active players and two handcuffed observers.

"Heather, don't," her sister croaked. "It's over."

"Shh, Shelly, you don't know what you're talking about."

Heather motioned with the gun to Sasha.

"Give me the tape."

"Sure thing," Sasha said, nice and calm. "I'm reaching into my bag to get it."

She slowly raised her hands to show she had a tape recorder. She popped the cassette deck and removed the little tape.

Then, she showed Price the tape. "See? Here it is. Let's trade."

Price threw back her head and howled with laughter. "Let's not."

Sasha shrugged and tossed the tape at the woman's feet.

Price looked around the circle. Russell and Connelly both had their weapons trained on her now, but she seemed not to notice.

Spangler, having fully accepted her fate, decided to try to help her sister come to the same conclusion.

"Heather, honey. Put the gun down. It's all over. Our deals, the commissioner job, everything. We're a disgrace. No different than dad."

"Don't you say that, don't you dare!" Price waved the gun at her sister.

"It's true, Heather. We're finished. Just, put down the gun."

"No."

"Heather, you know I *was* at my front window Tuesday afternoon?"

Price's head snapped back.

"What?"

"I was. And I did see someone in the alley."

Spangler was shaking now, tears flowing.

"Stop it," Price said.

"It's true."

"Stop it."

"I saw you. With Lewis's old hunting rifle. Your truck was parked in front of the alley, blocking the street side, but I saw you. I *saw* you, Heather. One perfect shot. Then you picked up your shell, put Lew's gun back in the gun rack, and drove away. *I saw you!*" Spangler was screaming and shaking.

Price jerked the gun, and Russell dove in front of Spangler.

But Price's target wasn't her sister.

She turned Stickley's gun around and aimed it at the roof of her mouth. Sasha turned her head.

One echoing bang later, the white tile wall behind Heather Price was a mist of red blood and gray matter.

45.

Two weeks later
Harrisburg, Pennsylvania
Day two of grand jury testimony of
Sasha McCandless, Esquire

SASHA PAUSED AFTER SHE DESCRIBED the wall, covered with Commissioner Price's brain matter and bits of skull. She took a slow sip of water from the heavy glass on the witness table before continuing.

"At that point, Special Agent Connelly and Deputy Russell secured the scene and called the state police to take Sheriff Stickley and Doctor Spangler into custody."

She caught the eye of her attorney, Will Volmer, and he nodded his reassurance. Although Chief Justice Bermann himself had promised her she didn't need counsel and, under the Investigating Grand Jury Act, her attorney wasn't permitted to make objections or address the grand jurors, Sasha had known from the minute she'd received the witness subpoena that she wouldn't be walking into the grand jury room alone. When the head of Prescott & Talbott's white collar crimes practice had volunteered for the role, she'd agreed in a heartbeat.

The special prosecutor, Aroostine Higgins, looked down at her notepad and then asked, "Why do you think Heather Price killed herself?"

"I don't know. Her sister had just implicated her in the murder of a sitting judge; maybe she didn't want to face the scandal and criminal proceedings that would follow. Maybe she couldn't stand the thought of losing everything she'd worked for. Maybe there's a suicide gene, and she had it. I honestly don't know. I just know that she did it, and she did it too fast for any of us to have prevented it."

Aroostine had made it clear to Will that she just wanted information from Sasha so she could develop her case against Griggs and Stickley. Spangler was Drew Showalter's problem, as he had been appointed special prosecutor by Judge Canaby to investigate the Orphans' Court issues in Clear Brook County.

Will trusted the young Native American attorney who Chief Justice Bermann had appointed to dig into the misuse of the Attorney General's Office and the county sheriff's office. That was good enough for Sasha.

"She's a real up-and-comer," Will had told Sasha. "And her name means sparkling water."

Sasha figured it was only fitting that someone named sparkling water was responsible for cleaning up the mess in Clear Brook County.

"Ms. McCandless, let's go back to the tape and the declaratory judgment action. Can you explain to the grand jurors what the judge's opinion held and why it was important?"

"Sure, after the county commissioners fast-tracked Springport Hospitality Partners' request for a liquor license for the café, Commissioner Price realized how easily she could control the process. Keystone Properties owns a large parcel of land in Firetown that it rented to a nutritional supplement company as a distribution center. When the landlord hosted a campaign event for Commissioner Price, she recognized the value of the land. But, it was too late. Keystone had already signed a memorandum of understanding with Big Sky. They were going to work out a way for Big Sky to tap the shale below while VitaMight continued to operate the distribution center above."

"And VitaMight was your client?" Aroostine prompted her.

"Right. The client whose discovery motion I had just argued when Judge Paulson appointed me to represent Mr. Craybill."

"Thank you. Please go on."

Will patted a hand on the table. His signal that she should slow down, walk the grand jurors through it step by step.

Sasha took a long breath before she continued. "She wanted that land, though. She and her sister, the two partners in Springport Hospitality Partners drew up a bid to buy it outright and build a resort hotel. The kind of place that would appeal to all the outsiders coming to Springport for the gas. It would be a cash cow."

"Go on."

"Keystone Properties wasn't interested. So, when Danny Trees showed up with his petition, Commissioner Price pushed it through, then used it to convince Keystone Properties to break its lease with its tenant, back out of the mineral rights deal, and sell the land to her. And, of course, she also pushed the hotel plans through and got her fellow commissioners to approve them. She wasn't count-ing on Big Sky suing, though. It asked Judge Paul-son to declare the approval of the hotel plans invalid and to reinstate the deal it had with Key-stone Properties."

Aroostine asked, "So, first she had someone threaten Judge Paulson to try to get him to rule against Big Sky?"

"Not exactly threaten. As I understand it, she harassed the county solicitor, Drew Showalter, to 'do something' to convince the judge he had to up-hold the hotel deal. To be honest, I think Mr. Showalter was actually trying to warn Judge Paul-son with his quote from *The Godfather*. He was sig-naling that this was a money grab. He was in a difficult spot, with a difficult client, but he did try to let people know that she had a hold on the com-missioners."

"He also did this by asking you to return a doc-ument?"

"Yes, by raising the issue of inadvertent disclo-sure, he drew my attention to a flyer that showed Keystone Properties had held a fundraiser for Commissioner Price on the property at issue. Again, he had ethical obligations, and perhaps le-gitimate fears, that were boxing him in. So, there were limits to what he could do."

"So, we're in agreement that he was no Atticus Finch?" Aroostine smiled.

"Right." Sasha smiled back. "Not a Sir Thomas More either, for that matter."

Showalter would be okay. The citizens of Springport understood what it had meant to be under Heather Price's thumb. After her death, the stories about her hard-nosed negotiating tactics and fondness for arm-twisting started to flow forward from all corners of the county.

And, according to Russell, Showalter was doing a decent job of investigating Shelly Spangler.

"Moving on, despite the warnings, Commissioner Price feared Judge Paulson might rule against her?"

"Yes. And, Drew had explained the judge's routine. So, she decided to preempt the opinion by killing him. She set up in the alley, shot him through the window, and drove away, unseen by anyone except her sister. Sheriff Stickley's job was to get the tape with the judge's opinion on it. But, when he got to chambers, the dictaphone was empty. So Attorney General Griggs, stepped in to help cover up the murder and get that tape."

"Why would he do that?"

"Apparently, Heather Price had determined she needed to have someone high up in her pocket. Her sister said she bought off the attorney general once she realized all the state representatives were bought and paid for by Big Sky."

"How did he try to cover up the murder?"

Sasha cleared her throat. "He convinced the chief justice to appoint an outsider to investigate the judge's murder. Someone with no prosecutorial experience and no understanding of the town's culture. Someone he was certain would fail."

Aroostine smiled again. "And who was that?"

"That was me."

"How'd that work out for Mr. Griggs?"

"Not as planned," Sasha said.

A soft chuckle rose from the grand jurors.

"Where was the missing tape?"

"Gloria Burke, the judge's secretary had it."

Sasha and Will had rehearsed this part of her testimony carefully. Sasha wasn't willing to say anything that would implicate Gloria. So she hoped to gloss over how Gloria came to possess the tape without lying.

"For safekeeping, would you say?"

"I would."

Sasha shot Will a grateful look. She didn't want to know what conversations he and the special prosecutor had had, but they'd worked.

"So, this decision that Commissioner Price was so desperate to prevent? I take it in his opinion,

Judge Paulson granted Big Sky's motion and unwound her precious deal?"

Sasha turned to face the grand jurors directly. "No. In a reasoned, detailed opinion, Judge Paulson denied Big Sky's motion and affirmed the council's decision to approve the hotel plans."

Aroostine let that statement ring through the room for a full minute before she said, "Thank you, Ms. McCandless. You're excused."

46.

One week later
Pittsburgh, Pennsylvania

CONNELLY'S QUESTION WEIGHED ON SASHA. She thought about it when she was running, sparring, and doing yoga. When she was showering, driving, and falling asleep. She just didn't have an answer.

It was time to do the decent thing and let him know. Face whatever the consequences would be.

She spent the morning working out—running, punching, and kicking until every bit of nerves had drained out of her, replaced by the welcome calm that accompanied physical exhaustion.

After a very long, very hot shower, she dressed in yoga pants and her softest hooded sweater and headed to the Strip District. She wandered the wholesalers' stalls and picked out a good Italian cheese, some fresh pasta, a handful of earthy mushrooms, and a bar of dark chocolate.

Then she walked along the cobblestone streets, dodging shoppers and tour groups, until she came to Wholey's Fish Market. She considered the live lobsters, but they waved their long antennae at her like they were greeting a friend and she didn't have the heart. The containers of lump crabmeat elicited no feelings of guilt, so she had the fishmonger dig one out of the ice for her.

She almost never cooked. And when she did, it was always from a recipe that she followed religiously, more like it was the instructions for deactivating a bomb than the steps for making a casserole or a roast. But, today, she had no recipe, no shopping list.

She floated from store to store, staying present in the smells and sounds of the Strip. Using them to keep her nervous worry about the upcoming talk with Connelly at bay.

She finished her shopping at Prestogeorge for some coffee. Russell's face flashed in her mind unbidden, as she inhaled the scent of the oily dark beans. She dismissed him from her mind and picked out some espresso beans.

On a whim, she stopped outside the coffee roaster's shop to buy a bouquet of tulips from a street vendor.

Finally, she headed for the car, her arms laden with packages, and tried to come up with a menu for the night's dinner. She was about twenty-five yards away when, without warning, the skies opened up and fat drops of rain pelted her. She broke into an awkward half run, the best she could manage with all her groceries.

The rain picked up as she reached the car and fumbled for her keys. She tossed her soggy bags and now-wilted flowers in the back seat and hurried into the driver's seat.

She was soaked. Water streamed off her hair and ran down her face. She flipped on the wipers. A scrap of paper stuck under the left windshield wiper waved wildly.

Great. She hopped out and freed it from the wiper. It was a parking ticket. Of course.

She returned to the car, tossed the ticket into her center console, and wiped her hands on her pants. She turned up the heat to stave off the chill and cranked the radio. A jagged line of lightning zigzagged across the sky and, almost immediately, a tremendous boom of thunder shook the car. April in Pittsburgh. The weather could turn in an instant.

Just as she popped the car into gear, someone banged a palm on her driver's side window. She jumped. Connelly's face peered in through the glass. She unlocked the passenger side and motioned for him to go around.

He ran around the front of the car and jumped in, slamming the door shut behind him.

"Hi," he said. He gave her a watery kiss then shook his head like a wet dog.

"What are you doing here?"

He'd planned to spend his day in the office, catching up on paperwork.

"Getting drenched, mainly. I finished up early and decided to grab lunch. It seemed like a nice day for a walk, so I thought I'd get a bite here. Glad I ran into you."

The sky was dark now, and the rain came in steady sheets.

"Me, too. I'm not driving anywhere until this lets up, though."

Connelly twisted in his seat and eyed the ripped and sopping wet bags on the back seat.

"Did you get anything good?"

Her earlier confidence in her ability to whip up a meal evaporated as she looked back at the random collection of food.

"I don't know. Maybe?"

She reached back and dug out the chocolate bar. She unwrapped it and snapped it in half.

"Want some?"

They ate the dark squares in silence and watched the rain cascade off the front of the car. A PAT bus rolled by, sending up a wave of standing water that splashed over the hood.

"What's the occasion, anyway?" He waved a hand at the groceries.

Her cheeks burned through the damp cold. What could she say? I was going to make a special dinner and then tell you I don't know if I love you? The idea, which had seemed flawless just that morning, suddenly struck her as lame, if not cruel.

"Ummmm..."

Connelly's eyebrows shot up.

"Sasha McCandless, at a loss for words? Inconceivable!"

She attempted a weak smile. Her stomach flipped. Just get it over with, she thought. She gripped the steering wheel with both hands and stared hard at the dashboard.

"Connelly, I've thought really hard about your question. You know, where this is going and how I feel about you. And, I'm sorry, but I just don't know."

Forcing the words out flooded her body with relief. He'd take it however he took it.

She peeked over at him. He was staring at her.

She opened her mouth, planning to tell him what they had did matter to her, but stopped when he burst into loud laughter.

He was laughing at her. Really laughing, like it was hilarious.

"Ummm?"

He tried to stop. Wiped a tear from his eye and caught his breath.

"I'm sorry, but you do know."

A spark of anger flared in her stomach.

"No, Connelly, I don't know."

He reached over and took her chin in his hands.

"Actually, you do. Ever since we got back from Springport you've been talking in your sleep."

"What?"

"Yeah, pretty much every night."

He gave her a crooked smile.

She sunk into the seat, almost afraid to ask, but she had to know.

"What do I say?"

He tilted her head up, forcing her eyes to meet his.

"One thing you say is that you love me."

"I do?"

He nodded.